THE FORGOTTEN MAN

A Q.C. DAVIS MYSTERY

LISA M. LILLY

SPINY WOMAN PRESS

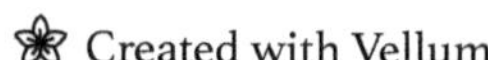
Created with Vellum

1

A LIKELY SUSPECT

IT'S NOT every day you interview the man who might have murdered your sister. I leaned into the airport restroom mirror and dotted concealer over the dark circles under my eyes, then brushed lint from the jacket of my suit. It was my best suit. The one I saved for appellate arguments and pitches to gain new clients. Its warm brown color set off my olive skin and nearly black hair nicely.

I wanted the man I was meeting to answer questions about his daughter's death. Like my sister, his daughter was kidnapped and killed at age five. The two girls were found in a grave together. Evidence showed the same person committed both crimes.

My phone buzzed.

"You wore the Armani with the red top, right?" my friend Lauren said when I answered. "Tell me you did."

"White top." I pulled my rolling bag alongside me as I left the restroom.

Lauren's my unpaid fashion guru, especially when I desperately need to impress. Which doesn't mean I take all her advice.

Lauren sighed. "Seriously, Quille, there's nothing wrong with color."

"Neutrals are safe. No one finds them jarring."

"I do," Lauren said. "Did you at least rent the BMW?"

I veered toward an exit, following the rental car shuttle signs. "I asked for one."

"Good. It'll make even you like driving. Good luck. With the meeting, not the car."

Automobile exhaust and cool, humid air hit me as I stepped outside. I put my hand to my hair, which I could almost feel tightening into frizzy curls rather than the long, loose waves I worked so hard to achieve every morning. I ought to have wrangled it into a bun. But I felt more at ease with my hair down.

My phone rang again as I waited in the rental car facility. It was my boyfriend. He'd planned to come with me on this trip. But at the last minute he was asked to take over a four-month project in Dubai when his boss became ill.

"Isn't it after midnight there?" I said.

"Eleven-twenty. Night's barely started." Ty's voice with its trace of Jamaican lilt sounded warm and upbeat, making me miss him more. "Good flight?"

"Yes." I wound a few strands of hair around my fingers. "I rewrote my questions for Ted Kev twice on the plane."

"Sorry I'm not there to help."

"You helped." Through one of his wealthiest commercial real estate clients, Ty knew someone who introduced me to the person who got me onto the calendar of Ted Kev, the man I was seeing today.

While I appreciated Ty using his contacts, and I missed him, I felt secretly relieved he couldn't join me. His efforts to assist in person when I looked into crimes didn't always work out.

"Still not thrilled you're starting with Kev," he said now.

"He knows the most about that part of the case." I put a

hand over my left ear. Five feet away a man yelled at a rental agent. "If I can get him to talk about it."

Over three decades after my sister's and Kev's daughter's bodies were found, the two murders remained unsolved. My parents were seen as the most likely suspects. At the very least, I hoped talking with Kev would help me understand why.

"People with his level of wealth think everyone's angling to get something from them," Ty said. "Because usually they are. Don't sound like one of those people and I bet he'll talk more."

"Don't sound like those people who want something? But I do. Want something."

"Figuring out who killed your sister means finding whoever killed Kev's daughter," Ty said. "You're not asking. You're offering to help solve his daughter's murder."

"He won't want my help if he's the killer," I said.

"But he'll want to keep tabs on what you're doing," Ty said.

A young, freckle-faced agent in a purple coat waved me over.

"Gotta go," I said. "Call you later. Tomorrow, I guess."

I was still getting used to the time difference.

"Be careful."

"I'll be fine," I said. "I've done this enough times."

I had. But I'd never had so much riding on it.

I NEVER MET my sister Q.C., but she's why I exist. Her full name was Quille Catherine Davis. Less than a year after her body was found, my mother got pregnant with me. A new baby was supposed to make her happier.

Though my dad disagreed, she named me Quille Catherine Davis II. My mom insisted on calling me Q.C. She taught me to sing and act, just as she had the original Q.C. Davis. I thought of my murdered sister as the "real Q.C." until I went to therapy in college. That's when I started asking people to call me Quille. My mother had the most trouble with the shift.

I talked to the therapist again before agreeing to look into the first Q.C.'s murder. That came about because after my former boyfriend died, I was drawn into the investigation of his death and helped solve the case. After that, people started coming to me when they didn't trust the police to find the truth about a crime. Or when the authorities got nowhere.

My mother rarely showed interest in anything I did. But she'd surprised me nine months ago by demanding to know why I helped strangers and ignored my own sister's death.

My odds of finding Q.C.'s killer must be next to zero. It was a decades-old case that had stymied local police and the FBI. But if I succeeded, or if my mother felt I did everything possible, maybe she could finally put Q.C.'s spirit to rest. And so could I.

At least that was what I hoped.

2

THE INTERVIEW

TED KEV'S corporate headquarters were in an old brick building, one of many in the warehouse district of St. Louis, Missouri. I wanted to talk in his office to see if he kept photos or mementoes of his daughter.

Instead, a receptionist took me to a glass-walled conference room that smelled of furniture polish, though there was no wood in sight. The conference table had chrome legs and a marble top that felt cool under my wrists. I set my file and legal pad on it next to the glass of water the receptionist brought me.

Kev joined me ten minutes later. He took a seat across from me, elbows on the table, hands folded. At sixty-seven, he was a contemporary of Steve Jobs and Bill Gates. But he could pass for late fifties despite salt-and-pepper hair and fine lines around his eyes. His light gray collared shirt unbuttoned at the neck to show a fitted slate gray turtleneck. His narrow-legged black jeans stressed his athletic build.

I asked if any of the authorities were still looking into his daughter Vanessa's murder.

"The police and FBI stopped knocking on our door a decade ago." Kev's voice was pitched mid-range, neither a tenor's high nor a baritone's low. "I still get calls and emails. Mostly from psychics. And people who claim they have tips about the killer. They all want to share what they know. For a small fee."

"I'm not asking for a fee," I said.

"Good. Since, as I understand it, you're not a licensed investigator. Or a criminal attorney."

"No," I said. "I handle business-related lawsuits. My criminal investigations are for select clients. Word of mouth only."

He tilted his head as if listening to a voice only he could hear. "And now you're your own client? Isn't there a saying that the lawyer who represents himself—"

"Has a fool for a client." My lips felt dry. I sipped my water. The glass, when I set it down, clinked on the marble tabletop. "But I'm not representing myself. I'm doing this for my mother."

That was only partly true. I wanted to find out who killed the original Q.C. for myself, too.

"Doesn't sound much different to me," Kev said.

"Did you ever hire a private investigator to look into Vanessa's death?"

"Twice. No luck." Kev ran his fingers along the edge of the computer tablet that lay in front of him. The screen lit, flashing his corporate logo. "And you're not here because you want to solve my daughter's murder. You want to end the cloud of suspicion over your parents."

"Don't you want the same for yourself and your family?"

He spun his thick silver wedding band around his finger. "There's no cloud over us. My wife and I proved where we were at all times. Your parents didn't."

"A dozen people saw my mother at Q.C.'s birthday party."

Q.C. disappeared from a local pizza restaurant and arcade on her fifth birthday.

"But not your father."

I couldn't deny that. My dad never accounted for his time well enough to satisfy police.

"They both have alibis for when your daughter was kidnapped," I said.

"Only from each other," Kev said. "And my wife was in a crowd of people when Vanessa was taken."

"And you?"

The newspapers from the eighties reported only that witnesses confirmed Ted Kev's whereabouts far from the school where his daughter was last seen.

He waved his hand as if physically swatting away my question. "I don't have to answer your questions."

"You don't," I said. "But no alibi is perfect. And until the killer is found, there will always be questions about you. And your wife."

Kev shifted, swinging his chair and legs to one side while keeping his body and face angled toward me. "Say I agree with you. You're hardly neutral. My lawyers tell me if you find anything that proves your parents' guilt, you don't have to turn it over to the police. Or to me."

"I'll follow every lead. Wherever it points. But you're right in one way." I folded one hand over the other. Both felt clammy. "As an attorney I have a duty to protect my clients. Including my parents. It'll be up to them what I share if it points to them."

Kev frowned. "As I said. One-sided."

"But if I learn anyone else killed the girls, including other relatives or friends of my parents, I'll turn over the information to the police and prosecutor."

I didn't add that the family members closest to me were already ruled out. My Gram, who raised me, had been in the hospital with my grandfather in Chicago when Q.C. disappeared. And both had been at work when Kev's daughter was taken. Family members on my mother's side had been home in

Pennsylvania. And my oldest sister, Kendra, was seven when all this happened.

Kev studied me. "My wife and I — going through all this again, I don't see the value. It's taken a long time, but we let go of the past. Accepted not knowing."

"My parents try, but they haven't been able to."

"You have to or it eats you alive." His lips clenched into a straight line for an instant, then he let out a breath. "I can't risk my wife going back to that so you can play detective."

"I'm not playing. I can't promise success, but I've solved crimes before where the police got nowhere."

"I know. That's the only reason you're here. My lawyers did a lot of digging on you."

"Then help me," I said, forgetting Ty's advice. But there was no point in pretending. "If I find the truth it might bring you and your wife peace."

"Peace?" Kev's sigh sunk his body low in the chair. His jaw loosened. His hands flopped into his lap. "Not sure peace is possible. Nothing can bring Vanessa back."

I almost stretched my hand across the cold marble table toward him. But I didn't. He might not want comfort from me because he was right. My main goal wasn't to help him.

"I'm sorry about what happened to your daughter," I said. "And sorry if my investigation will cause you or your wife pain. But I can't help my parents without looking into your daughter's death, too. I wanted you to know before I started calling anyone you know. So you wouldn't be shocked."

He nodded. "I appreciate that."

I'd thought about not contacting the Kevs before looking into their daughter's murder. I might be able to take more witnesses by surprise that way. But as soon as I questioned anyone close to them, the Kevs would hear about it. And they were more likely to cooperate if they didn't feel blindsided.

Also, though I saw them as murder suspects, a lot of people

saw my parents that way, too. As much as I could, I wanted to treat the Kevs with respect. The way I wished the police treated my parents.

Ted walked me back to the reception area where more chrome chairs grouped around a low table. He said he needed time to talk with his wife before deciding if they'd answer my questions.

He opened the glass door for me. "The odds are against your learning anything useful."

"Everything's against me. Including time. But I need to try."

He asked that I not contact his wife until I heard back from him. I agreed. But I didn't plan to wait forever. If I didn't hear back in a few days, I'd find a way to get in touch with her.

For now, though, the person I needed to get in touch with was my mother.

3

PARENTS TWICE OVER

THE SKY SPIT rain as I parked in front of my parents' house in Edwardsville, Illinois. I waited on the wide porch until the BMW's headlights turned off, listening to the rain hit the eaves. My friend Lauren had been right about the car. It handled well, especially on the expressway. And if Ted Kev noticed it when he walked me out, it might have made him more likely to see me as an accomplished, successful attorney he could trust.

I let myself in the front door. "Mom?"

The house, an old Victorian my dad's always working on, smelled of wood, dust, and fresh paint. I sat on a narrow wood bench in the foyer to take off my boots. A giant gold-framed photo hung above me. In it, the original Q.C. wore a flouncy white dress and cradled a pink stuffed bear in her arms.

She and my oldest sister take after my mother. Blondes with peaches and cream skin and rounded cheeks. I got my father's olive skin and wiry, wavy-to-curly black hair. His is mostly gray now.

"Mom? You awake?"

Still no answer.

My stockinged feet slipped on the worn hardwood as I

hurried to the living room. My mother lay curled on the couch in a fetal position. But her hair looked combed and her powder blue sweatsuit clean. I stepped closer. Her chest rose and fell in an even rhythm.

More framed photos of Q.C. as a toddler sat on the end tables, angled toward the couch. I loosened my grip on my phone and started back toward the foyer to get my rolling suitcase.

"Q.C.?" my mother said.

I swung around. "Quille."

She sat and rubbed her fingers over her eyes. "You know I meant you."

"Sure," I said, though I didn't.

When I was a kid and my mother bragged about the singing and acting talent of the daughter she called "my Q.C.," she never meant me. And with my coming to town for this investigation, she might easily have been dreaming about my sister.

My mother smoothed her sweatshirt. "Did you bring tea?"

I pulled a green striped paper bag from my shoulder bag. "Chocolate spice crème."

"Not the chai?"

"No, sorry. They don't make it anymore."

From around when I turned five, I made hot tea for my mother every Saturday morning. On good days my mother gave me a voice lesson after tea, then played piano for another hour so we could sing together. Sometimes after that she watched TV or read magazines with my dad, my sister, and me. A few Saturdays she even joined us for pizza and board games at night.

On bad Saturdays, she went back to bed after tea and stayed there the rest of the weekend.

I thought the tea flavors caused my mother's moods. I carefully compared the descriptions of each tea before choosing one, asking my Gram the meaning of words I didn't know.

There was a four-week stretch of good days one April after I switched to Imperial Earl Grey.

As an adult, I know it wasn't about the tea. But it's a hard habit to break. Before this visit, I'd spent twenty or thirty hours combing websites and visiting tea shops in Chicago. But no one sold chocolate chai latte tea like the one my mother loved that was discontinued.

Now she shook her head. "Too late in the day for caffeine."

"I brought herbal, too. Cherry blossom."

"It'll give me acid reflux."

"I'll make it half strength."

She sighed. "Just make the chocolate."

I kept an eye on the clock as the tea steeped. It filled the kitchen with the smell of dark chocolate and cinnamon. My mother squinted when she tasted it. "I suppose you can leave some when you go."

I put the tin in the cabinet over the sink. Her latest medication must still be working. Usually, she's harder to please.

My mother pushed her mug aside. "What're you doing today? For the investigation?"

"Talking to the retired police chief." I glanced at my phone. "In twenty minutes."

"Chief Highbottom? But he thinks we did it."

"I know." I sat across from her and tasted the tea. It was spicier than I expected. "But he remembers a lot about the case. Things that weren't in the newspapers."

"Tell him to send you his notes. Then you won't need to talk to him."

"He's not willing to share them. And I can't force him."

My mother's lower lip puffed out. "Well, that's not a very good start."

"It's not the start. I already talked to other people. And researched." I topped off my mug and stood. "I need to get ready for the call."

"I still don't know why you need the chief. Nothing he says will be helpful."

"You might be right," I said, my stock answer to difficult clients. "But I need to know why he thinks what he does. And I can't only talk to people who are on your side."

I SHIFTED the camera so my laptop screen showed the closet's slatted folding doors rather than the double bed in my parents' attic guest room.

"He already agreed to talk, Quille." My friend Danielle, a criminal defense lawyer who shares an office with me in Chicago, was already signed onto Zoom. "How the room looks won't change his mind."

Danielle used to be a cop — one of the first Black women patrol officers in Chicago — and then a prosecutor before switching sides. I asked her to help because she knew so much about police procedure and criminal law.

"How much is the chief allowed to tell me?" I said.

"Nothing that could hurt the investigation since the cases were never solved. But this late in the day I'm guessing he'll be pretty open."

My laptop dinged when Retired Edwardsville Chief of Police Donald P. Highbottom entered the waiting room. He still lived in town but spent January through March in Florida.

I straightened my suit jacket. Then I clicked the button to let in the man who led the investigation into my parents.

4

THE CHIEF

Highbottom's hair was dull gray. His face looked more rounded than in the photos I'd seen from when he investigated Q.C.'s case. But his navy-blue crew neck shirt fit snugly across a broad chest and muscled upper arms. I wouldn't count him out in a fight. His virtual backdrop mixed American flags and police shields, giving him an official look.

I wondered how he felt about being retired.

"Sure you're ready for this, Miss Davis?" he said, his voice tinny.

"As I can be."

As I filled him in on why I asked Danielle to join, his eyes shifted to look at her on screen. "With your experience, you know when a child's killed, it's nearly always a parent. Or a parent's partner."

"But there are two sets of parents here," Danielle said. "And no hint of abuse in Quille's family."

The school and medical records I'd been able to get for Q.C., my sister Kendra, and me showed no sign anyone thought we might have been abused. I looked into it because my research showed that when children are killed, it's usually by their parents. Often it's escalating child abuse.

But there are other reasons, all of which horrified me.

So-called altruistic killings, where the parent sees the world as too harsh and decides to "save" the child by sending them on to an afterlife. The killing of an unwanted child the parent views as standing in the way of their happiness. And murder as revenge on a spouse who cheats, or pays too much attention to the child, or does anything else that, in the mind of the killer, warrants punishment.

Though I wasn't exactly a neutral observer, as Ted Kev pointed out, I couldn't believe any fit my parents.

"There isn't always a record of abuse," Highbottom said.

"But no neighbor, teacher, or relative I called so far saw any sign of it," I said.

"And Quille's mom has a strong alibi," Danielle said.

"That doesn't mean she couldn't have helped plan. Brenda Davis stays in view of dozens of people while Cliff Davis lures their daughter away from the party." The chief's eyes shifted again, this time toward me. "Your sister would trust her dad."

"My sister trusted everyone. My aunt said she was always giving out hugs at tiny tots choir concerts. Or at preschool or the shopping mall."

Highbottom's jowls shook as he nodded. "I did hear that. But your dad would have the easiest time getting her to leave her own birthday party. And your mother didn't need to be part of the plan. He could have committed both murders and your mother covered for him."

I kept my face blank, grateful for all my practice doing that as a lawyer. Going into the call I knew Highbottom saw my parents as capable of cold-blooded murder. It didn't make it easier to hear it aloud, but most cops would see the case that way.

Over the last month, I'd read everything I could find about

JonBenét Ramsey, the child beauty pageant winner killed in the nineties in Colorado. DNA evidence had recently suggested a stranger did it. But for decades, detectives and most of the public felt sure one family member or another killed her and the others covered it up.

Danielle's eyebrows raised. "After he killed her daughter? Pretty extreme."

"Not if Brenda Davis believed someone else did it and didn't want her husband to get in trouble."

"My parents cooperated with police," I said. "Answered questions. Agreed to all your searches without warrants, waited forever to get a lawyer. That doesn't sound like people hiding something."

Highbottom scratched his cheek. "I'm sure your friend has plenty of guilty clients who did all those things."

I glanced at Danielle. She sighed. "He's not wrong. If stupidity were a defense, I'd win ninety percent of my cases."

"My mother's not an easy person to deal with," I said. "If my dad asked her to lie for him when Q.C.'s and Vanessa Kev's bodies were found, she'd ask why. Not give him an alibi no questions asked."

Highbottom shrugged. "By that time your mother probably didn't remember what either of them did the day the Kev girl went missing. If your father claimed he also didn't remember, she wouldn't find it strange. They'd talk. Sort it out. And surprise, surprise, once they do, both tell the same story."

I noticed Danielle give a faint nod and knew she'd argue exactly that if she were the prosecutor. It didn't help that as late as when I was in middle school my mother spent entire days curled in the corner on the couch, hair oily and flat, wearing pajamas. Though she held a script to help me run my lines, she usually seemed unaware of me. Sometimes I flubbed a line on purpose to check. She never noticed.

There must have been many days like that after Q.C. disappeared.

"Still, it's a lot of guesswork." Danielle brushed a stray fringe of dark hair from her forehead. "Any evidence against Cliff or Brenda?"

"The killer bound both girls' wrists and ankles with purple duct tape. Same type Cliff Davis's bluegrass band used. The local hardware store sold it."

"That can't be the only place that sold purple duct tape." I clicked to Google and started to run a search. Then I closed the screen. You could order anything online today, including duct tape in all the colors of the rainbow. That wasn't so in the 1980s.

"It wasn't just the color," Highbottom said. "The weight, the fiber count, the adhesive all matched. None of that is unique. But it's not common."

"Anything else?" I said.

"Your parents cooperated on some things. But they blocked us on others. They went to a local reverend for marriage counseling before and after Q.C. was kidnapped. But they and the reverend refused to say what they talked about."

"Counseling's confidential." I gripped the handle of my empty mug, hiding my shock. My mother didn't believe in talk therapy. She told me that over and over when I saw a therapist in college. "That's like asking what they talked about with their lawyer."

"And it's not a good enough reason to target the Davises more than the Kevs," Danielle said. "What am I missing?"

Highbottom inched his chair closer to the screen. His face loomed large. "Cliff Davis, Quille's father, is the only one connected to both murdered girls."

5

CONNECTIONS

I PACED in the small area in front of the desk as Highbottom explained. During the nine months before Q.C. and Vanessa were killed, my dad's bluegrass band, the St. Louis Bluegrass Boys, played in bars, coffee houses, and universities in the St. Louis area. According to Highbottom, two of the bars and one coffeehouse were in Clayton, the small city where the Kevs lived at the time.

I stood still, rested my hands on the back of the chair, and bent toward the camera. "That's it? His band played all over the country."

"But during those nine months he played in the St. Louis area twice as often as the entire year before. Could've met the Kevs. Or the girl herself."

"Could have," Danielle said. "No proof he did?"

Highbottom admitted there wasn't. He also didn't know if the Kevs were bluegrass fans.

I took a seat again and scrolled down Ted Kev's company profile. "Ted's company biography says he enjoys classical and jazz. His wife's lists her as CFO and co-founder, but no personal details."

"It's a possible point of contact," Highbottom said. "And there are none between the Kevs and Q.C."

"I thought you didn't handle that part of the case," I said.

"Kept my ear to the ground. And had a friend on the St. Louis police force."

I wished I could talk to the man who spearheaded the Kev side of the case. But he died five years before my mother asked me to investigate. And no one from the Missouri state police or the FBI was willing to talk to me because it remained an open investigation. At least in theory.

"What about the Kevs' alibis?" I clicked over to my spreadsheet about the case.

"The wife, Gail, was in plain sight at a dance recital the whole time her daughter was taken," Highbottom said. "But the day Q.C. was kidnapped she was at home alone."

That fit with what I knew from the news reports.

"And the husband?" Danielle said.

"At a fishing cabin with a man named James Smith the day his daughter disappeared. Also when Q.C. was taken."

"Same person alibied Kev both times?" Danielle said.

Highbottom nodded. "Smith is married to Gail Kev's sister. Makes the alibis weaker. But the two families owned the cabin together. The men went there often on weekends."

I scribbled notes on my yellow legal pad. I find it easier to listen when I handwrite instead of typing, plus there are no clicking keys to distract others on the call. Later I'd enter everything into the spreadsheet.

"Any other girls kidnapped and murdered around the time Vanessa and Q.C. were found?" Danielle asked. "Or after?"

"After?" I said.

A door banged and the hardwood floor vibrated under my feet. I guessed my dad was home. He parks in the garage and comes in the back door. It slams if you forget to ease it shut.

"Serial killers typically don't just stop," Danielle said.

Highbottom rubbed his fingers over his mustache. “None around here. But about a year after the Davises moved to the Chicago area a seven-year-old girl went missing. Never found.”

“You’re blaming my dad for that?” I pressed my palms together in my lap, out of sight of the camera. “Over 2.5 million people live in Chicago. A lot of children must go missing.”

“Not as many young ones each year as you might think,” Highbottom said. “Older kids, teens, they go missing. Mostly they run away. Little ones, not so much.”

The question of later kidnappings and murders had never occurred to me, though it should have. But none of what Highbottom said proved anything about my parents. I pointed that out.

“That’s why they were never arrested,” Highbottom said. “And to be clear, I’m not saying I’m convinced they’re guilty. But they’re the only viable suspects.”

“You never interviewed the Kevs?” Danielle said.

Highbottom shook his head. “Not personally. Until both girls were found in the same grave, no one connected the crimes.”

“Why not?” Danielle said. “St. Louis and Edwardsville are in different states, but they can’t be more than twenty-five miles apart. The girls were the same age. Both taken from a public place. Both performers.”

“Lots of little girls sing in choirs or dance in recitals,” Highbottom said.

He shouldn’t tell my mother that. According to her, Q.C. had been unique. A rising star.

“What about after the girls were found together?” I said. “You still didn’t interview the Kevs?”

Highbottom frowned. “I’ve got no jurisdiction in Missouri. And the state police and the FBI took charge right off anyway.”

“Anyone tell the police in St. Louis about Q.C.?” said Danielle.

Highbottom crossed his arms over his chest. "Talked with the chief there myself. But we both pegged Q.C. as a domestic matter. She was taken from her own party, a family event. Cliff Davis claimed he was strolling the neighborhood during it. Plenty of time and opportunity to grab his daughter."

I bit my lip. Highbottom had made up his mind about my dad and his certainty probably swayed the St. Louis chief. I longed to confront him about it. But I wanted him to keep helping me. Putting him on the defensive wouldn't make that likely.

"So the police never looked at the Kevs for Q.C.?" Danielle said.

"Sure, but only after the girls were found together."

"Any evidence that shows a serial killer — a stranger — killed both girls?" Danielle asked.

I expected the chief to say No. Instead, he told us the killer might have taken some sort of memento from each girl. He wouldn't tell us what, as it was information the police withheld from the public. But that could suggest a stranger serial killer. He added, though, that the missing mementos might have simply gotten lost, especially since the killer moved the bodies from wherever the murders took place to a single grave.

After he signed off, I asked Danielle what she thought of Highbottom.

"You won't want to hear this." Behind her, the outer hallway lights in our office suite dimmed as they switched to energy saver lighting. "But he's not entirely off base for thinking your parents are more likely than the Kevs."

I nearly dropped my pen. "Why?"

"Think of it as KIS — Keep It Simple. Simplest answer here is one of two scenarios. A stranger starts with Q.C., gets a taste for killing, moves on to another girl. Or someone who knew Q.C. killed her, then killed Vanessa and buried the girls together to make it look like a serial killer if they were found.

The second's more likely because in real life stranger killers are rare."

I rolled my pen forward and back on the desk. "But couldn't someone on the Kev side plan to kill Vanessa and try it first with an unrelated girl? Less chance of getting caught if there's no personal connection."

"A practice run."

"Right." The smell of green peppers and olives sautéing drifted up from downstairs. My dad must be cooking.

"Possible," Danielle said. "But more complicated."

"But I — you think my parents — I can't believe they could do that."

"You asked me to be an objective sounding board."

"As my friend, though?"

"As your friend who's a criminal defense lawyer, murderers come in all shapes and sizes. Lots of them don't look or sound or seem different from anyone else. And rage, jealousy, grief — they can make anyone do anything. But knowing you, it's hard to believe anyone who raised you could go out and murder another girl in cold blood."

I appreciated the attempt, but Danielle's words didn't make me feel better. My parents didn't raise me. Not really.

6

RELYING ON THE FACTS

My mother's frown deepened the faint lines around her mouth and between her light blond eyebrows. "Why a contract? It's not like we're paying you."

After dinner — my favorite, skillet macaroni and cheese with green olives and green peppers — I had cleared the dishes and loaded the dishwasher. Now I sat on one side of the dining room table. My parents sat on the other, cups of decaf coffee steaming in front of them. Next to my dad, with his olive skin and wiry gray and black hair, my mother looked paler than usual.

"It makes clear we have an attorney-client relationship," I said. "That way anything you or Dad tell me, unless it's about an on-going crime, stays between us. I share it only if you want me to."

More photos of Q.C. stood on the built-in antique buffet alongside photos of my oldest sister, Kendra. In her baby photo Kendra smiles. Her peaches and cream skin glows. As a grade-schooler, she laughs as she pushes Q.C. on the swings and then climbs out of a treehouse my dad built at their first house in Edwardsville.

But in her eighth-grade graduation photo, one of two from after Q.C.'s death, Kendra stares into the camera, expressionless. Her shiny blond hair is pulled into a tight ponytail. Her high school graduation photo is a candid shot, though she still wears her cap and gown. I'm ten, and I cling to her side, my wavy, messy dark hair flying in the wind. Kendra ignores me, smirking at something or someone off to the side.

My dad pushed the sugar bowl toward my mother.

She stirred two teaspoons of sugar into her coffee. "You make it sound like we're hiding something. We told the police everything."

"It's not about hiding things. The formal contract is so clients can say what they want to their lawyers without being afraid the other side, or the police, will learn about it. And turn it against them. So if there's anything you were worried about sharing with the police —"

"There's nothing." My mother put on her reading glasses, a new pair with tiny crystals along the top rims.

Wearing pretty glasses and reading the contract added to my sense that my mother was doing well. I hoped the investigation wouldn't undo that.

"Great. But if anything comes to mind later, you can tell me."

"That won't happen." My mother pointed to the third paragraph. "What's this about our duties and relying on the facts we tell you?"

"It's in all my contracts. Sometimes clients don't tell me what I need to know. They forget something. Or think a fact doesn't matter. This reminds them I work based on what they tell me."

My mother took off her glasses and glared at me. "You're talking to other people, too. Shouldn't you be more worried about them?"

"I will be. I am. But they're not my clients."

"Brenda." My dad closed his hand over my mother's. "Quille's doing us a favor. Putting in a lot of time and effort. Let's do things her way."

He was trying to help, but he made it sound like I was being difficult. "It's not my way. The Illinois bar requires —"

"Favor?" My mother folded a corner of the contract. "This is her sister. She ought to care what happened to her sister."

I opened my mouth to speak, but my dad shot me a look, his graying eyebrows lowered. I nodded and glanced out the window. The neighbors' yard lights highlighted my parents' cherry tree, which would be budding soon. At home in Chicago the trees in the nearest park remain bare until mid-April or later. But spring comes earlier in southern Illinois.

Dad took the last page, signed it, and handed my mother the pen. "The sooner you sign the sooner we can all relax. And talk about something pleasant."

"All right, all right. I just wanted to know what it meant."

"I'm glad you asked," I said. "I want you to understand it."

I slid the contract into my accordion folder. And tried not to think about how easily my dad got my mother to sign.

The rest of the evening I focused on legal work, most of it relating to a brand new case. My phone rang as I finished typing an email to the client, who failed to mention when he hired me that there was a court date next week. That meant flying home to Chicago unless Danielle could cover it. I'd hoped to stay in Edwardsville for at least two weeks before popping back for a couple days.

Everything Highbottom said churned through my mind as I lay in bed that night. In my loft condo at home sirens, rumbling elevators, railroad bells, and clacking L trains blur into background noise that lulls me to sleep. Here, the lack of city street sounds meant my ears caught each yard noise. A little after two in the morning a shuddering sensation woke me, as if that door downstairs slammed again.

But when I crept out to the stairwell, I heard only the buzz of kitchen appliances, my mother's cuckoo clock ticking, and a few random creaks. I returned to the guest room and peered out the dormer window. But with no moon and no high rises or all-night convenience stores to cast spillover light, I saw only darkness.

I fell asleep sometime after that. The phone startled me awake in the morning. It was Gail Kev. She wanted to meet in person before deciding whether to help me investigate.

7

QUILLE GETS QUESTIONED

THE HIGH-CEILINGED coffee house in Clayton, Missouri, smelled of dark coffee with an undertone of woodsmoke. An elegant silver-haired woman in a pink Chanel suit waved at me from her seat near a stone fireplace.

She'd told me she needed to leave by nine-thirty for a board meeting. It was eight forty-five now.

"Mind grabbing my hazelnut latte, dear?" she said after we shook hands. "I saw this spot and snagged us seats. For privacy."

"Of course."

Gail Kev's haircut exposed small, perfectly shaped ears with diamond studs in them. Like her husband, she was nearly seventy. But unlike him, the fine lines around her eyes barely showed. Jewels embellished her Manolo Blahnik satin flats. I guessed they ran close to a thousand dollars.

Not shy about letting the world know she had money.

I felt grateful I'd worn one of my more upscale business casual outfits — Kate Spade cuffed denim jeans and low-heeled boots, a white button-down shirt, and a tailored gray blazer. Still, its total cost probably ran less than a tenth of Gail's ensemble.

She insisted on ordering a drink for me from her phone and paying. I returned a few minutes later with two steaming mugs.

"Thank you, Miss Davis."

"Please. Call me Quille." I sank into an armchair, then immediately straightened my back. This wasn't a social visit, and I wasn't with a friend.

"Like your sister." She smiled, but didn't suggest I call her Gail.

"She was Q.C.," I said. "I'm Quille."

"It's important to differentiate yourself, I imagine. Where did you go to high school, Quille?"

The question surprised me. "I did independent study."

As a lawyer some people ask where I went to law school. Occasionally I'm asked about college. But rarely high school. I suppose if I attended near St. Louis it would tell her something about neighborhoods and, with that, social status and income level.

"Homeschooling?" Gail said.

I nodded, though I don't call it homeschooling because people tend to assume that's for religious reasons. I did it to leave enough time for acting. If Gail got the wrong impression, though, I didn't mind. I haven't noticed religious people being more honest than anyone else, but a lot of people assume they are. Which could make her more apt to open up to me.

Gail asked if I had belonged to a sorority.

"No. The Chicago campus of University of Illinois didn't have much Greek life. And those of us who commuted rarely joined."

She pressed one hand to her chest as if about to say the *Pledge of Allegiance*. "I'm from Dallas."

"Oh?"

"Sororities matter there. You grew up in Chicago?"

"No, in LaGrange. A suburb about twenty-five minutes west of downtown."

"I don't know it. A nice place?"

"Most people like it. Lots of local shops and restaurants. And Victorian houses with big yards."

I hadn't lived in one of those houses. I drifted between my parents' apartment and my Gram's across the hall, spending more time in the latter. But if Gail was looking for common ground, I doubted apartment living fit the bill. And she'd asked about the town, not my home.

"Didn't your husband have me researched?" I said.

"Oh, yes. We learned plenty about your law firm. And your job at the accounting firm before that. A little about your acting career. But your childhood information couldn't be vetted."

I shifted in my chair. I wasn't sure I believed Gail. My Gram owned the entire apartment building where I grew up, so my parents' names wouldn't be on it. Plus, Davis is a common last name. But I didn't buy that the vast world of public records and algorithms couldn't connect us.

Gail folded her hands in her lap. "What can you do, Quille, that the police, or the private detectives we hired so long ago, can't?"

"It's more that I'm not either of those. Being questioned by police, or by a licensed investigator, can make people tense. The way your heart rate might go up when your doctor checks your pulse. Or just when you walk into the doctor's office."

Gail Kev tapped a manicured finger against the edge of her mug. "White coat syndrome."

"Yes. People relax more with me. And when they relax more, they remember more."

A wide archway separated the area where we sat from a music room. It had smaller tables and more chairs. A harpist set up at the long end of it, plinking a few strings.

"And say things they shouldn't?" Gail said.

"Sometimes."

I didn't want to tell her much more. Partly because there's no real trick to it. Or, there is, but it's just that I listen and do my best to respond in a kind, thoughtful way to what people tell me. Part of why legal clients hire me is that I'm good at understanding the other side of each case, which means I can do a better job arguing against it. And as an investigator, that's almost my entire secret.

That and being willing to take too many risks, at least according to my boyfriend Ty. And a few other people who care about me. But, of course, they're wrong.

The harpist's smooth tones echoed through the room, adding a calming feel that contrasted Gail's tense shoulders and posture.

Gail took a long sip of her hazelnut coffee. "Do you pretend you're there for another reason? So they don't know you're investigating?"

"Not with most people."

"But some? How do you decide?"

If Gail Kev was the killer, telling her too much might give her an edge. But if she was smart enough to get away with two murders for decades, I wasn't telling her anything she didn't know.

"Partly what's right, partly what keeps things simple."

A shiver went through me as I recalled Danielle's Keep It Simple theory and what it suggested about my parents.

"For example?" Gail said.

"To me, it wouldn't be right to pretend to be someone else to get you to talk about your daughter's death. You had a terrible loss. So did all the people who loved your daughter. But if I'm talking to, say, your mail carrier, that's different. If it's simpler, I might give another reason for my questions. Or just say I'm working on a case."

"But can't you get more information by, let's say, browbeating witnesses?"

"The police did that to my parents and their friends. It didn't solve my sister's murder."

"They didn't browbeat us." Gail's face paled as she gazed into the unlit fireplace. "But they searched our house, our yard, our company headquarters. Twice. And questioned us. Many times. And our families. And our friends. Still, I was surprised. They were polite."

I sipped my chai latte, which tasted like it had an extra pump of sweet syrup, wondering how much the police's treatment of the Kevs related to their position in society. They'd barely launched the business in the mid-1980s. Ted Kev didn't become uber-wealthy until decades later. But he and Gail belonged to the local Jaycees and Lions Club. Plus, her family owned property not only in Dallas but all over the country, including in the St. Louis area.

My parents, on the other hand, were a bluegrass guitar player/part owner of a music store and a grade school teacher who gave piano lessons on the side.

I stayed silent, waiting to see if Gail would say more. She did.

"Then after Nessa's body was found the FBI came and did all the same things."

"That's what you called her? Nessa?"

"Everyone did. Vanessa seemed too adult somehow. Though I thought when she grew up, if she became a dancer...." She shifted on the loveseat and cleared her throat. "Vanessa Kev sounds like a dancer's name, doesn't it?"

I thought about the list of motives for parents who kill their children. It didn't sound like Gail Kev hadn't wanted her daughter. And nothing I'd found in my research suggested Vanessa was abused, though that might never have been made public.

I didn't know if Ted Kev had wanted a child.

"She was taken from a dance recital, correct?" I said.

Gail placed her mug exactly in the center of the table and squared her shoulders. "Don't think I haven't thought about that. That if I discouraged her from dancing, she might be alive today."

"Oh, no. No. I didn't mean that. I'd never think that."

"I would. I do. Just as I imagine your parents wish they never had that birthday party."

"They never hosted a birthday party after that. And didn't let me or my other sister attend them."

"See?" Gail twisted her wedding band on her finger. "I feel for your mother. Everyone blames mothers. Like that poor girl JonBenét Ramsey's mother. People acted as if it was her fault her daughter was killed. All because she let her daughter compete in child beauty pageants."

I thought that oversimplified the press coverage a bit. But I had seen entire video segments devoted to the beauty pageants.

"Did people blame you? Or criticize you?" I said.

"For not being home enough."

"But you left the company."

"I still put in five or six hours a week. Consulting. Back then that was considered neglecting my child. Especially one so young as Nessa."

"I'm so sorry."

Gail drank the last of her coffee. "My husband talked to that Detective Sergeant you work with in Chicago. He said good things. But Ted thinks it'll be too hard for you to learn anything new after all this time. And it'll be too distressing, especially for me, to revisit all of it."

"What do you think?" I said.

8

REVELATION

My dad sat on the wooden swing on my parents' wide front porch fingerpicking his Martin D35 with bare fingers rather than metal fingerpicks. The Martin is a large-bodied acoustic guitar with deep, rich tones. His has a few scratches across the back from decades of use.

I climbed the stairs and sat across from him in the old wood rocker. The song he played was familiar, but I couldn't place it.

"Any luck?" he said.

"If you define few answers and plenty of delay as luck. Gail Kev's not sure yet if she'll help." I set my shoulder bag on the porch floor. The early-blooming snowdrop flowers near the stairs gave the air a faint honey scent. "No work today?"

"Going in late. Bad night for your mom. I'm surprised you didn't hear her pacing."

"I got up around two. I thought I heard someone in the yard." I told him about the sounds.

"Raccoons. The recycling bin was knocked over last night."

"They like plastic and glass?"

"Probably trying to get into the garbage. I'm better at remembering to seal that."

The strings squeaked as he slid his fingers down the guitar neck.

"*Fair and Tender Ladies*?" I said.

"Yep."

It's a traditional song that warns young women not to trust men who court them. I could only remember one line: *First they'll appear, and then they're gone.*

"Is Mom having a lot of bad nights?"

"A few more than usual. Talking about Q.C.'s death — it's hard. She wants you to go ahead, though."

I leaned forward, clasping my hands together. "You're sure?"

"She'll be all right. She upped her anti-anxiety meds." My father dampened the strings, cutting off the last note he played. "I've been thinking about what you said last night."

"Which part?"

"Things we might not have told police. There was something. Doesn't change anything, so I'm not sure I — well, not sure I should say anything. It's not only my secret."

"There's a secret?"

"But we asked you to do this thing. To investigate. It doesn't seem right to put you through all this and keep things from you." He tapped his fingers on the guitar's body, making light thumping sounds. "And your Gram and Aunt Cathy know. I don't want them worrying what's okay to tell you or not."

Gram is my dad's mother. Cathy's his sister. She and my dad both attended Southern Illinois University and settled in Edwardsville after graduating. But Aunt Cathy stayed when my parents moved to LaGrange to live in Gram's building. She's been a huge support for my mom since my parents moved back into town. Sometimes I thought she was closer to my mom than my dad.

"What is it?" I said.

My dad shifted his guitar so it lay flat on its back across his knees. "I didn't want Q.C."

9

THE UNWANTED CHILD

I PRESSED my feet flat on the porch to stop the rocking chair's motion. My dad had just calmly told me he fit into one of the five categories of people who kill their children.

"Didn't —?"

"Not at first." He rubbed his hand over the strings near the sound hole.

I walked to the porch railing and gripped it. And reminded myself not everyone's excited when they learn a baby's on the way.

"Were you and Mom having problems?"

"No. Things were great. Kendra was four. Finally in preschool. The band was getting gigs all over. We decided in the summer your mom would go on the road with me."

"Mom?" I turned around to look at him. "But her teaching — didn't she always —"

" — teach summer school. We decided this time she'd take summer break. And pause the piano and voice lessons."

"Could you afford that?"

Dad shrugged. "The band's income doubled that year. And the store was doing pretty well."

My dad and a partner run a music store together, but it's never been much of a money maker. When we lived in LaGrange the partner took care of everything.

"And you'd take Kendra, too?" I said.

"We were going to send her for a month and a half to your grandparents in Pennsylvania."

"Really?"

I talked to my grandparents on my mother's side when I began rounds of phone calls to get background on the murders. But I barely knew them. My mother had never spoken to them during my lifetime. They gave me as little information as possible when I called. It didn't matter much for the investigation. They were in Pennsylvania when Vanessa Kev disappeared.

But on the call, they didn't ask anything about my parents, Kendra, or me.

"The rest of the time she would have stayed with Cathy," my dad said. "Kendra was excited about that."

"She never told me."

"Probably doesn't remember. She was four. And it never happened." Dad propped the guitar against the house. The yellow siding looked especially worn and chipped next to its polished wood body.

"So Q.C. wasn't — planned?"

"Not planned. Not unplanned. Your mom never felt right on birth control pills. We tried other methods on and off. I thought about a vasectomy. But neither of us wanted to say No forever to more children."

I glanced away and studied the front lawn, a mix of green and brown grass and mud, as he spoke. My dad and I didn't talk about sex or birth control. Neither did my mother and I. When I became a teenager, Gram had those conversations with me. And Kendra filled in the blanks.

"Was Mom unhappy about being pregnant?"

"If you ask her now — and I hope you don't — she'll say she was thrilled. But she was looking forward to going on the road. Sang back up and practiced for months so she could join us for some songs."

I drummed my fingers on the wide railing as my mind raced, barely taking in my dad's words. I worried I wouldn't recall them later. Normally I remember everything anyone says word-for-word. A leftover skill from years as an actor.

I wished I had asked to record him. I wished I could write down what he said. I wished I'd never started this investigation.

"Quille?" His voice, from behind me, sounded far away. "Should I not have told you?"

I shifted to face him again. He still looked like my dad, with his shoulder-length wavy hair, now mostly gray, and short trimmed beard, all the way gray.

"It's fine. I'm fine. It's good you told me. Why do you not want me to ask Mom about it?"

"It must haunt her like it does me. When you lose a child the way we did...when you lose a child, you feel guilt. You know you could have stopped it. If you just did one thing differently. One thing. For years I lay awake nights thinking about that. What one thing might have changed it."

"Chief Highbottom said you and Mom went to marriage counseling. Was that when you were having problems?"

His forehead creased. "We never went to marriage counseling. Your aunt thought we should. But your mom — well, you know. She thinks it's a waste of time. Talking to a stranger about your problems."

I nodded. "When you found out Mom was pregnant did you — I mean, how unhappy —" The worn railing pressed into my lower back. In my law practice, I ask people uncomfortable questions all the time. But this was my father.

He shook his head. "Never thought of ending the pregnancy. We accepted that life needed to go forward a different way."

10

ANOTHER VIEW

"YOUR DAD'S life went forward the same way." Aunt Cathy shifted her briefcase to her other hand and nodded toward the right fork on the path. "Your mom had to do the accepting. A lot of accepting."

We veered toward the pond on the east side of the medical complex where my aunt works. She's a vice president in charge of finance.

"It had to change things for him, too," I said.

My shoulders dropped and I let out a long breath as we settled on a bench under a leafy willow tree. In one way I don't know my Aunt Cathy that well. My parents moved away from Edwardsville not long after I was born. I only see her on holidays and occasional visits.

But I feel at ease with her. It's not just that we look alike, sharing the same coloring from my dad's side of the family. It's that the need to sort through each word before I speak, to choose exactly the right one, falls away when I'm with her. I can be myself.

And I know she's there for me. Like today. When I texted, she immediately made time for me.

"When he was home, sure, another child changed his life." Cathy slid her phone out of her briefcase and set it face up on the bench. "But he was on the road for eight or ten weeks at a time."

"Even in winter?" I didn't know the bluegrass world all that well. My dad stopped playing other than for fun before I was born. But I thought it revolved around summer festival season.

"A little less November through February." The sun shone down on us. Cathy unbuttoned her light wool coat. Underneath she wore a long-sleeved sweater and black dress pants. "But you know how performing works. You work when other people are off. Cliff's band played every weekend all year round. Lots of weeknights too."

I nodded. One reason I chose not to pursue full-time work in the arts was the schedule. Combined with low pay and uncertainty, making a life of it required greater love for the craft than I possessed.

"But Dad took care of Kendra and Q.C. during the day, right? If he was in town?" I said.

"Now and then. But Brenda took care of your sisters every day. Ran them back and forth to the sitter, or my place, before and after she taught."

A large goose followed by four smaller ones sailed across the pond. I shifted my weight, uncomfortable on the hard bench. I didn't love this picture of my dad.

"He spent time with me when I was a kid," I said.

Gram had done all the practical things. Making sure I studied, taking me to auditions, shopping for clothes or school supplies. But Dad and I watched movies together. And he came to the openings of all my plays until he and my mother moved back to Edwardsville.

"Different times. Different life." Cathy's phone buzzed with a text. She typed a quick response. "Sorry."

"Did Mom ever think about not sticking around?"

"I don't think so. She used to say it wasn't marriage. It was life."

"Meaning?"

"She wanted your dad to succeed with the band, make a good living at it, and have equal time for his family. In the real world, that rarely works."

The sun shifted so it shone right into my eyes. I put my sunglasses on. The leaves on the trees turned darker. "Is that what they argued about the day of the party?"

During the last two months I'd talked to everyone in my family by phone or video chat about that day. But there were gaps.

"What makes you think they were fighting?" Aunt Cathy wound her fingers into her hair, a habit I share with her. Sometimes for me it's an afterthought. Sometimes it's because I'm uneasy about something.

"Well, as I heard it, you and she sat at the counter drinking martinis at two in the afternoon at Q.C.'s birthday party. And Dad took a walk in the middle of the party, supposedly to get cake and balloons. Things you'd think he would've picked up ahead of time. Also, my mother was already taking pain pills because she strained her back. So why martinis?"

"That last one's easy. The pain pill wasn't doing much. She wanted a drink to kick it into gear."

"And my dad's walk?"

"He meant to get the cake earlier in the day and forgot. Then he stopped for more balloons, too. Your mom was not happy."

"How do you forget the cake for a birthday party?"

"That's what the police wanted to know. Your mom thought he did it purposely. To give himself a break from the party."

Despite being a musician my dad's pretty introverted, which isn't as unusual for performers as a lot of people think.

"Was she mad at him about it?" I said.

"You bet. I was, too. She got that he didn't like parties. But she had the girls day in and day out, and he couldn't stick around a few hours for a birthday party?"

"Who watched the kids at the party? All of them. Not just Q.C.," I said.

Cathy scrolled through email on her phone, answered one, and set the phone down again. "Everyone. There were nearly as many adults as kids."

My aunt told me a couple adults sat at each table when pizza was served. Then the kids scattered to play arcade games and it became a bit of a free-for-all. My cousin Abel, who was Aunt Cathy's only child, Q.C., and a handful of other children jumped around in a big wire cage full of colored plastic balls. According to Abel, whom I'd talked to by phone a week ago, Q.C. left to use the restroom.

"But you didn't see Q.C. head for the Women's Room?" I said.

"Girl's Room," Cathy said. "It was a very child-centric place. But no, I didn't see her. No one but Abel did."

That fit with what my parents' copy of the police report said.

I took out a small lined notepad and a pen. "What's your last memory of Q.C.?"

Cathy drummed her fingers on her thigh. "Her running around at the party. She wore a pretty purple dress I'd bought her with a flouncy skirt. She loved that dress. Your dad had put matching ribbons in her pigtails."

I put a star by the ribbons. No one had mentioned that detail before. Vanessa Kev's body was found with her hair dyed blond and put into pigtails, a style she didn't usually wear. They were tied with purple ribbons.

"How do you know my dad put the ribbons in her hair and not my mother?"

"Oh. Guess I don't. Your mom told me her back hurt so much Cliff got Q.C. ready for the party. I assumed that included the ribbons. But it could have been your mom."

Cathy told me the Girl's Room was just off the hallway that led to the glass back door that opened into the parking lot. The police believed someone watched from behind a parked car until they saw Q.C. alone in that hall. Then they lured her out and grabbed her.

My parents' car sat where they parked when they arrived — in the spot closest to the door. My parents checked inside the car and the trunk for Q.C. before calling the police. They also called a neighbor to see if Q.C. might have decided to wander home. She hadn't.

"How good is your memory of that day?" I said.

"A mix. Some crystal clear moments, most of it a blur."

A breeze that smelled of freshly cut lawn cooled my face. "What's clear?"

"Your mom screaming Q.C's name when we couldn't find her. I heard that a million times in my dreams over the next few years. Still hear it sometimes. And the second the two police officers pushed through the glass front door. My heart started skipping beats. Like I knew it meant we'd never get her back. Crazy, right? Most kids, they just wander off. The cops said that. But the uniforms, the badges, all in the middle of those kids sticky with pizza sauce and a table full of presents waiting to be opened." Cathy put her palm over her stomach. "I knew it in my gut. That she was really gone."

I asked if she remembered what Kendra did during the party, but she didn't. And my sister had almost no memory of it. She was seven years old then.

"What about other kids at the party? Anything stand out to you?"

She shook her head and her long, dark hair, so much like

mine, swung around her face. "Can't even remember all their names."

I opened the list of party guests on my iPad. Most I'd already talked to or tried to reach without success.

Cathy pointed to one I hadn't tried to call yet. "He's back in town. And he's Kendra's age. He might remember something. His little brother was one of Q.C.'s favorite playmates. Lived right down the street from your parents. In the church on the corner."

"In a church?"

"Their father's a reverend. Your parents knew him. The home was on the second floor, the church on the first. Probably still is."

My aunt's phone buzzed again. She glanced at it and started gathering things together. I zipped my long leather jacket and we retraced our steps around the lake.

"I heard my whole life about how talented and fun Q.C. was," I said. "I grew up with her photos all around me. It's hard to believe my parents didn't want her."

"They did. It just took them a bit to get there. Which isn't all that unusual."

Dad had seemed pretty clear about the not wanting part.

We paused as the path forked. One way led to the parking lot and the other toward a group of squat red brick buildings.

"What did Mom say when she found out she was pregnant? Did she tell you?"

I had waited to ask my aunt this until the end of our talk. I thought she might be more relaxed and less on guard. While I trusted her more than anyone else to tell me the truth, everyone has their biases. I felt sure hers was to believe the best of both my parents. I wanted to believe that, too, but it wouldn't help me understand the case against them.

"I was with her when she got the call." Cathy shifted her sunglasses higher on the bridge of her nose. "Your dad was in

Chattanooga at some bluegrass festival. Hadn't been home in six weeks. Didn't even know she was late."

"And?"

"She sank down on the couch and stared at the phone. Said maybe the doctor made a mistake. If she was lucky."

11

SISTER TALK

Saw Aunt Cathy. Can you talk?

I SAT in the parked car, trying to answer a client email while I waited for my sister Kendra to answer my text. But my aunt's words kept sounding in my head.

My mother's feelings on learning she was pregnant didn't mean she hadn't later wanted her daughter. But for the first time I wondered if all the talk about Q.C., all the photos of her, came from guilt. My mother's constant praise of Q.C. might be a way of insisting that yes, she had been excited about her second daughter.

I deleted my draft email. It made no sense. Before I could try again Kendra called. She was at work but could talk for a few minutes. I spilled out what I'd learned.

"All parents have mixed feelings, Quille," Kendra said when I finished. "If you had children, you'd know that."

I pressed my lips together. My sister loved to play the you-wouldn't-understand-because-you're-not-married or you're-not-a-parent card.

"Right," I said. "But we practically grew up in a shrine to

Q.C. It never occurred to me they weren't thrilled about her."

"Well, Dad might not have been right off. But believe me, Mom was. Everything was about Q.C. from Day One. Whether it would be a boy or girl. What the name should be. When Q.C. was a baby, she clapped her hands once when Mom played piano. Mom said she had the soul of a musician. Q.C. hummed when Mom taught voice lessons and Mom knew she'd be the future female Bill Monroe."

Bill Monroe, the father of bluegrass music, was an idol of my father's.

"That fits my theory, too," I said. "That she was overcompensating."

"Or she just liked Q.C. best. You had to burst out with that whole John Fogarty song before Mom noticed you could sing. And learn all the lyrics by heart. What was that song? Something about TV."

I searched my mental catalogue of Fogarty songs. "*I Saw It On TV.*"

"Yeah, that. You were three when you started singing it straight through. On the line about all the girls screaming you used to wave your little hands. Sorta cute. Almost made me like you despite the whole baby Q.C. thing."

I shifted the phone to my other ear. "The what thing?"

"Baby Q.C. That's what they called you. It was better for Baby Q.C. if we moved to LaGrange. Be quiet, Baby Q.C. needs to sleep. Gram came home from the store at lunchtime every day to take care of Baby Q.C."

How often Kendra ignored me when we were kids was starting to make more sense.

"She must've taken care of you, too," I said.

"Well, I was there. Obviously. But I made my own lunch. And Mom's. And Gram fed you."

Kendra was nine when the family moved to LaGrange. It

didn't seem terrible for a nine-year-old to make her own lunch and her mother's. But it wasn't ideal.

"Sorry. Never knew that," I said.

"At least you weren't a crier. The first Q.C. had colic and Mom got almost zero sleep the first nine months."

Parents of babies and toddlers who cry and cry sometimes lose it and shake or hit the child. But Q.C. was five years old when she was killed. Surely being colicky didn't play into her death.

"Quille? Still there?" Kendra said.

"Just thinking."

"Look, you know it wasn't Mom or Dad who did it. Focus on these Kev people."

"That's not how investigation works."

"Well, sure. But this is to make Mom feel better, not solve the case."

I pulled the phone away from my ear and stared at it. "Why would I do it if not to find the killer?"

"To make Mom feel better." She enunciated each word as if I might not have gotten it the first time.

"Right. Okay, I should go," I said. "I want to talk to our mother before Dad gets home."

"So touchy."

"It's fine. You were helpful. Talk later."

"Come visit," she said.

It took me a few minutes to get the car started because I forgot I'd put the parking brake on. The Chicago area's so flat I almost never use one.

When I pulled out of the parking lot, I really did mean to head back to my parents' house. Instead, I drove the opposite direction.

12

STORE STALKING

VANESSA KEV HAD NO SISTERS. No siblings at all. But she did have two cousins that the articles I'd read said she was close to. One worked as a sales manager at Nordstrom in St. Louis.

Her name was Kimberly Byerly, formerly Kimberly Smith. Daughter of the man who alibied Ted Kev for the disappearances of the two girls.

A faint aroma of expensive perfume hung in the air as I walked into the department store. Quiet piano music played overhead, sounding almost as if it were live. I asked a twenty-something young woman in the designer fashion department where I might find Kimberly Byerly. She directed me to Women's Attire.

After buying some new low-heeled pumps so I could carry a trademark metallic gray Nordstrom shopping bag, I headed for that department. Square-shaped cushioned armchairs were arranged near dressing rooms. I sank into one that angled toward Kimberly's section.

Shopping bag at my feet and peering at my phone, I hoped I looked like a tired friend waiting for someone to finish trying on outfits.

Kimberly was in her mid-fifties and her social media posts were few and careful. Mostly photos of woods and lakes in southern Illinois and western Missouri. Nothing about her son and daughter, though I knew from other research they lived on the West Coast and had two children each. Kimberly herself appeared only in group photos. She stood a head taller than those around her and looked fairly thin.

Her profile listed her as divorced but gave no details.

I didn't spot any employees who looked to be the right age and gender. After about fifteen minutes I moved to a chair at the other end of the department.

Twenty minutes later, on my third stakeout, someone behind me told a customer she'd call Kimberly, the manager. A moment later a tall, slim woman emerged from a side door. She wore fashionable black-framed glasses that added width to her narrow face.

I meandered to a rack of dress pants priced at over three hundred dollars for no reason I could see. I hadn't yet prepared questions for Kimberly, so on the drive over I'd decided to merely watch her to get a sense of who she was. But now that struck me as foolish. The landline number I had for her might be out of date. And if it wasn't, it's easy to say No to someone on the phone and hang up. An in-person ask is harder to avoid.

I inched along the rack, closer to Kimberly.

"Like I said," Kimberly told the customer, "I'm sorry about it being discontinued. Not sure what all the manufacturer was thinking. It's our most popular blazer. But alterations will fix it up for you. No charge."

Kimberly spoke with a southern drawl and sweetness more pronounced than most I heard in the St. Louis area. Had I not seen her first, I would have pictured a short, slightly plump woman with white hair wearing a flowered dress.

The customer thanked her. I was next to Kimberly before the customer got three steps away.

"Excuse me," I said. "Kimberly Byerly?"

"That's right, hon. What can I do for you?"

"I'm Quille C. Davis," I said. "And I'm very sorry to bother you at work. I'm hoping to set a time when we can talk later. About your cousin. Vanessa Kev."

Her eyebrows, which had been plucked into thin lines, drew into a V. "Vanessa? Wait, you're who again?"

"Quille C. Davis. I'm —"

"The lawyer Aunt Gail warned me about."

"I spoke to Gail this morning." Already that felt like an impossibly long time ago. "I hope I didn't upset her. I'm just trying to find answers about both crimes. To help both families."

Kimberly raised her hand, palm out, in a Stop gesture. "It's fine. I've been wanting to talk with you."

13

THE PHOTOGRAPHER

I HOPED Kimberly might want to talk later, after she finished her work day. That way I could sketch out some questions. But she led me straight to the wine and coffee bar inside Nordstrom.

"Don't tell anyone we spoke," she said as we wound our way to a table near the polished wood railings that enclosed the seating area. "Sometimes Aunt Gail takes a long time to make up her mind. If she hears I went ahead before she gave an okay, she'll be mad."

After we ordered I shut off my phone and stowed it in my shoulder bag. I made sure Kimberly saw me do it. People so rarely get undivided attention these days that when they know they have it, they talk more.

"Why are you so willing to talk to me?" I said.

"Well, for one thing, no one's looked at Nessa's death in forever. The police don't seem to care any longer."

"They think my parents did it. Or my father did, and my mother covered it up. You should know that up front."

A server set down our drinks. Mine was dark cocoa. I

ordered a pain au chocolat and a fruit plate as well. With any luck, Kimberly would feel she needed to stay until I finished.

Also, it was two p.m., I'd missed lunch, and hunger's a migraine trigger for me.

Kimberly sipped the foam off her cappuccino. "Hard to believe. Your parents seemed like good Christians."

"Did you meet them?"

My mother's Methodist and finds comfort in attending services. My dad joined her church when they married, though he never spends much time there. Neither talks much about religion. But maybe they did in the past.

"No," Kimberly said. "But they were interviewed on TV with their reverend when the girls were found."

I made a mental note about the reverend and waited for an espresso machine to stop whirring so we could hear each other. I asked what my parents said in the interview. I hadn't been able to find it online. But Kimberly didn't remember anything specific.

"Any thoughts on the perpetrator?" I avoided the words killer or murderer in case, like my family, the Kev clan liked to avoid the ugly imagery.

Kimberly's eyes drifted to the rows of wine glasses that hung over the bar, gleaming in the recessed lighting. "I don't want to accuse anyone. Especially all this time later."

"But?" I said.

"I had a bad feeling." Kimberly waited while the server set down my fruit and pastry. "Told the police. Well, I didn't. I told my parents. They told the police."

"But no one interviewed you?"

She shook her head. "No. When Nessa was taken I was out of town. With my mother at a Mary Kay event. No one thought I had anything to do with it. And I was thirteen. My parents said I was too young for the police to talk to me."

"They interviewed your brother, though?"

News articles stated the brother was at the Kevs' house that day. He was supposed to go to Vanessa's dance recital but fell ill. I couldn't find any information about where he'd been when Q.C. was taken.

"He was older," Kimberly said. "Seventeen."

"You mind if I make a few notes?"

"Go ahead. I want you to figure this out, hon."

I took out a notepad, wrote the brother's name, and starred it to remind me to come back to him. "Who did you have the bad feeling about?"

"A man who worked with my mother. His name was Klaus."

The name sounded vaguely familiar but I couldn't recall why. "He worked at Mary Kay?"

"No, no. She was a typist at a local construction company for, I don't know, ten years? It was while she was getting her Mary Kay business off the ground."

"Klaus. First or last name?" I opened my iPad and scrolled through my research chart. It showed each person who might be connected to Q.C.'s or Vanessa's murders. But no one named Klaus.

"First. Not sure about his last. Williams? Wilson. Or Williamson. Maybe. I never called him by it. He said I could call him Klaus. It made me feel grown up."

Her teenage longing to feel like an adult reminded me of my own adolescence. Nearly everyone around me was older than me at home and in my acting work. I forever felt the need to catch up.

Kimberly told me she was thirteen when she met Klaus at an open house at the construction company. He was the one-man computer department. She guessed he'd been about twenty-five.

"Still remember that computer." Kimberly's eyes shifted upward as she spoke. "Took up a whole room. Had its own air conditioning unit. Very chilly in there."

"Why its own air conditioner?"

"That's how it was in those days. Computers failed if they got a little too hot. Or if dust got into them. Klaus told me how hard it was to find the right environment." She pointed to her smartphone, which lay on the table near the crystal salt shaker. "Crazy when you think of it now. Probably they all had less power than our phones do today."

Kimberly told me for about a year — the year before Vanessa was taken — Klaus stopped over at her parents' house for drinks with her dad every few weeks. He also joined in family cookouts or picnics.

She pressed her napkin to her mouth, wiping foam off her upper lip. "He called me 'babe' in a way that made me feel pretty. Not like an awkward beanpole who towered over all the boys."

"Is that what made you feel there was something off about him?" I bit into my pastry, enjoying the buttery crust and dark chocolate filling.

"Strangely? No. He called all women that. The way someone older might have said 'dear'. But one day he asked if I wanted to work for him part-time."

"At the construction company?"

"No. Not for Uncle Ted either. A side project. He wanted me to do some keyboarding. But I didn't know how to type yet, and he kept saying he could teach me. That's when it started feeling off."

I scribbled notes. "You said not for your uncle. Did Klaus normally work with Ted Kev on something?"

"Oh, didn't I say? My mom introduced the two of them. That was a few years before I met Klaus. Uncle Ted was developing all these programs for businesses. Klaus was his partner."

My research didn't reveal Ted Kev having any partner other than his wife, Gail, before the company incorporated. The two had a series of employees, but no other partners. "Klaus was a partner in your uncle and aunt's company?"

"Hmm." Kimberly ran her finger around the rim of her mug. "Doesn't seem right now I think on it. But Klaus worked with Uncle Ted on something. Then Klaus got hired by some giant company. Not IBM. But somewhere like that."

Kimberly thought Klaus started his new job about six months before Vanessa's death.

"He was an amateur photographer, too," Kimberly said. "Took photos at all the family events. And Nessa's dance recitals."

"Really?" In the JonBenét Ramsey case, police focused for a while on a photographer who took pictures of JonBenét. I assumed the St. Louis police likewise looked into Klaus. But I made a note to check.

"Aunt Gail loved it. Such beautiful portraits and he refused to charge for them."

"Was he at the recital when Vanessa was kidnapped?"

"Not sure. He'd stopped coming around much by then."

"But Nessa would have known him?"

"Oh, yes. She called him Klaus, too."

"Did you ever tell Gail or Ted that you got an odd feeling about Klaus?"

"After Vanessa disappeared. But not before. I feel guilty about that. Guess that's why I'm talking to you now."

"Why didn't you tell them?"

"The adults thought he was all fine so I figured it was me. Imagining things. Then someone took Vanessa and I thought I ought to tell my parents at least."

Kimberly didn't remember anything else about Klaus.

I asked about Vanessa's dance teacher and other students and parents. All Kimberly recalled was the teacher's name, which I already knew. Michelle O'Brien. The problem was there were way too many Michelle O'Briens in the world.

So far, I'd found a legal assistant, a speech therapist, a pediatrician, two lawyers, a retail clerk, and a construction worker. And that was only in the St. Louis area. But no retired dance instructors.

Kimberly told me she and her brother saw Vanessa a few times a month. With the age difference, though, it was less a friendship and more Kimberly and her brother keeping an eye on their little cousin.

"My brother was great with her," Kimberly said. "Had the patience to play Candy Land over and over. Or paint little designs on her nails."

"I'd love to talk to him."

Kimberly's online presence was careful. Her brother's was non-existent.

Kimberly looked sideways. "That might be a problem."

14

THE OLDER COUSIN

"LAST TIME JIMMY and I spoke was the day he left for college," Kimberly said. She added that he attended Boston College.

Quick math in my head told me James Smith Junior, who Kimberly called Jimmy, went away to school about two months after Nessa's death and never returned. Possibly coincidence. Maybe significant.

"He never came to visit?" I said. "Or called?"

"No. Don't even know if he graduated."

In these days of social media, I couldn't imagine no photos anyplace of a college graduate. But in the eighties it must have been easy to disappear if a person wanted to. The question was why.

"Do you know if he's still alive?" I said.

"Yes. He sends postcards. Couple times a year from all over the world."

"And that started when?"

"About a year after he moved away."

Kimberly told me the messages said things like "Hope you're well" or "Just to say Hi" and were unsigned. But she recognized her brother's writing. The postcards came to her at her parents' house in the beginning. About six months after she married and moved out they started arriving at her new home.

"So Jimmy's keeping track of you."

"Must be."

That took some effort in the eighties as well. A skip tracer I shared office space with sometimes shared stories of Herculean efforts to find people back when he started in the business.

Kimberly agreed to send me photos of the postcards. There were about sixty-five total. Not much for three decades.

"I couldn't find Jimmy online," I said. "But there were a lot of James Smiths, so maybe I missed him."

"Probably not," Kimberly said. "I'm sure he's not on social media. I've looked on and off over the years. Never any luck."

I'd checked various people finder databases, both free and subscription, and gotten nowhere.

"So he doesn't want to be found." I sipped my hot chocolate, careful not to finish it. An empty mug might remind Kimberly how long we'd been talking.

"Maybe," Kimberly said. "But we're all of us cautious. Because of what happened to Nessa."

"My family's the same," I said. "My mother encouraged my acting career when I was a kid. But she worried about the publicity. These days with social media I don't think she'd have let me get on stage."

Kimberly nodded. I asked if her parents tried to reach Jimmy after he went away to school.

"Dad called him a few weeks after the semester started. But Jimmy told him he didn't want anything more to do with us or our hick town."

"I'm so sorry. Why would he say something like that?"

"No idea, hon. Mom cried for days. She wanted to call him again but my dad said to wait. Let Jimmy make the first move. Apologize. He didn't."

"Did you call Jimmy?"

"I called the payphone in his dorm. Students didn't have their own phones then. The boy who answered didn't know Jimmy. Tried two more times and the same thing happened. You better believe I got in trouble when the long distance bill came. Also a big deal back in the day."

I almost asked Kimberly if she emailed her brother. Then I remembered the timeframe. "Did you write letters to him?"

"A few. Never got an answer. Last time I tried was his junior year. It came back unopened."

I ate the last kiwi slice on my plate. "Odd that he sent a letter back when he was mailing you postcards."

"The school sent it back. Said they had no record of him in the dorms. I thought he moved off campus. Or dropped out."

Or something worse happened to him. Kimberly seemed sure her brother's handwriting was on the cards. But that could be imitated.

"Did you or your parents talk to his friends?" I said.

"He didn't really have friends. Not that I knew, anyway. I think my mother talked to a few of his high school classmates. Or their parents. But no one had heard from him."

I pressed, thinking he must have had some friends, but Kimberly definitely didn't know any of them if he did.

"Did your brother and father get along?"

Kimberly tapped her index finger against the corner of her eyeglasses. "Oh, honey, you know. Fathers and sons."

"I don't. Not really. No brothers."

"Well, not a great mix. They argue about everything."

"Such as?"

"Best place to get a hamburger. How much to salt your food. Cars. My dad bought a new Ford without test driving it. Turned out to have all these features Dad didn't like. Jimmy brought that up every chance he got. How foolish a person must be to buy a car without test driving it."

"Did they clash over anything more serious?"

"Jimmy got in fights at school. He was suspended twice. Did not make my father happy."

Clumps of cocoa congealed in the bottom of my mug. Kimberly had drained her cappuccino. "Did Jimmy start the fights?"

"No clue, hon."

"What were they about?"

She moved her empty mug an inch to the right. "Also no clue. Jimmy didn't talk to me much. To anyone, really."

I wrote a J and a question mark on my notepad. Kimberly had every reason to be jealous of her little cousin's relationship with Jimmy. Whether that had anything to do with Vanessa's death was a whole other question. Because she was only thirteen when Vanessa was killed, Kimberly seemed like the least likely suspect on the Kev side.

Jimmy was definitely someone I wanted to talk to. He spent time with his little cousin but ignored his sister. And Vanessa spent a lot of time with him, making it likely she'd trust him if he asked her to go with him somewhere. Plus he had a history of violent behavior and trouble forming relationships. At least according to Kimberly.

As with Kimberly, though, Jimmy's age gave me pause. At seventeen I doubted he had the resources to kidnap and hide not one but two little girls. I also couldn't imagine how he might have homed in on Q.C., who lived one state over.

"Was Jimmy a bully?" I said.

"He didn't pick on me. Or Vanessa."

I asked if she could email me anything she remembered that might help find Jimmy.

"Of course," she said. "To be honest, that's a big part of why I wanted to talk with you. Maybe in your investigation you'll find Jimmy."

15

TO BE HONEST

IN LAW PHRASES LIKE "TO be honest" or "to be frank" can be red flags. A signal that until now, the witness has been lying. Or it can mean just the opposite. That now they're hiding something and to cover they stress that they're being forthright.

Other times, though, it's just a verbal tic. I didn't know Kimberly well enough to guess which, if either, might be true for her.

She glanced at her watch, an old-fashioned clockface with a plain silver band. "I should get back."

"Could you look at these quickly?" I opened a file on my iPad that showed photos of everyone in my family from around the time Q.C. was taken. I asked if Kimberly remembered any of them. My parents both looked familiar to her, but the others didn't. If there was a connection between the two families, and if Kimberly was being honest, she wasn't it.

I closed the iPad and slid my arms into my jacket sleeves. "You think your parents will talk to me?"

"My dad will if my uncle says he can. My mom? Maybe. She doted on Nessa. Both my parents did, really."

Interesting that she thought her father, related to the Kevs only by marriage, needed an okay from Ted Kev. But her mother, who was Gail's sister, might not.

Kimberly led the way out into the shopping area. "I'd put in a word for you with Mom and Dad, but I don't want them to know I talked with you if they think it's a bad idea. No point getting them all upset. You understand, hon?"

"Sure," I said.

Though if I didn't get a return call, I'd be back to plead my case with Kimberly. I walked with her to the designer fashion department and thanked her again.

"You're talking to your family, too, I guess?" she said.

"I spent the last two months on the phone doing that," I said. "And there are people I'll talk to again in person now."

"I feel for your poor mother. That's who everyone blames when anything happens to kids, isn't it? The mother?"

"Why do you say that?"

I wondered if Kimberly and Gail Kev talked about that together or if they separately reached that conclusion.

"Oh, I don't mean little Nessa and your sister. But all around. Mothers get the blame." She shook my hand. "Good luck."

I stared after her as she wove her way around circular clothing racks. She and Gail weren't wrong about blame. When the news reports a baby abandoned or a child locked in a car, I never hear anyone ask where the father was. They ask how the mother could do something like that.

But Kimberly and I had just spent over an hour talking about Nessa and Q.C., not social issues or the way of the world. Something made her link that to blaming mothers. Since she didn't know mine, she must be talking about her own mother.

Or Gail Kev.

I headed outside. And nearly got into a silver four-door sedan parked near my rental car because they looked so much alike. I noticed at the last second the license plate started with AG, while mine started with CD, my dad's initials.

Inside the vehicle, I fiddled with the music settings until I found something I liked and finally put the car in gear. I couldn't put off talking to my mother any longer.

Our relationship had challenges enough without my making what could only sound like an accusation that she hadn't wanted Q.C. But I'd promised to investigate, and I meant to do my best at it. One way or another.

MY MOTHER CHOPPED a deep red tomato into quarters and then eighths. "Really, Quille. What kind of question is that?"

"It wouldn't be strange to have mixed feelings," I said.

"How would you know? You've never been pregnant." She grabbed another tomato from the pile in the center of the table. "Have you?"

"No. Had a scare a few years ago."

"Well, it's not a scare when you're married. I wasn't some single girl barely scraping by."

"I wasn't —" I made myself stop. "I'm not scraping by."

I was lucky in that my work experience plus accounting and law degrees put me in high demand when I finished law school. That helped when I started my own law practice, too. Every few months I sent my dad extra money to help with my parents' bills. The mental health benefits were limited under my dad's policy.

My mother didn't know any of that.

"It's still not the same," my mother said as she handed me a block of cheddar.

I started grating it. Thin orange strips collected on the plate. "Weren't you about to travel with Dad's band for the summer, and then you couldn't because you got pregnant?"

"Who told you that?"

"Aunt Cathy."

I said a silent apology to my aunt for throwing her under the bus. But it seemed better for my parents' marriage if my mother didn't think my questions came from talking to my dad.

"Really. Aunt Cathy. Probably said I was unhappy I couldn't go on the road. But I wasn't." My mother dropped the tomato wedges into bowls. "Honestly, can you see me living out of the back of a van?"

I couldn't.

My mother was particular to say the least. My whole life my Gram and later I made sure to buy the exact seven-grain bread my mother liked. Never multigrain or white or whole wheat. She needed soap with the faintest lavender scent but no hint of lemon, caffeinated tea before ten in the morning and herbal after, and plenty of magazines in the house in case she felt like reading. But not so many it left her feeling overwhelmed and as if she'd never get through them all.

"No. But you love singing," I said.

"That doesn't matter when you have children. Plans change. I was thrilled about Q.C. Your dad was thrilled. And Kendra was excited about being a big sister. It was all good. Whatever Cathy says."

Or my sister said. Or my dad. He'd hidden his true feelings well from my mother.

Or my mother was lying. To me or to herself.

16

BETWEEN THE LINES

AFTER A DINNER of oven baked chicken with fingerling potatoes — my go to meal when I need to cook for more than two people — I ducked into the enclosed back sun porch to research. My mother did a crossword puzzle in the kitchen while my dad loaded the dishwasher.

Their voices carried through the heat vents. I kept one ear out for whether either of them told the other about my conversations with them. They didn't.

I found nothing more online about Jimmy Smith. If Kimberly wanted me to track down her brother, she needed to send me something more to work with.

My luck was no better with Klaus. Despite adding that name to my searches, no one other than Gail came up as a business partner to Ted Kev. Reading between the lines, her efforts more than her husband's got early investors on board. When she returned a year after her daughter's death, she spearheaded the drive to take the company public.

But the articles I found, and there weren't many, featured Ted Kev.

I wondered if Gail wanted her role to be in the background or if Ted did. Though it might be neither. In the eighties, the press might have assumed a wife's role in her husband's company must be little more than window dressing.

An email ping interrupted my thoughts. The message was from Dylan Sabatini, the boy — now a man in his mid-forties — Aunt Cathy suggested I talk to. I'd emailed him before starting my research.

As I sent an answer to Dylan, my dad joined me, a whiskey sour in each hand. Black plastic stirrers shaped like quarter notes adorned the drinks. I'd given them to my dad on Father's Day the year he and my mother moved back to Edwardsville.

"Thanks." I tasted my whiskey sour. Fresh squeezed lemon, egg white, simple syrup, and a hint of bourbon. Just how I liked it. "Remember Dylan Sabatini?"

Dad settled onto the wicker couch near the windows. Behind him shadows shrouded the back yard. "Dylan?"

"Kendra's friend. He lived down the street from your old house. Above the church."

"Oh, right. The Sabatinis."

"Dylan's in town. I'm meeting him tomorrow."

"Can't think he'd remember much about Q.C.," my father said. "He must've been, what, six?"

"Seven," I said. "Is his father the reverend —"

My mother popped her head into the room. "Who're you meeting?"

She wore pajama pants and a pink tank top, her hair combed and pulled away from her just-washed face with a brightly colored scrunchie. Very unlike the mother of my childhood who wore the same gray sweats morning, noon, and night unless my Gram ordered her to change them.

"Dylan Sabatini."

My mother crossed her arms over her chest. "Because he

played with Kendra? How will that help? You should be talking to the Kevs."

"I have been."

"And their friends."

"I will. But Dylan was at Q.C.'s party. And he lives here again."

"Waste of time." She headed for the stairs. Over her shoulder she said, "But I suppose you know what you're doing."

Her tone implied she doubted it. But that was nothing new. In a way I found it comforting. If everything about my mother changed it might be too unsettling.

A half hour later, I sat on the edge of the double bed in the guest room and texted Ty. No answer. Not a surprise. It was eight in the morning in Dubai, and he was a late riser.

Then I texted Lauren.

Harder than expected here. Not the Kevs. My mom. Wish you were here.

She answered immediately.

Seriously? I'm on the next plane.

No, no. Might be back soon anyway. And I'm fine.

Say the word. Got a million reward miles.

She probably did. Her parents take her on three trips a year, always first class. They pay, she keeps the points. But I could talk with Lauren in a few days when I flew home for court. And I didn't want to get in the way of her work. She's a real estate agent and the spring sales season was about to take off.

The stairs creaked, one after another, as if someone were climbing them. But my dad had already followed my mother up to bed. I flicked on the hall and then the stairwell light. No one.

I put on a Pandora station that played white noise and searched the Sabatini family online. Some of what I learned was ordinary, some tragic. None of it explained why both my parents seemed to want me to stay away from Dylan Sabatini.

But talking to him tomorrow might answer that.

17

NEGOTIATING

THE HIGH SCHOOL hallway smelled of disinfectant, chewing gum, and sweaty teenagers. Across from a row of metal lockers, I paused in the doorway of Dylan Sabatini's classroom.

He sat, back straight, behind a plain wood desk. A black sport jacket hung over his chair. His collared purple shirt gave his pale face color. His high, almost sharp cheekbones and dark slanted eyebrows made him striking.

A blond student splayed her brightly polished nails across the other side of the desk. She looked down at them as she spoke. "I know I left some questions blank. But I'm not lazy. I focused on the others, the ones I knew."

As she spoke, Dylan glanced at me and raised one eyebrow. But he shifted his gaze to the girl again, expression serious, the instant before she peered at him from under her long lashes.

"My dad says that's how to succeed in life. Lean into your strengths."

"I'm sure your dad is right. In his business." He smiled and held up a hand as the girl started to speak. "Which is not teaching Algebra."

"No, but —"

"And I'm guessing it's been a while since your dad learned Algebra."

"Well, yeah." She rolled her eyes. "He's ancient. But he says it's always better to work smart than hard."

Dylan spread his arms wide. "Absolutely. And working smart in Algebra means working the problems. Otherwise, you're just learning a bunch of rules without knowing why. No point in that, is there?"

She bit her lip. "I guess not."

"I'd never want to drone on about rules just so I could test you on them. That'd be boring."

"Rules are boring."

"Very." He slid her exam booklet across the desk. "Tell you what. Want to make your dad happy and raise that grade? Tomorrow after school you can have thirty minutes to take a makeup test. Attempt every problem you skipped, showing your work, and your F turns into a D. Just like that." He snapped his fingers.

"A D?"

"But wait. You'll get one point for each correct answer, half a point if the answer's wrong but your work's on track. Could bring you into C territory. B if you ace it."

She tilted her head and smiled. "How about an A? For acing it?"

He tapped the booklet and ignored the half-flirt. "Then you'd get the same score as your friends. And they didn't get a second try and thirty extra minutes. You don't want to be unfair to your friends, do you?"

She pressed her lips together, no doubt searching for an answer that didn't make her look bad. Finally, she took the booklet. "Can we make it Thursday after school instead? I've got a thing tomorrow."

"We can make it Thursday."

"Thanks Mr. S."

She bounced past me out the door, head down to look at her phone, thumbs flying over its keys. Dylan waved me in.

"Want to handle my next settlement negotiation?" I said.

"High schoolers. Most don't want to learn, but it's my job to teach them. And coach them."

One side of his mouth quirked into a half smile. On some men, especially a lot of young male lawyers I know, it would have been an arrogant smirk. But on Dylan it looked playful, as if we were both in on a joke he'd made about himself. If he flashed that smile in class, I bet a lot of high schoolers had crushes on him.

"What do you coach?"

"Wrestling. Q.C. Davis the second, I take it," he said.

"Quille." I held out my hand to shake. "I go by Quille."

"Sorry. That was probably in your email." His long, slim fingers closed around mine as he met my eyes. His irises were the palest blue I'd ever seen, encircled by black. "Had Q.C. on my mind since that's what you wanted to meet about. Shall we get a drink?"

"Before five?"

"Or coffee. But four student conferences in a row calls for whiskey at some point in the evening."

I glanced at the open classroom door. "You aren't worried your students will hear you say that?"

"Unless I'm on social media or text them nothing I say registers once they leave class." He grinned. "Sometimes while they're in class for that matter. So? Coffee? Soda? Whiskey?"

"Whiskey works," I said.

18

THE NOT SO GOOD SON

"I REMEMBER YOUR MOM. Yelling for Q.C. Then she and your dad racing around looking for her." Dylan sipped his Maker's Mark, which he'd ordered neat. "Oh, and Kendra crying."

"After Q.C. disappeared?" I said.

A whiskey sour light on the whiskey sat on the bar in front of me. I agreed to try the buffalo wings, which Dylan said were the best choice. They came from a food truck the bar partnered with. Recess Brewing featured exposed brick walls, gleaming hardwood, and many types of beer and cocktails but no kitchen.

"Before. When she saw all Q.C.'s presents."

My sister had never told me that. But she recalled next to nothing about the party. "She knew how birthdays worked, right?"

He rubbed his finger around the rim of his whiskey glass as he thought. "She always thought Q.C. got better presents."

"Better how? More expensive?"

"More — personal. One Christmas she and Q.C. got identical dollhouses. But only Q.C. liked dolls. Kendra wanted roller skates. Another time your mom surprised them both with batons."

"Because Q.C. wanted to twirl."

He shrugged. "Kendra tried. But not really her thing."

"My mother treated them the same. But not equally."

"Exactly. And Kendra saw it how you might think. That your mom liked Q.C. better."

"Was Kendra mad at Q.C. about it?"

That might be the source of Kendra blocking out the whole party. If she felt angry at Q.C., her seven-year-old self might have feared she caused the terrible thing to happen.

"More at your mom. Maybe at Q.C. Had to suck feeling that way and then your sister ends up dead." Dylan raised his glass. "This is a cheerful conversation. Lucky we've both got whiskey."

"And wings," I said as I rolled one that was dripping barbeque sauce in the bleu cheese crumbles that came on the side. "You remember a lot about how Kendra felt."

"Let's just say my feelings about my brother were not unlike Kendra's about your sister."

Dylan and I ate a few wings before talking again. I wiped the tangy sauce from my lips then asked how often he and his brother played with Q.C. and Kendra.

"Every day almost. At least, before Q.C. disappeared."

Yet my dad acted as if he barely remembered the Sabatinis. Aunt Cathy must be right. He barely spent any time at home.

I rubbed the back of my neck, which felt stiff. "Only before Q.C. disappeared?"

"After that all our parents watched us like hawks. Hardly let us out of the house. And your mom stopped coming over."

"To your house? When did she come over?"

"All the time. Went places with us, too. School plays. Local choir concerts. She and my parents drank cocktails on the porch on Friday nights. And played bridge Thursday afternoons."

"My parents played bridge?"

"Your mom played bridge. Your dad was on the road. She partnered with a widow from the church." He drank the last of his whiskey and waved at the bartender. "Which, now I think of it, is a weird way to talk about the woman. Like that's all that mattered about her. That her husband died. But that's what my parents always said. A widow from church."

"Is she still alive?"

"Died before I went to college. She and your mom played well. Intuitive my dad called them. He and my mom just shouted. He never read my mom's bids right. Blamed her."

"You remember all this from when you were seven?"

"Shouting's how I knew they were playing. But the bidding, all that, my mom told me later."

"I'm sorry about your mother." My online research had turned up her obituary. That and the church social media pages told me she fought a six-year battle with pancreatic cancer. She died a little over a year ago, two days after Valentine's Day.

"And I'm sorry about your sister." Dylan ate the last celery stick from the plate of wings.

"Thank you," I said. "What brought you back to Edwardsville?"

"My mother. Came to help take care of her. The last three years were a lot tougher than she made it look. She was the consummate PW to the end."

"PW?"

"Sorry. Preacher's wife. Whereas I failed at being a PK — Preacher's Kid."

"By coming back to take care of your mom?"

"By leaving in the first place. And getting divorced after an entire eleven months of marriage. Then there's not taking over the church, but not having the decency to do something my parents could brag about. Not like my younger brother. He became a surgeon."

"Your dad didn't see being a successful musician as respectable?"

One dark eyebrow arched. "You did your homework."

"Studio musician in New York, member of a classic rock cover band that played all over New York City. What led to teaching?"

"I majored in education. Dad's requirement if he was going to pay for college. Did some student teaching in New York but got enough work as a musician that I never did it as a career. Until I came here and needed a job."

"And you're still doing it. Does that mean you like it?"

"Hate to admit it and give my dad the satisfaction. But yeah. Though I might like teaching college better. So I'm thinking about that."

"No more music these days?"

"I play with a blues band on and off. Do some studio work in St. Louis. In the summer. What about you? Your parents steer you away from acting and towards business and law?"

It was my turn for raised eyebrows. He'd done homework too. But there was next to nothing online about my acting, as it predated social media. It was one thing for Ted Kev's private investigator to find out about it. But I doubted Dylan had those types of resources.

"You know I used to act?"

"Asked my dad about you. He said you were in some musicals. Your acting career impressed him. Which sort of irks me."

"I can see that," I said. "Given how unimpressed he is with your creative work."

"Exactly."

I tapped my fingers on the table. I didn't get my first real acting job until nearly a decade after my parents moved away from Edwardsville. The productions I acted and sang in were all in Chicago area theaters.

Yet Dylan's father knew about my acting and singing. Knew about me.

19

CREDIT

Dylan touched my wrist. "Quille?"

I looked over at him. "Sorry. What?"

"I asked if you still sing."

"Not as much as I want. Two of my friends and I sing together a cappella."

"But?"

"One of them had kind of a bad break up and went MIA for a while. Now he's back. But not quite all the way. He started seeing my other friend Lauren. And really likes her. Unlike his previous girlfriend, I guess. His free time's kind of limited these days."

Dylan nodded. "Always a trick fitting everything in when it's not your full-time gig. You miss it? Singing?"

"Lots. It's how I unwind. Reminds me to stop working and have fun."

"You need a reminder?"

"Sometimes."

The aching in my neck morphed into an all-too-familiar tightness at the back of my skull. It happens most often when I spend too much time at the computer, don't get enough sleep, or feel stressed. Or all three.

In another few minutes my head would start pounding. I fished three Advil from my shoulder bag. After I swallowed them, I asked if Dylan remembered any more about my parents, Kendra, or Q.C.

"No, sorry. Hardly saw your family after Q.C. was taken. And then they moved away."

I rubbed my fingers into the sides of my neck as I thought about Dylan's words. My mother spent all kinds of time with his parents. Then she stopped when Q.C. was taken, which also was when my Dad quit the band to stay home more.

"A retired cop I talked to said my parents had marriage counseling at their church. Any chance they went to your dad?"

"Could've."

"I'd like to talk with him. Will he be more likely to agree if you ask?"

"You might have more luck on your own. You may have guessed that I am not the favorite child."

"I know that feeling."

Dylan clinked his glass against mine. "To things in common."

"I might be my Gram's favorite," I said. "Kendra thinks so."

"Everyone should be someone's favorite."

I asked if he recognized any of the Kevs in the photos on my iPad. He didn't. He also didn't recall anyone named Klaus hanging around.

"But at seven, not sure I knew adults had first names. Everyone was Mr., Mrs., Miss. No Ms. That was for those hippie radical women who didn't shave their legs and were hiding whether they were married or not."

I laughed. "Did you know women like that?"

"No, but my dad was convinced they existed. Somewhere up north. Maybe Chicago where you live."

A deejay started setting up in the corner. Once the music began, I suspected it'd be too loud to keep talking. I tried to think what I most wanted to know. I asked Dylan about photographers at Q.C.'s concerts or school events. Maybe Klaus had been there, too.

"Hmm. Local paper covered community events. Concerts. Fun fairs. The pumpkin decorating contest at the courthouse on Halloween. They might have sent a photographer."

"Oh." An eighties technopop song blasted over the sound system. "That's a great idea."

"What is?" Dylan leaned closer to hear me.

"He's a photographer, maybe he's credited somewhere." I gestured to my iPad. "Mind if I do a quick search?"

"Have at it. I'll try calling my father. I'm not the favorite, but it saves you telling your whole story again."

Dylan stepped outside so he could hear. I was still scrolling through photos with no luck when Dylan returned.

"What'd your dad say?"

"He wants to talk to your mother first."

20

OTHER CRIMES

DYLAN WALKED me to my rental car. "Any idea why your father won't just talk to me?" I said.

"Dad's all about the politics of life. Probably wants to be sure he doesn't offend your mother if you're looking into Q.C.'s death all on your own."

I clicked open the lock. "Yes, because that's my idea of fun."

"If it is you really do need reminding."

Dylan waited on the sidewalk as I got into the car. He knocked on the passenger side window just before I pulled away. I buzzed it down.

"Text any time if I can help." He flashed that half-smile again. "Or if you need a guide to fun in Edwardsville."

By the time I got home, my parents had already eaten. I wanted to ask about what I learned from Dylan. But I had too much legal work to do.

On the sun porch again, I read through documents for the new case with the upcoming court hearing. Two cousins who owned a factory together disagreed over whether to sell it. And over which employees to keep if they didn't. It looked like the disputes could be sorted out if both sides were reasonable.

Maybe I could avoid the need to return to Chicago so soon.

But when I emailed as much to the lawyer on the other side, who must also be working late, he didn't think so. His answer was quick and fast:

Have you met your client?

After setting a time to talk with my client over Zoom, I turned to my Klaus research again. An hour of trying various search terms and databases finally yielded results. A photo sharing website included grainy digital images from a 1980s St. Louis Community College - Meramec photography exhibit. Meramec was less than ten miles from Clayton, Missouri, where the Kevs lived when Vanessa was killed.

I couldn't see the photos well. But the credits included Klaus Erickson.

A cell phone rang somewhere in the house. I ignored it as I switched to another database. My next searches made me think the credited photographer was the same Klaus Kimberly remembered. And her thirteen-year-old instincts had been right on.

Six years after Vanessa's and Q.C.'s deaths, Klaus Erickson pled guilty to possessing child pornography and possessing and distributing marijuana. He had to register as a sex offender and served eight years in federal prison. According to the newspaper article I found, the original charges included transporting a minor across state lines for immoral purposes. And producing child pornography.

21

GUILT

KLAUS ERICKSON, now divorced, lived in Pontiac, Illinois, about halfway between Edwardsville and Chicago. That put him about forty miles from my sister Kendra in Normal, Illinois.

My mother appeared in the doorway from the dining room. "Why are you hounding Reverend Sabatini?"

"Hounding? I never met him."

"Using his son to get to him. Honestly, Quille, you're so unfeeling. That's not how I raised you." She spun and left the room.

I gripped the edge of the table to keep myself from following her and saying something I might regret about her parenting.

My Gram raised me. My dad helped. My mother might have wanted to, but other than the voice lessons she had nothing to do with any choices about schooling, friends, or how I spent my time. Then, just before I turned sixteen, she and my dad moved back to Edwardsville so she could be closer to Q.C.'s grave. I stayed with Gram. And did my best to tell myself my parents' decision to leave had nothing to do with me.

After a few minutes, when I felt calmer, I found my mother

in the kitchen paging through a gardening magazine. I paused in the doorway. "Why is it unfeeling for me to talk with Reverend Sabatini?"

"Rev has nothing to do with Q.C.'s death."

"Rev?"

"It's what everyone called him. Leave the man alone. His wife just died."

"Over a year ago," I said.

My mother's lips pursed. "Oh, and you think he should just be over it."

"No. But I'm not planning to ask about his wife. Why don't you want me to talk to him?"

"Don't yell at me."

"I didn't yell."

She stood. "But you want to." Her flip-flops clomped on the tile floor as she stomped past me and out of the room.

I took a step after her, then stopped. I couldn't think of anything to say that might shift her mood since I didn't know why she got so upset. I was about to go back to my research for now when my dad poked his head in from the living room.

He suggested I make tea while he started the gas fire pit in the back yard. I brewed a raspberry hibiscus blend meant to calm frazzled nerves. Outside, my mother sat near the firepit, her back to the cherry tree. Its thick branches forked into a Y only a couple yards above the ground. If I'd grown up here, I might have climbed it.

I sat across from my mother. She wore a jacket and the fur lined moccasins I sent her for Christmas. My dad kissed her forehead and nestled a wool blanket around her. "Relax. Talk with Quille. Enjoy the fire under your favorite tree."

My mother's lips twitched into a smile.

"Why is it your favorite?" I said.

"Never you mind." My mother's eyes darted toward my dad.

He grinned. "Well, it was her favorite the night we moved in here anyway."

My mother playfully swatted his arm with the edge of the blanket. "Shush, you."

Dad squeezed her shoulder and disappeared inside.

It was nice — and completely new to me — to see my parents as a couple with inside jokes who still flirted a bit after all these years.

"Your questions reminded me of the police." My mother looked at me across the crackling fire. "One minute suggesting your dad and I had problems, so one of us hurt Q.C. out of spite for the other. Then saying I might be covering for him."

"I'm sorry I made it sound that way," I said. I didn't think I had. But after decades of being suspects, I could see my mother taking all questions that way. "I don't believe either of those things."

All the same, a tiny voice in the back of my head noted that sometimes people get angry about questions because they're guilty of something. Though not necessarily what they're being questioned about.

"Then why the third degree?" my mother said.

I also didn't think I'd given her the third degree. But it was better to explain than argue. "When I've done this before, looked into crimes, often a little thing is key. A moment a witness never thought to mention. A few words a suspect said that meant nothing at the time but revealed a motive."

"You think I'm going to reveal a motive? For who? Me or your father?"

"I don't —" I stopped and drank some tea, letting the warm liquid coat my tongue and ease down my throat. "Look, Mom. If you want, I won't ask you or Dad anything else. I won't look into our side of this at all. Just the Kevs."

Crickets chirped in the darkness. Lots of them lived under the outdoor steps leading down to the basement.

"What's the catch?"

"I probably won't learn anything the police didn't. Because what I need is to find the overlap. Who's in common to both sets of people. Why Q.C. and Vanessa both were taken. And I can only do that if I learn as much as I can about everyone. Not just the Kev family members and friends."

My mother finally tasted her tea. She frowned and set it on the bricks again. "Needs honey."

My mother doesn't like honey. But I fetched a plastic bear full of it from inside and placed it with a spoon on a napkin next to her mug.

"I didn't need the whole thing," she said.

"You're welcome," I said. "Why don't you want me to talk to Reverend Sabatini?"

She squeezed a drop of honey into her mug and stirred. "Why are you obsessed with him?"

"I'm not obsessed. He knew all of you. And other people in the neighborhood. Maybe he saw something. Or met someone from the Kev side and doesn't know it."

Blue tinged the tips of the flames. My mother sighed. "He knows how guilty I felt when I got pregnant with you."

22

UNHAPPY TRUTHS

My hand froze as I lifted my mug to my lips. "With me?" I'd expected my mother to say something about Q.C. or my dad. "Guilty?"

If my mother had been involved with Sabatini, it could explain a lot.

"After Q.C.'s — what happened, your dad and I hoped a new baby would brighten our world. Give Kendra something to be excited about. But when it was real, all I could think was how could I bring another baby into this world? With all the terrible things that happen."

"That's when your depression got worse? Not when I was born?"

The story I grew up with was that my mother's post-partum depression on top of her grief over Q.C. sent her into a spiral. She never recovered. It made me feel like the camel-breaking straw or the final coffin nail of my mother's life.

"It was all hard. I'm not strong, Quille," she said. "Your dad's not strong. We didn't know how to cope."

I inched my chair around the circle a little closer to her and reached over to squeeze her hand. "No one's that strong, Mom. No one ought to lose a child like that. Or at all."

She pulled her hand away, but it took a second for her to do it. "Your Gram would have soldiered on. She did soldier on. That's why we moved. You needed more. Someone who could be strong. And it's good. You take after your Gram, and it's good."

"What about Kendra?" I said. "You moved for her, too, right?"

"For her, too. But you were so tiny. Barely five and a half pounds when you were born." My mother clutched the blanket across her chest. "I tried to take care of you as best I could. Protect you."

"You did," I said. "I'm fine. I grew up fine."

She nodded without looking at me. "I'll think about Reverend Sabatini. Talk to your father. We'll see."

Deciding a Maybe was the best I could get, and a little thrown by my mom's words, I went upstairs to the guest room. I was catching up on my law email when a message came in from Kimberly Byerly. It included a PDF of the scanned postcards she was sure came from her brother Jimmy.

To my untrained eye, the handwriting looked consistent from one to the next. Though, as Kimberly told me, the messages were short. No personal information. No clues other than the postmarks. Those ranged from the eastern United States to various European countries and, in the early 2000s, Japan.

Kimberly attached three photos from the 1980s. One showed Vanessa Kev as a toddler wearing a black leotard and turquoise tights. A preteen boy held her in his arms. His slim build, narrow chin and the slant of his nose made it easy to see the resemblance to Kimberly.

Both the boy and the toddler smiled into the camera, looking so happy to be with one another. I studied the boy, thinking of what Danielle said about how murderers looked. If Jimmy Smith posed a danger to Nessa Kev, you couldn't tell from this photo.

The background showed a storefront, but sun glared off the picture window so I couldn't see inside. The camera angle cut off part of the sign, but the business's name started with "Little Li". After checking my notes for the name of Vanessa's dance instructor I searched the words Dance, Michelle O'Brien, Little, and St. Louis. There weren't many hits, but it was enough.

Little Lilies dance studio closed thirteen years after Vanessa's death. Its owner, Michelle O'Brien, retired. A few more searches, this time in paid databases, explained why I hadn't found her sooner.

Not only did she now live in Wisconsin rather than Illinois or Missouri, she'd married a second time two years after closing the dance studio. She took her new husband's last name: Zamorski. He was a dancer, too, and together they ran a folk dancing studio in Milwaukee.

Milwaukee is about two hours north of Chicago by car, making it about a six or seven hour drive from Edwardsville. Or a flight plus a drive or train ride. But it looked likely I'd need to be in Chicago for court in two days. If I could persuade Michelle O'Brien to talk to me around the same time, I could squeeze in a trip to meet her in person.

With Ted and Gail Kev not ready to talk and my mother stonewalling me on Reverend Sabatini, the dance instructor might be the best person to tell me about Klaus Erickson. And about the day Vanessa Kev disappeared.

23

TRACKING

THE NEXT MORNING, I failed to convince my new client to turn over documents the other side was entitled to, which meant a court hearing. I emailed the other attorney. He emailed two words ten minutes later.

Told you.

On the upside, I reached Michelle O'Brien. She sounded eager to help once I explained who I was and what I was doing. Her only free time was the next morning. I got lucky and booked the last open seat on a 7:05 PM flight that night. It was a center seat. But St. Louis to Chicago flights are only about forty-five minutes in the air, and there are worse things.

Hoping to build on success, I called James and Therese Smith, Vanessa's aunt and uncle. I'd tried them twice the day before and gotten voicemail. I got it again now, but finally left a message.

Mr. and Mrs. Smith, this is Quille C. Davis. You may already know from Gail Kev that I'm investigating the deaths of

> Vanessa Kev and my sister Q.C. Davis. To do a good job I need to talk with one or both of you. I believe I can help sort out what happened to your niece. Please call me back.

After making my mother a grilled cheese sandwich for lunch, I sent Chief Highbottom an email with a few questions, then left separate voicemails for Ted and Gail Kev, asking if they'd talk to me again. Or at least tell their family members it was all right to speak to me.

I spent the rest of the afternoon writing a legal brief and following up on current and former TG Kev Computer Solutions Inc. employees. Most of those I'd found over the last two months ignored my emails and calls. Today I got through to eleven of them. Six declined to talk but offered polite apologies. Five gave less polite responses.

One of those, though, called me back from a burner phone twenty minutes later. A programmer, he only shared information I already knew about the company from its public filings. But I did learn something. The man claimed an NDA — a non-disclosure agreement — barred him from talking about anything more. Including the company environment, what Ted and Gail were like to work with or for, and anything touching on the personal life of Ted, Gail, or their daughter.

Standard NDAs protect business information. Trade secrets, computer algorithms, the recipe for Coca Cola. One lawsuit I defended involved drafts of company logos. But I'd never seen an NDA that covered as much as this employee felt sure his did.

At least now I knew why it was so hard to get ex-employees, normally a great source of information about any company, to talk.

In between working, I went down to the kitchen for more tea, mainly to check on my mother. She dropped onto the couch and watched TV all afternoon, which worried me. But she waved me away when I asked if she needed anything.

After dinner, my dad walked me to the BMW. I'd decided, much as it was fun to drive, I'd get a less pricey rental when I came back. It would help offset the extra flight costs.

I set my laptop backpack and my shoulder bag, which I planned to carry on, on the passenger seat as my dad put my rolling bag in the trunk. He hugged me. "Mom will be all right. She'll calm down about the Sabatinis."

"Do you care if I talk to the reverend?"

"I don't see the point, but — this yours?" He retrieved something from the passenger seat floor mat. It looked like a key ring with a shiny metal circle attached.

It felt cool in my palm. "Never seen it before."

Dad peered at it. "Looks like a bag tag. You know. E-luggage tracker. You sync it to your phone and it tells you where your bag is at all times."

"Or where I am." I flipped it over. The tag had no company logos or serial numbers.

I shone my phone's flashlight over the front and back seats and floormats, then rifled through the glove box. My dad checked the trunk and the undercarriage of the car. We didn't find any other devices. I took out everything in my shoulder bag and backpack and found nothing. I'd check my rolling bag at home. I didn't want to delay too much and risk missing my flight.

"Could've fallen off the bag of the last rental car customer," Dad said.

"I didn't notice it before."

"Want to ask the car company when you drop it off?"

My thoughts flew. "No." I handed it to him. "Keep it. In your pocket if you don't mind. If someone's tracking me, let's confuse them."

"I can take it to one of those cell phone repair places. See if they recognize the brand. Or know how to find out what it links to."

"Great." I slid my laptop into its sleeve in the backpack.

"Think the Kevs are tracking you?"

"Seems low tech for them." I zipped my wallet into the side compartment of my shoulder bag. "But the car's been parked on the street a lot. Here and other places."

"Someone needed to get in to put it there, though."

I thought about the night before. Dylan flashing that half-smile as he offered to help. Resting his arms on the open passenger side window.

24

WHO SAW HER LAST

A LONG LINE at the rental car return made me nervous I'd miss my flight. I checked the time every few minutes, and did the same when I finally got on the shuttle bus and later into the security lane, though I knew it didn't make the process faster. I kicked myself for not following through with getting the TSA Precheck status. But before this, I flew once or twice a year at most.

Despite four texts telling me the flight was leaving on time, the display at the gate showed an hour delay. I found a seat across the corridor where it was less crowded and called Danielle.

"Highbottom vaguely remembers the task force interviewed a photographer, which was probably Klaus." I moved a seat over as a family of four squeezed into the seats next to me. "But he thinks he had an alibi. He's going to ask around. I'd love to talk to Klaus, but I can't think why he'd want to help."

"If I were his lawyer, I'd tell him forget it," Danielle said. "With his background, the police might try to pin it on him whether he did it or not."

"But I should try."

"No question. Plenty of people don't listen to their lawyers. Though you might want to talk to the prosecutor first. Get some background."

"Is it normal to reduce the charges so much? From producing child porn and selling drugs to possession of both? Especially the marijuana part. It's such a minor offense."

"Not in the eighties. Pot was illegal. People saw it as a gateway drug."

"Right." I often forgot that. For years before Illinois decriminalized it, Chicago treated most marijuana offenses more like traffic tickets. But in the seventies and eighties, even Chicago likely went after offenders.

My next call was to my friend Lauren to see if I could drive her car to Milwaukee the next morning. Driving is the worst and most expensive way to get anywhere in Chicago. Walking or public transportation isn't always faster, but it's cheaper. And less stressful. I work or read or let my thoughts wander and someone else gets me where I need to be. No veering around taxis that dart through red lights or paying a fortune for parking.

All of which is why I don't own a car. I do, though, own a parking spot. It came with my condo, one of a few available spots. Lauren lives in the same converted warehouse building but has no parking spot. She does, though, own a Volvo. It's over ten years old but still handles well.

So we share.

It took some effort, but Lauren agreed I could drive the Volvo to Milwaukee. She didn't mind my taking the car, but she wanted me to wait until she could come with. But Michelle Zamorski, formerly O'Brien, had one day free this week. After that, she was traveling overseas.

I wasn't about to miss my window.

I arrived the next morning at the Zamorskis' dance studio

as a class let out. Boys and girls streamed out of the studio chirping good-byes to Michelle.

She was about my height and slimmer, almost wiry. Her hair, the color of iron filings, was pulled into a bun at the top of her hair. Wavy strands sprung out on the sides. Fine lines creased her neck and face.

Michelle told me the school focused on ethnic dances from eastern European countries as she ushered me into an interior stairwell. The building looked as old as my parents' home but smelled of varnish and lemon polish.

"No Irish dancing?" I said.

Her smile reached her eyes. "I'm not Irish. I'm Scandinavian. O'Brien was my first husband's name. I kept it because we divorced at a crucial time in my career. I didn't need a name change."

I followed her up a set of steep stairs. "But you didn't mind one later."

At the top of the stairs, she flipped through her key ring. "Wasn't planning to keep teaching when I closed Little Lilies." She opened the door and motioned me to follow her in. "Then I flunked retirement. Took on a private student here, taught a class there. Pretty soon my husband and I are buying this building and opening this studio. He's also very bad at retirement."

"My Gram says it's overrated," I said.

Michelle and her husband lived in a beautifully furnished apartment above the studio. Antiques with rich, upholstered fabrics, striking pieces of art, and leafy plants and trees.

In her kitchen, she made lemongrass tea for me and black drip coffee for herself. I perched on a counter stool at a table made from a heavy wooden door. I asked what she remembered about Vanessa Kev.

"Talented girl. Motivated. But not competitive."

"Meaning?"

"If she didn't get a solo, it disappointed her. But she was thrilled for the girl who got it." She hopped off her stool. "Forgot the cookies."

I told her it wasn't necessary, but she took homemade chocolate thumbprint cookies from a pink tin and arranged them in a spiral on a crystal plate. "From a student's dad. He's an aces baker. Never did learn myself. No time."

"What about Vanessa's parents? Were they upset if she didn't get a solo?"

If they were anything like some of the stage parents I met growing up, they would have been.

"No idea about Ted. Never met him. Her mother wanted Nessa to get lots of experience. She was pleasant, though. Understood how little the girls were. How important it was that they all get to dance. Plenty of time for competition later."

Michelle remembered Klaus Erickson as a photographer with reddish hair and a nice smile. "He was friends with Gail Kev. Took tons of photos. Even gave me a few to use as publicity." She rubbed her lower back. "Mind if we move to the living room? Told my husband these backless stools aren't for septuagenarians. But we're both more about look than function. You know how that is."

I nodded, though I wondered about the long explanation. And if the topic, not the counter stool, made her uncomfortable.

But once settled on a worn leather couch she returned to it without prompting. "I offered to pay Klaus for the photos. He wouldn't hear of it."

Her warm tone suggested she knew nothing of his crimes. I decided to keep it that way for now so I didn't distract her from my next questions.

"Did the police ever question him about Vanessa?"

"Must have. They questioned everyone."

"Including you?"

"Oh, of course. Not aggressively. I was happy to answer. Wait, no. Not happy. Nothing happy about any of it. But I wanted to help however I could."

"I'm a little surprised you never met Ted Kev. He never attended a recital?"

"Not one I was at." She crossed to a grouping of plants on an antique side table. Brown leaves lay on the floor beneath them. Michelle started collecting them. "You don't mind if I tend the plants while we talk, do you? I'm hardly here. Then when I am I see how sad they look."

"Not at all. Did Gail ever mention why her husband didn't attend?"

I didn't know if my questions made Michelle nervous or if she was one of those people who can't stay still. A dance instructor might be the best person to arrange for a kidnapping of a student dancer. Though I couldn't think why she'd do it.

"She said Ted worked a lot. Gail did too when she was at the company. Being a startup and all."

Michelle disappeared for a moment and returned with a green plastic watering pitcher.

"How about the rest of the family? Anyone else attend the recitals?"

"Her cousin. Came to nearly every one. Some rehearsals too."

"Jimmy?"

She watered each plant, careful not to let any spill over. "Yes. Forgot his name for a second there. Jimmy. Always cheered her on. The other kids loved him, too."

"Was he at the last recital, the one Nessa was taken from?"

"No. He was sick. Otherwise he never would have missed it."

"How do you know he was sick? Did someone tell you?"

"Hm." She paused near a tall ficus. "You know, I'm not sure. Can't remember. It was so long ago."

"If he surprised Vanessa backstage and asked her to go somewhere with him, would she?"

The jeweled earrings that ran up the side of Michelle's ears caught the light as she nodded. "No question. But there's no way Jimmy would hurt Nessa."

"Did the police consider him a suspect?"

"No idea. They weren't exactly chatty about their theories."

"Who saw Nessa last that day?"

Michelle set the watering pitcher on the side table and wiped her hands on her heavy brown leggings. "That's the thing. Nobody knows."

25

THE TIARA

THE STAINED glass windows cast a colorful pattern across the floor. Michelle moved through it as she picked dry leaves off plants and told me about the day Vanessa Kev was taken. Hues of blue, magenta, and pink danced across her arms and face.

"A dozen dance troops performed that day. Three from my school. My tiny tots went on first, then my early grade schoolers. Nessa barely made it into that group. Age-wise. Not talent-wise. Talent, she fit right in. But normally I waited until they were six."

"When did you first see Nessa that day?"

Michelle inspected a bamboo plant with brown-edged leaves. "Police asked that. I had no idea even back then. It was chaos backstage. Too many girls. Not enough dressing rooms."

"You didn't check the students in?"

"Someone from the charity hosting the event did. They ran the whole day, got the proceeds. I toggled between my students. It was the toddlers' first performance. It was like herding cats. Excited cats. A few crying cats. But cats."

"Any parents backstage?"

"For the tots and early grades. We could never keep them on track otherwise. For the older kids, no."

That meant a lot of adults with access to the kids before and during the recital. Michelle estimated at least thirty-five parents, a handful of teachers, and about ten older student volunteers. She said she'd given a list of names to the police.

"Was Gail backstage?"

"If she was, I didn't see her." Michelle closed her fingers around a dry vine from a spider plant. Bits of it drifted toward the floor. "But Nessa was self-sufficient for a child her age. Doing things herself made her feel like a real ballerina. As she put it."

"Did you see Nessa before she went on?"

"That I remember. Because I asked her to take off this pretty little tiara someone gave her for luck."

That was new information. "Someone? Who?"

"Wish I'd asked. Believe me. But there was so much going on. I just told her she couldn't wear it on stage. It didn't match the costumes. She ran to put it in the dressing room, came back without it."

"And then went on stage?"

"Yes. I was sweating, though. Worried they'd all miss their cue because of it." Michelle brushed past a plant with what looked like tiny cactus buds on its vines. A dozen fell onto the floor. "Oh, this one. Breathe near it and it falls apart."

"Did Nessa's group get on stage on time?"

"They did. It was all good. Except that, I don't know if you know this, the tiara is why it took so long for anyone to know Vanessa was missing."

26

AFTER THE RECITAL

"I NEED TO BACK UP." Michelle pushed aside a plush purple pillow to make space on the sofa and sat still at last. "The school's auditorium had a terrible design. Had to climb two flights of narrow metal stairs to get in or out of backstage."

"What about students on crutches? Or in wheelchairs?"

"They couldn't take part. Not in a choir concert. Or a play. Or a graduation ceremony for that matter." She sipped her coffee, which must be as cold now as my tea. "Well, I suppose they could if they could get up the stairs on the auditorium side. There were only about ten steps there."

"But the ADA — oh." I vaguely remembered from law school that Congress passed the Americans With Disabilities Act in 1990, years after Q.C.'s and Nessa's deaths.

Michelle nodded. "The not-so-good old days. Acoustics were awful, too. Very echoey. After they finished performing, each child had to stay dead silent as they tiptoed up the stairs and out. Until they got to the Multipurpose Room, really. Then they could talk, jump, dance. Whatever they wanted."

"The what room?"

"Multipurpose Room. That's what the school called it. Used

it for everything from ice cream socials to gymnastics to PTA meetings."

Michelle told me a local ice cream shop and bakery provided treats in the Multipurpose Room for the dancers and their parents. But the parents were encouraged to stay in the auditorium and watch the other dancers, not simply leave once their kids got off stage. Otherwise, the older girls performed to a half empty theater.

"And those acoustics again. Too much noise if people came and went." Michelle glanced at my nearly empty mug. "More tea?"

"I'm fine," I said. "So parents stayed in the theater while their little kids were alone in this Multipurpose room?"

"The older girls, the volunteers, kept an eye on them."

"Hard to believe more people didn't check on their kids. That Gail didn't."

Michelle pulled on a loose thread on the plush pillow. "Different times. Five-year-olds walked to kindergarten alone. Kids rode bikes without helmets. One day, probably, oh, a few months before Vanessa disappeared, it was pouring. I pulled over and offered a teenage girl without an umbrella a ride. Didn't know her. I was being kind. She accepted. I dropped her at school. I'd never do that now. And she'd never accept."

"You think something like that happened to Nessa?"

"Not exactly like that. But the police kept saying a child wouldn't go off with a stranger. But that girl got in my car. Someone who seemed kind, they might be able to lure Vanessa."

"And the tiara?"

"Oh, yes. Gail came to the Multipurpose Room about forty-five minutes after Nessa's performance ended. Stepped in to relieve one of the volunteers serving ice cream."

"And didn't look for Vanessa?" I said.

"I'm sure she looked. Or meant to. But I stopped to tell her how thrilled I was with Nessa's performance. And I pointed out a little girl wearing a tiara with her back to us. And told Gail the story about almost missing our cue."

"You both thought the girl was Nessa?" I said.

"Yes. All the early grade girls wore the same costumes. It was a crowded room. The child had her back to us most of the time. She was also brunette and about Nessa's height."

So Michelle, according to her own account, told Nessa to take off the tiara. Then suggested to Gail that the girl wearing it was her daughter. Maybe an honest mistake. Maybe.

Michelle told me Gail's volunteer shift ended about twenty minutes later. That's when she realized the girl wasn't Nessa.

I imagined the scene. Crowded or not, knowing what happened it seemed impossible that both women mistook a different girl for Vanessa. I tried to make allowances for 1980s parents being a lot more laissez faire than today's.

But it still felt off.

"Where did Gail think the tiara came from?"

"She thought Nessa's cousin Jimmy might have slipped it to her before they left home. Because he felt bad that he couldn't attend the recital."

"But wasn't he home sick?"

"Not home. At the Kevs. He stayed overnight there."

"Why was the other girl wearing the tiara?" I said. "Do you know?"

"She said she found it with her things after the performance. She thought Nessa left it for her."

"Could that have happened?"

"It was like Nessa. She wanted the other girls to be happy. If one of them admired her hair clips or earrings, Nessa gave them to her. Once I had to politely get a bracelet back. I could tell it was expensive. Didn't think her parents would be happy if she came home without it."

"Had the girl admired the tiara?"

"No. She said she didn't see it until after the performance. And she didn't see Vanessa after the performance."

"But she assumed Vanessa left it."

"Right. The girl wasn't one of the better dancers. Nessa always wished her luck and told her she did a good job even if she stumbled. That's why she thought Nessa gave it to her — as a 'good job' sort of prize."

Michelle gave me the girl's first name, but she didn't remember the last. She promised that the next time she went to her storage locker she'd see if she still had records of her students.

"When she realized Nessa wasn't in the Multipurpose Room, did Gail call the police?"

"Not right away," Michelle said. "That was partly my fault, too."

27

THE SEARCH

Michelle twirled a half green, half brown leaf. "I thought Nessa must still be backstage. Sometimes the younger girls hung around the older ones while they changed. Sort of a bask in the limelight thing. But Gail checked, and she wasn't there."

"Was she worried?"

"Not too much yet. We checked the playground. A few older girls were there. Surrounded by cigarette butts, smelling like smoke and chewing gum. They hadn't seen Nessa."

"Or anyone else?"

"You know, I don't know if we asked that." Michelle rubbed the leaf between her fingers. Dried bits fell onto the coffee table. "But I told the police who they were. I'm sure they questioned them."

I felt less sure. In the best circumstances, things slip through cracks. Michelle didn't remember the girls' names. They were from other dance schools.

"How did Gail seem at that point?"

"Clutched her purse so tight I thought she must be crushing everything inside. But still keeping it together. Speaking slowly and calmly. Like if she did everything would be okay. She started to lose it when we didn't have change for the payphone so she could call home. I got some from a volunteer."

"Did Gail talk to Jimmy?"

If Ted Kev was at the cabin, no one other than Jimmy should have been there.

"Don't know." Michelle cocked her head. "I was checking the auditorium balcony. When I came back, Gail said Nessa wasn't home and that she'd called the police."

Michelle guessed about two and a half hours elapsed between Nessa's dance performance and when the police arrived. Plenty of time for someone to get far from the school by car. Or on foot.

While waiting for the police, Michelle called a school administrator who came with master keys. Volunteers searched classrooms and offices with no luck.

"Volunteers who could have been involved in the kidnapping," I said.

"We still thought — hoped — Vanessa wandered off. Lots of kids thought it was fun to be in a school building when it was closed. They snuck into classrooms. Wrote on the chalkboards. Stole the chalk."

"Gail thought Nessa might be doing that?"

The formal, reserved woman I met didn't seem likely to have a five-year-old who broke into classrooms for fun. But who knew what she'd been like before the crime changed her whole life.

"She was desperate to believe it."

I asked if Michelle heard about my sister's disappearance before Nessa was taken.

"Seeing as it was decades ago, hard to say for sure. But I don't remember knowing about missing girls before the recital. We all would have been more careful. And more panicked right off when we couldn't find Nessa."

My mother complained there was too little publicity about

Q.C.'s disappearance. She thought if there had been, Q.C. might have been found alive. But unlike the JonBenét Ramsey case a decade later, the national press never focused on Q.C. or Vanessa.

Day after day in the nineties, my mother watched news coverage about JonBenét. One second, she cried for the parents. The next she threw shoes at the TV because police handled those parents with kid gloves. And because JonBenét was on the news in the first place.

It made me think about Ted Kev's non-disclosure agreements. The Kevs might have somehow tamped down on the media, preferring privacy. Or maybe it was just one of those things. The way these days one video went viral and another like it faded into the ether.

"So you first heard about Q.C. when —"

"When they found the bodies together." Michelle smoothed the edges of the throw pillow. "It was — shocking. That another girl was with her. Less so that Nessa was dead. By then I thought she might be."

"Why?"

"Nothing in the news about ransom. I knew police might've kept that quiet. But after the first week I thought if there'd been a ransom demand Vanessa would've been back."

"You think the Kevs had the money? I read that the company started on a shoestring."

I'd found surprisingly few articles about the start of the company or about Ted Kev personally. But those few referred to him as a self-made man.

"Maybe. But Gail's family had plenty of money."

"Did everyone know that?"

"It wasn't a secret. Her family owned oil refineries in Texas. If someone asked for money, the grandparents would have put it together to save that child."

I got names of students Michelle remembered from Nessa's

class, but Michelle didn't have any contact information. Before I left, I told her about Klaus Erickson's criminal record and sentence.

Her distress seemed genuine. She rocked back and pressed her palm against her chest. "I can't believe I let him around all the children."

I reassured her that she couldn't have known there was anything dangerous about him.

In the car, before starting the drive home I called Highbottom. I caught him as he was packing for his return home from Florida. I asked whether the police saw Michelle O'Brien as a suspect in Vanessa Kev's disappearance.

"Everyone there that day was a suspect. Never heard much about her, though. Might've been ruled out early. You think she was involved?"

"Gut level? No. But it'd be a lot easier for someone to grab Vanessa if the dance instructor smoothed the way."

With a tiara, for instance. But I couldn't quite see it. For one thing, if Michelle O'Brien was a serial killer of little girls, with all the daily opportunities, she wouldn't have stopped with two.

"What was the theory on how my dad got Vanessa to go somewhere with him?" I said.

"Posed as a parent of one of the other dancers. Got backstage."

That part was plausible. "And then? How did he supposedly get her to leave with him?"

"No idea," Highbottom said. "I was out of it by then."

"And no one remembered seeing my dad backstage."

"No. But no one remembered Ted or Gail Kev anywhere around Q.C.'s party. Or saw them around town for that matter. Another reason these cases never got solved."

My phone buzzed as I hung up. Danielle had found me the name of the prosecutor in the Klaus Erickson case.

28

COURTING QUESTIONS

NOT WANTING to take time for lunch but wary about hunger triggering a migraine, on the drive to Chicago I ate two of the emergency power bars I keep in my shoulder bag. Then I called Ty with the phone on speaker. Because I don't drive much, I don't like multi-tasking while doing it. But we hadn't spoken in days.

He was just back from an evening wining and dining clients after a long day at his office. He sounded exhausted. I decided not to mention the tracker my dad found in my car. Ty could do nothing about it from Dubai. At least we got to talk, and he said he'd text me good times for a Zoom call. I tried not to think about how hard it might be to find a time that worked for both of us.

When I got to my office I wrote and filed two motions and answered client emails. I also tried calling Klaus Erickson. The odds of him talking to me were next to zero. But in both my acting and law careers I learned it pays to take the long shots. Try enough of them and you'll get somewhere you wouldn't have gotten without the attempts.

Not this time, though.

Klaus answered the phone, more than most people do these days if they don't know the number. But once I told him who I was and what I wanted, he hung up. And didn't answer my follow up call.

My luck with the prosecutor of the charges against Klaus wasn't much better. The Illinois Attorney Registration and Disciplinary Commission listed him as retired. His current address and phone number were in Belleville, Illinois. Almost all the way back to Edwardsville.

The automated voicemail that answered didn't say his name, so I was unsure if I reached a current number for him. I crossed my fingers and left a message.

I was about to dive into the file for tomorrow's hearing when someone banged on the outer door of the office suite.

TWENTY MINUTES later Lauren and I sat along the windows at a round white marble table at Café des Livres. It's the café and restaurant on the ground floor where I work. Though Lauren practically had to drag me there from my office, the break felt good. It was after seven, I was exhausted, and I was starving.

We ordered goat cheese salads, chicken and mushroom crepes, and a half bottle of Pinot Noir.

"Seriously a good call not telling Ty about the tracker." Lauren squeezed a lime slice into her water. "He feels bad enough already that he couldn't go to Edwardsville to help."

"I wouldn't say it to him, but in some ways it's easier without him. Not that I don't miss him like crazy."

"Well, seriously, he hasn't been your best back up for investigations," Lauren said. "Though I messed up that one time. But otherwise, I'm awesome."

She was awesome. As for Ty, it was a bit of a sore spot with me how often he reminded me to be careful. More than once he was the one who added to the danger I faced. Not purposely. But his efforts to help didn't always turn out the way he meant them to.

"You are. But it's not your job — or Ty's — to look into crimes."

"But I like it," Lauren said. A server set down our salads but still hadn't brought the wine. "And my money's on the teacher musician guy who was chatting you up. Or on his parents."

"He wasn't chatting me up. And I've thought about that. He was seven when Q.C. was taken. Obviously, he didn't kidnap and kill two girls. That'd be like blaming Kendra."

Lauren shook her head, sending her blond bob swinging. "Right, but his dad could have done it. Or his mother. Like if there was something going on between the reverend and your mom. She does it for revenge."

"There's something about my mother and the reverend. But the Sabatinis were out of town when Q.C. was taken."

"Were they? You've got absolutely no idea how thorough the local police were in verifying that."

"I've got absolutely no idea how thorough they were about anything," I said. "Besides hounding my parents."

"Have you asked your mom yet? If she had an affair?"

I started to wind my fingers into my hair, then let go and let my hand rest on the table. "Much as I'm longing for another heart-to-heart, no. I'm hoping to talk to Rev first. Questioning my mother feels a lot like talking to a hostile witness. I figure the more I know beforehand the better the odds I'll get her to tell me what I want to know."

Carole Ports, the French proprietor of the café and my long-time friend, set an uncorked bottle of Pomerol, rather than the Pinot Noir we'd ordered, in the center of the table. "On the house."

Lauren checked the label. "Ooo, I love this one. Seriously, thank you."

Even the least expensive Pomerol was pricier than any wine on the menu. I echoed Lauren's thanks but protested that Carole didn't need to dive into her private collection for us.

"*Mais oui*, I do," Carole Ports said. Her long earrings dangled as she poured the wine. "You have both done so much for me. And risked your lives to do it."

A little over a year before in the midst of a blizzard, I helped her search for a missing neighbor. A college girl to whom Carole was like a second mother. Just as she was to me.

"You can't give us free food and drinks forever," I said.

"*Bien sur que je peux.* And I want to." She rested her hand on my shoulder. "Enjoy. Unwind. Forget crime, and your family, for tonight."

After Carole walked away Lauren lifted her glass. "You're not going to forget crime, are you? You need to finish filling me in."

"So long as you drink most of the wine. I still need to get ready for my court hearing."

"YOUR HONOR, everything the plaintiff claims my client did falls within his duties as president of the company." I rested my hands on the ledge in front of the judge's bench. It helped me ignore my phone, which was vibrating in my inner suit jacket pocket.

The judge's heavy black eyebrows raised. "That may be so, Ms. Davis, but the LLC agreement allows both brothers to see the books. Don't you agree?"

My opponent, who wore a rumpled suit, wisely stayed silent. He knew, I knew, and the judge knew that the answer to that question was Yes.

The phone buzzed twice fast. Someone had left a voicemail. I hoped it was Klaus. Or the prosecutor.

“The right to inspect has limits,” I said. “For the record, my client objects. But, of course, we’ll make the books available if the court requires it.”

“For the record” is lawyer speak for “I agree but this client is difficult so I can’t come out and say I agree.” Judges, most of whom once practiced law themselves, mostly get it.

“I’d expect nothing less, Ms. Davis. Seven days.”

I asked for ten. I wanted to review the records when I next got back from Edwardsville instead of before I left. But the judge, not happy he had to hear us argue for no real reason, stuck with seven.

In the hallway outside the courtroom, I finally checked voicemail. Christopher Taflinski, the retired prosecutor of the case against Klaus Erickson, was willing to talk to me. By phone or in person near Belleville, Illinois, where he lived.

He wasn’t that far from my parents’ house. After a lot of cajoling, my client agreed to download the books to a shared drive so I could start reviewing them right away. I left a message with the prosecutor suggesting dates to meet.

It took me twenty minutes to walk back to my office. Despite the snow flurries and wind, I enjoyed the exercise. And the chance to let my mind wander. By the time I got there, the prosecutor returned my call. He remembered Klaus’s case well and agreed to meet me tomorrow afternoon.

“I think you’ll find it fascinating,” he said.

29

NOT THE BRIGHTEST BULB

THE NEXT DAY I drove straight from St. Louis Lambert Airport to Belleville. Former U.S. Attorney Christopher Taflinski met me at a diner three blocks from the town square. Over fountain colas and apple pie he told me the story.

Danielle wasn't kidding about the stupid things people did.

Six years after Q.C.'s and Vanessa's deaths, Klaus Erickson became involved in what he called an affair with his wife's sister. The sister was sixteen when it started, seventeen when it ended. The night before her birthday, he took nude photographs of her.

Two years later, for other reasons, his wife filed for divorce. She knew nothing about Klaus and her sister. Klaus told her and threatened to send the nude photos to the wife's family and friends if she didn't agree to no alimony. The wife called the FBI. A sting was set up. The wife asked Klaus to drop off copies of the nude photos in her mailbox so she'd know he was telling the truth about having taken them.

An FBI agent watched him do it. The photos were direct proof of child pornography and indirect proof of statutory rape.

The sister told law enforcement Klaus also gave her marijuana and took her to parties across state lines in St. Louis.

Christopher finished the story as the waitress set down the bill. I slid it toward my plate.

"I can't believe he tried to blackmail his ex with evidence of his own crime. And thought it would work," I said.

Christopher's hands trembled as he cut what was left of his pie in two. A thin man in his mid-sixties, he had told me when we sat down that he had Parkinson's disease. He said he always explained that to victims and their families when he was still working. If he didn't, he feared they might think the shaking came from issues like drinking or drug use.

He ate a forkful of baked apple filling. "Sadly, in some families it might have. But not this one."

"The case against Klaus sounds strong. Why reduced charges and a plea deal?"

"Same reasons as always. Saves time and resources compared to trying the case. Avoids emotional distress for the victim. And any chance of a not guilty."

"Juries are unpredictable. But you really think they'd say Not Guilty?"

"All it takes is one person to hang a jury. Someone who feels a girl at sixteen-going-on-seventeen is old enough. And remember, not as much awareness back then about predators and age differences."

I finished my pie, which was delicious. "How bad were the photos?"

"Sounds horrible to say they weren't bad. But I've seen things that'd make you vomit. That make the jury ask not 'is he guilty?' but 'can we lock him up forever?' That's not what these were. The girl was nude. But no sex acts, no exposed genitals."

"Did you find any other photos? I assume you searched?"

"The FBI turned his home and business upside down.

There were other nudes, but no one else underage. And no one who claimed they were forced or coerced."

Christopher didn't think the FBI agents who handled the matter contacted the task force on Q.C. and Vanessa, but he didn't know for sure.

"You think this later crime makes it more likely Klaus killed Q.C. and Vanessa?" I said.

"More likely than someone without his background. But in my experience, a twenty or thirty-year-old man involved with a teenager — doesn't mean he preys on young children. That's a very specific predilection. Not saying they can't cross over."

"I wish I knew if Klaus ever met Q.C.," I said.

"I'd say there's no chance he'll admit it if he did, but he's clearly not the brightest bulb."

"Bright enough to hang up on me. Any chance I could see the photos the FBI found? To check if my sister appears in them?"

"They're not in the public record. You might try talking to his ex-wife. She may have seen them."

I took down the ex's name and paid the check at the counter on our way out. Dessert and soda for two cost barely a dollar more than one latte at home. Back in my rental car — a Hyundai this time — I took out my iPad. I found an address easily enough for the ex-wife. She lived in southern Indiana now.

But her phone number was no longer valid.

I texted my paralegal to ask her to hunt for a current phone, then called my mother to tell her I'd be there soon. She was back in her irritable mode and snapped at me when I asked about Reverend Sabatini. I sent off a text to Dylan Sabatini.

Maybe I could get more information out of him. I sighed and started the car. Ty might not be the ideal person to help me investigate. But he was a great buffer between my mother and me. With him, she smiled and unwound. Once she even danced.

Half an hour later I turned the corner onto my parents' street. And discovered I might have a buffer after all.

30

THE SURPRISE GUEST

"You didn't seriously think I was letting you handle this whole investigation alone?" Lauren waited as the Lyft driver took her rolling suitcase and leopard print Dolce & Gabbana overnight bag from the trunk.

I hugged her. "Did Ty put you up to this?"

"I was totally already booking my flight when he texted me. Someone's got to get your mother to let you talk to the reverend."

"If you can do that, I'll owe you big time." I carried her bag up the steps. "Leave your coat on. Mom's bound to order us out somewhere."

Lauren and I stepped into the kitchen.

"Mom, you remember Lauren."

My mother had been to Chicago twice for Thanksgiving since she and my dad moved away when I was sixteen. She met Lauren the second time, when I was still in law school.

"You should have told me you were bringing a guest." My mother closed her magazine. "Dad's not going to want to cook for four."

"I don't want to be any trouble. I can whip something up," Lauren said.

"There's nothing here to make." Frowning, my mother handed me cash from her jar on the counter. "Get a vegetable platter, buns, and a pan of that Italian beef at the grocer. Dad can heat it. Make sure they don't put any peppers on it."

"You're sure I can't cook?" Lauren opened the freezer. "Frozen ravioli, vegetables, chicken thighs." Lauren opened the opposite door and inspected the refrigerator shelves. "Or if you don't want me to defrost —"

"If you told us Dad could have rearranged the music room." My mother pointed at Lauren. "You'll have to share with Quille. Or sleep between the instruments."

I grabbed my coat and we headed out.

"She does know the refrigerator's full of food?" Lauren said.

"Possibly." A text from Dylan came in as I got in the car. I read it, then pulled the shoulder belt across my chest. "How do you feel about meeting Dylan Sabatini after dinner instead of hanging around my parents' house?"

"Totally fine."

WE MET Dylan at a bar and grill next to a tattoo parlor off Main Street. An acoustic but still loud bluegrass band played in the corner. The music featured the traditional brassy bluegrass guitar leads, twangy banjo riffs, and thumping standup bass. We sat at the table farthest from the speakers but still needed to scoot close together to hear one another. I had no idea why Dylan suggested here instead of Recess Brewing.

"Motive's not an element of murder in Illinois. Or in most states," I said in answer to a question from him. "But showing why a defendant wanted to kill someone can help convince a jury."

"But here the why might be because someone's a sociopath," Dylan said. "Which, speaking of, sorry again about my father. He told me he wouldn't call your mom, then that's the next thing he did."

I sipped my whiskey sour. "Okay, there's so much in that statement I don't know where to start."

Dylan tilted his head and smiled. "Maybe with my implying my father's a sociopath? I meant it only in the most benign sense."

Lauren stirred the ice in her diet Pepsi. She was the designated driver tonight. "In what universe is that benign?"

"Dad's not really dangerous except that he's a born salesman. And not even the kind that makes you feel slimy."

"So the kind that makes you feel good?" I said.

"The kind people believe is their friend and invite to their Thanksgiving dinners."

"Shouldn't people feel that way about their pastor?" Lauren said.

"Not if he's only looking to fill the donation plate."

"You're saying he doesn't care about his congregation?" I said.

If Dylan planted the tracker on me for his father, he could be pretending to dislike his dad to keep me from seeing that they were working together. But I was less sure than before that he was responsible. Danielle told me a lot of tow truck drivers, and some of her clients, had electronic devices that opened electronic locks on doors.

Whoever placed the tag could have done it anytime.

"When I was a kid, he spent hours perfecting his sympathy face in front of a mirror," Dylan said. "Recorded himself saying comforting phrases, too. Until he got just the right tone."

"Before I got comfortable, I practiced introducing myself in court," I said.

"And I seriously worked on my handshake and how to greet people at open houses when I was a new realtor," Lauren said.

"Sure." Dylan drained his glass. "You should do that for businesses."

"But your dad's church is his business," Lauren said, surprising me a bit. She's religious and the only one of my friends who attends church weekly. She also sometimes invites the local priests for dinner. Maybe it gave her insight into the ins and outs of running a successful church. "It can't keep running if no one donates."

"But he insists it's not a business. While he works on his sympathy face in the mirror."

A few minutes later, Dylan headed to the bar for a refill. As soon as he was out of hearing distance, Lauren leaned closer to me. "You didn't tell me he was Bacon. Mm. And Eggs."

Lauren dated a lot more than I did over the years and used dating apps. She developed a shorthand when texting me from her first meetings. Lizards meant someone who creeped her out. Like feeling a lizard crawl across your bare stomach. Bacon stood for someone so hot, you could fry bacon and eggs on his stomach.

"It didn't seem relevant."

"Hotness is always relevant. And I notice you didn't disagree."

"No, but I'm seeing Ty. And you're seeing Joe."

"Oh, please. We can still appreciate. We're in relationships, not dead."

Dylan returned and slid onto the chair next to me. "All set."

"For?" Lauren said.

"Open mike at eight." He glanced at me. "You said you miss singing, so I signed us up. But I'll take the slot myself if you don't want to."

I wrapped my hand around my glass. "I'm not much for

winging it. Joe, Danielle, and I rehearse for weeks for every job."

"But you sing for fun at parties," Lauren said.

"Parties don't have stages."

Dylan nodded toward the corner where the band played. "One, barely a stage. Hardly two inches off the floor. Two, studio musician, remember? I'll follow you. And we can step in the back room. Run through things first." Dylan waved his hand at the room. "Three, not a discerning audience. Everyone here will be drunk in another half hour or so. If they're not now."

He wasn't wrong. Despite the volume, most people paid little attention to the band. Usually, I don't like that. There's no point in singing for an audience that doesn't care. But I was fine with it when trying out new material.

"Maybe," I said.

Dylan squeezed my lower arm. His fingers felt warm against my slightly chilled skin. "You look into crime but you're afraid to jump on stage?"

"Different things," I said. "And afraid's too strong a word. I just like being prepared."

"Let's see your set lists. Bet you a month's pay you've got them on your phone."

"You win the bet," Lauren said. "And they're color coded."

He gave that half-smile. "Of course."

"Go ahead, Quille. Have a little fun," Lauren said.

31

GETTING WHAT YOU WANT

LAUREN TOOK my phone and opened my master set list. Dylan's shoulder nearly brushed mine as he leaned over to see it. "Townes Van Zandt. Nice. How about *Rex's Blues*?"

"I almost never get to sing it. My friends think it's too dark."

Dylan knowing Townes Van Zandt's music surprised me. A lot of people have heard his songs because stars like Bob Dylan, Emmylou Harris, and Willy Nelson covered them. But almost no one I meet ever knows about him.

"Dark but beautiful," Dylan said. "You sing lead, I'll harmonize. Or the other way if you want."

"I'll sing lead."

We chose two more and ducked into a back storage room where Dylan stowed his guitar before we arrived. He knew the bartender here, too.

"Getting the sense you spend a lot of time in bars," I said as he twisted a tuning peg.

"Not as much as you might think. But they are one place my students can't go. Makes it easier to relax."

We strained to hear ourselves over the music filtering in from the main room. But after twice through each song I felt all right about the tempo and the key. I was less sure how well our voices blended given the din.

Dylan glanced at the time. "Once more through each? There's plenty of time."

I was tempted. But the longer we sang, the less time I could spend asking about Dylan's father. Which might be his whole reason for suggesting this.

"No, I'm good," I said.

"Works for me." He put the guitar back in the case. "Now I see why you like investigating crime. Everything else in your life is planned and predictable."

"Lawsuits aren't." I followed him into the main room again where, happily, the band had taken a break. "But I want to know more about your dad. Why does it bother you that he practices a sympathy face? He might want to be sure he can comfort people even if he's tired or burnt out."

"Because he turns on a dime to get whatever — or whoever — he wants."

Lauren had ordered a second whiskey sour for me. I sipped it. "For example?"

"One Sunday, I watched him console a woman whose husband just died. Deep voice, sympathy face, tears welling. Then he spots a big donor near the door. A second later he's lighting her cigarette, touching her arm, admiring her new dress. Inviting her for coffee. Where she no doubt handed over another big check."

I thought of Dylan flashing that half-smile at me then becoming again the serious though cool schoolteacher.

"What?" he said.

"You're not bad at switching gears yourself. Like at school."

"Sure, but I do it to keep things appropriate. My non-teacher self can flirt with a pretty lawyer lady who stops by. My teacher self needs to avoid anything students might see as social, let alone flirty."

Lauren poked my side and whispered in my ear. "Told you."

I kept my gaze on Dylan. "You're sure your dad's not doing the same thing? Being the side of himself that fits the situation?"

The emcee announced that the open stage started in fifteen minutes. I flipped to the lyrics to *Rex's Blues* on my phone to reinforce them once more before our turn.

Dylan sighed. "Maybe. No one wants to admit they're like their parents. No one I know anyway. But there is a difference. My father turns on the charm when he wants something. If there's nothing to get, he doesn't bother."

"And with you it's genuine?"

He tilted his head. "I like people. Like having fun. And, sure, I like to flirt. In my college days — maybe once or twice later — a girl took it more to heart than I meant. Made me more aware. And I don't flirt to manipulate people."

"Calling me a pretty lawyer lady wasn't to try to get anything from me?"

"How do you know I didn't mean the lawyer lady who stopped by last week? But seriously, I would like something. To buy you dinner while you're in town."

"I'd like that. But not as a date. I have a boyfriend."

"And where is he while you hunt for a double murderer?" He glanced at Lauren. "Nothing against your blond bubbly friend here, but shouldn't your guy be riding shotgun?"

"That was the plan. But he got a four-month work assignment out of town. It was almost impossible to carve the time out of my law practice to do this, so I couldn't put it off."

I didn't want to say Ty was out of the country. Dylan might think that left some sort of opening.

"Hmm. Well, what if the three of us have dinner? Not a date. And since I suspect you have ulterior motives, you can pay. If you want."

The emcee called us to the stage before I needed to answer.

I looked over the lyrics while Dylan retuned his E string and told the audience a joke.

We started with *In The Pines*, the easiest song I knew for singing with a stranger. Dylan sang lead. I kept my eyes on his fingers, getting a feel for how he played and when he changed chords. His voice was warm, with a slight vibrato, and right on pitch. On the first chorus, I watched his lips and matched how long or short he held the notes.

On the second chorus I hit the harmony perfectly. Our voices blended almost as if they were different registers of the same voice. We slid into the second song as the applause burst out. I relaxed enough to look at the audience. Many ignored us. But about a third seemed transfixed. I took that as a win in this place.

For *Rex's Blues*, which doesn't have a chorus, Dylan joined in on the last two lines of each verse. His voice wove around mine effortlessly. Our eyes locked, and though we hadn't talked about doing it in advance, we ended by repeating the last line. Dylan's pale blue irises, ringed with black, drew me in. We rounded out the last note at the same instant. There was a second of silence, then applause washed over us.

Dylan flashed that half-smile, and my pulse leapt.

"Fun, right?" he said.

I nodded and stepped away from the microphone.

Lauren hugged me with one arm when I sat at the table again. "Seriously, no way I'm telling Joe how good you two sounded. He'll worry you'll move here to sing with Dylan instead."

"No chance of that." I took a long drink of water.

Dylan clutched his stomach. "You wound me."

"Not because you're not a beautiful singer. You are. Because I am a die-hard Chicagoan."

"It's a great city," he said.

On the drive home, Lauren said, "This dinner. You know it's a date, right?"

"Not if you come with."

"You also know Ty might end up staying in Dubai, don't you?"

I stopped typing notes on my iPad. "He never said that."

"The cities growing at light speed aren't in the good old US of A."

"He talked to you about this?"

If he had, it surprised me. He hadn't said anything to me. Ty believed in enjoying life now, not worrying about later. And the work in Dubai was short-term. He was filling in for his boss.

Lauren parked in front of my parents' house. "No. But I know enough about commercial real estate to say categorically that to get ahead, Ty needs to think beyond Chicago."

"But he loves Chicago." I got out of the car, steadying myself with a hand on the door as I did. I'd finished the second whiskey sour after getting off stage and it made me a little unsteady.

"Sure, but think about it." Lauren followed me up the front stairs. "Everywhere he worked he was the only Black man in the entire firm. Putting together deals where no one who could green light them was Black. Yet he built a stellar career. You don't do that if you don't want to get ahead."

I faltered on the top step and grabbed the porch railing. "You do if you love the work for its own sake. And he does. Like me with looking into crimes."

"You could be right." Lauren opened the screen door. "But it's something to think about."

After fumbling a bit, I fitted my key into the front lock. "Right now, I'm thinking about whether Dylan asked me to dinner to keep tabs on me for his dad."

Because whatever he claimed, I bet Dylan got whatever he wanted when he chose to turn on the charm.

32

SYMPATHY

Despite what I told Lauren, as I took off my mascara and eyeliner I kept thinking about Ty. I checked the time. Eight in the morning in Dubai. Too early to call and expect a thoughtful talk.

The phone rang as I started to text him, making multiple mistakes due to those whiskey sours. To my surprise, it was Gail Kev, responding to one of many voicemails I'd left.

I sat on the edge of the bed. Hoping I sounded clear and not alcohol-muddled, I relayed the story of Klaus Erickson's arrest. I ended with the fact that the original charges included producing child pornography. There was one more charge that might relate to the murders, but I couldn't at the moment bring it to mind.

"Oh, no. The photographs — they weren't of girls Vanessa's age? You're certain?"

"The ones that led to his arrest were of a teenager. I haven't seen others yet."

The question reminded me that I needed to see if my paralegal found a current phone number for Klaus's ex-wife. I hadn't checked my law firm email since Lauren arrived.

"I had no idea," Gail said.

"Don't think anyone did. You didn't hear about the arrest when it happened?" My mouth and throat felt dry. I started down the stairs to get some water. "Seems like something one of your private investigators should've learned."

"They might have told Ted. He's shouldered as much as he can since Vanessa — since what happened. I don't want to hear unless something significant happens."

Apparently, a suspect arrested for producing child pornography didn't qualify. Or Gail didn't want to admit to knowing of Klaus's arrest since she didn't tell me about it when we met.

"Any idea if the task force followed up with Klaus?"

I passed the music room on the way to the kitchen. Lauren had rearranged my dad's guitars and computer to create a cozy spot for herself around the pull out couch.

"None," Gail said. "But would they? He had an alibi."

"From the girlfriend he later married." I poured a glass of water and tried to think what else I needed to know from Gail. I'd rather question her when I was bright, awake, and completely sober, but she might refuse to talk again. "Was Klaus ever Ted's business partner? Or yours?"

"What? No. Never."

I drank a third of the water. "Klaus worked in computers. I want to be sure there was no connection."

"Only that he took photographs. And he was friends with my sister and her husband."

"When we met you said you felt for my mother. What did the press say about her?"

"Nothing specific. That I remember. But lots about how similar the girls were. Their ages. Both pretty. Nessa being a dancer. Your sister being a singer."

"Was there talk of a serial killer?"

"Oh, yes. Lots of fear headlines. The 'Is your child next?'

sort of thing. As if people would only care if they thought their children were in danger."

I asked if the police told her anything about the killer keeping trophies or mementoes from the girls. Gail sounded shocked. "Never. In fact, I got the sense the task force didn't think it was a serial killer. A stranger serial killer, that is."

"What gave you that impression?"

"They said it was unlikely a stranger took your sister. With so many friends and family around."

"But they didn't think that about your daughter, too?"

"They said a family member or friend could have lured her away. But there were so many people at the recital, it'd be easy for a stranger to pose as a parent or teacher. Convince Nessa they had a message from me to meet somewhere. Or from Ted that he was waiting outside. Something like that."

That explained why the police thought my dad could have gotten to Nessa without being noticed. I wasn't about to admit it to Gail, but it made sense. As a child I was in two musicals with large casts. I didn't know everyone's family members or friends. If I hadn't been raised to be ever on the alert and didn't know my Gram, not my parents, was the one most likely to be looking for me, it wouldn't have been hard for a stranger to get backstage and convince me they had a message from my mother or father.

"At the time, did you think my parents did it?" I asked.

I wasn't sure why it mattered. But her impressions might tell me something about how the police focused their investigation.

"Ted and I never believed that."

I had the impression Ted did think that. But maybe he took a softer tone with his wife.

"Why not?" I said.

"In photos and on TV, their eyes — haunted. Like ours. I wanted to reach out over the years. Connect. But I didn't know how they'd feel. Ted thought it might not be appropriate. Said they might want to be left alone."

I made my way upstairs again. "Did he want to be left alone?"

"In a way. He didn't want to forget Vanessa. But the first time he met people who knew nothing about her, Ted felt relieved. He worried I'd think that made him a terrible person. But I understood."

I sank onto the desk chair. "When people ask if I have brothers or sisters, I never know what to say. If I say one sister, it's like writing Q.C. out of the family. But if I say two, the person might ask me more. Then I have to talk about her murder."

"Yes." For the first time Gail's voice sounded warmer and less strained. "Yes. I can't say I have no children. But I need to unless I want to talk about it. And I don't."

A text from Ted Kev pinged my phone. He must be listening to Gail's side of the conversation.

> She's almost in tears. This is why I don't want her to talk to you.

"I'm sorry if this is upsetting you," I said, wondering if Ted knew Gail and I had already met in person.

"It's not. It's nice to talk to someone who understands."

"Could you do something for me? If your family members are willing, would you tell them you don't mind them talking to me?"

After a long pause, she said, "Yes. Yes I suppose that's all right. I'll tell them."

She ended the call a few minutes later after Ted said something I couldn't hear in the background.

But she was true to her word. The next morning, Therese Smith, Nessa Kev's aunt, called me.

33

AN EX-WIFE SPEAKS

LAUREN MADE BREAKFAST — bacon, blueberry pancakes from scratch, and sliced grapefruit — as I set a time to meet Vanessa's aunt and uncle at their home. My dad was already at the store and my mother was asleep.

Sunlight poured through the window over the sink. Lauren and I ate at the kitchen table. I drank orange juice and ate too much, and for the first time felt relaxed in my parents' house.

Lauren left for a coworking space a few miles away. I worked in the guest room researching issues for two of my cases. And I left a message for Klaus Erickson's ex-wife Eva at a number my paralegal found.

I tried Eva a second time in the late afternoon. This time she picked up.

"He's not my favorite person," she said when I finished the shortest version I could manage of why I was trying to reach Klaus. "But he didn't kill your sister. Or Vanessa Kev."

I muted the notifications on my laptop. "You're sure?"

"He was at my place all day the day Vanessa was taken. We'd been dating about two months, and it's the first time he stayed overnight."

Klaus preyed on her sister and tried to blackmail her, making it unlikely she was lying to protect him. But people aren't always logical. Or consistent.

"If he wasn't involved in the murders, there's no harm in him talking to me, is there? He might know something about someone else in the Kevs' circle."

"Might," Eva said. "And the police might come after him again with you stirring things up. Try to pin the murders on him now that he has a record."

"But I'm not working with the police. And they haven't done anything on these cases in decades."

"Doesn't mean they won't."

"No. But if Klaus knows anything that might help me find the killer, that could be better for him, too. No more questions hanging over him."

I deleted a few junk mail messages, letting the silence drag on. The hall floorboards creaked behind me. I glanced over my shoulder but saw no one through the open doorway.

"What kinds of things are you trying to find out?" Eva finally said.

"For one, whether the police questioned him again about the murders after he was arrested or convicted of the later crimes."

"No idea. Wasn't exactly on good terms with him then."

"Are you now?"

"We speak. Not sure if that's good terms. We have children together. They're almost grown, but it's a bond. He wasn't a terrible father."

"Despite what happened with your sister?" I said.

"That's not your business."

"No. Unless it relates somehow."

"It doesn't."

"You're probably right. But I'm asking everyone I can everything I can. This has hung over my whole life." I walked to the dormer window and rested my forehead against the window pane. Talking about Q.C. and my childhood over and over was leaving me with an exhausted, heavy feeling that could sink me into a darker place. But Eva might share more if she understood what it meant to me. "I'm named for Q.C., and I grew up knowing she was murdered. Then I found out my parents are the only suspects anyone really looked at. You worry I'm working with the police? I'm working against them. All of them."

This time it took longer before Eva spoke.

"The police called Klaus a pedophile. I had to move. For the kids' safety. Our house got spray-painted and egged. Three times. People spit at me in the grocery store."

"At you?" I moved to the bed and sat, propping pillows behind me.

"There was no social media yet. But things weren't that different from now. People got a few 'facts' and lost their minds. All they heard was my husband was a pedophile. And I was dumb enough not to know it."

"I'm so sorry."

"Klaus wasn't a saint. He deserved his sentence. But my sister was underage by less than a month when they started sleeping together. And less than a day when he took the photos. He took advantage, no question. I never forgave him. But I wasn't blindly letting my kids live with a pedophile."

Frustration with the police was our common ground, so I asked if she was there when Klaus was questioned. Detectives usually talk to suspects or witnesses separately. But it pays to check.

"No. They talked to him twice. I didn't see why. But he told me it was fine. That they ought to talk to everyone as much as it took to find whoever did it."

"He wasn't nervous they'd pin it on him?"

"Why should they? He didn't have a criminal record. Then. He took some photos and knew the family. Big deal."

"No one complained about him or said they saw him anywhere near Q.C. or Vanessa?"

I didn't want to reveal that when she was thirteen, Kimberly Byerly told her parents she felt uncomfortable around Klaus. If he had anything to do with the murders it could put her at risk.

"Is there something like that? What do you know?"

"I don't know of anyone seeing him near the girls. I'm just guessing why he'd be questioned twice."

"Well, I think most people were. When Vanessa went missing and after her body was found."

"Did they talk to you twice?" I said.

"Yes. To ask where Klaus was when the other girl, your sister, disappeared."

"And where was he?"

"With me. He made lunch for me at his place."

Convenient, though not necessarily suspicious, that both times they weren't out in public where anyone else might see them. I returned to the desk to make a few notes.

"Klaus knew the family and Vanessa," I said. "Did he have any guesses about who might have taken her?"

"He thought maybe Vanessa's cousin. The boy. That he might've been jealous of all the attention Vanessa got. But after the two girls were found together, he figured someone in your family. Because your sister was taken first."

"Anyone in particular?"

It didn't matter much since Klaus didn't know my family. But it could tell me what the general public thought at the time.

"The police made it pretty clear they thought your dad. But Klaus said, well, he thought your dad, too. But later, after that famous case with the beauty pageant girl — Jon something —"

"JonBenét Ramsey?"

"Right. Klaus figured your dad did it but he was covering for your sister. The older one."

"Kendra?"

"If that's her name. With JonBenét, they kept looking at her older brother. Like he might envy JonBenét. Like what Klaus thought about Vanessa's cousin. And that's when Klaus said maybe your sister did it, got really mad and maybe did it by accident. And your dad covered it up."

Dylan's comment about Kendra crying over Q.C. getting all those presents ran through my mind. I stood again and paced the room. "But then why kill Vanessa?" I said.

"Make it look like a serial killer. Or at least like an adult did it."

Kids get jealous of their siblings. It doesn't make them killers. Still, if only Q.C.'s murder happened, and Kendra did lash out at Q.C. and kill her by accident, I could almost see one or both my parents lying to protect Kendra.

It wasn't just Dylan's words that made jealousy a likely motive. Kendra herself told me how my mother's constant Q.C. talk upset and angered her. And after Q.C.'s death, my mother and Gram focused on taking care of me, not Kendra, who was only eight. It fit a theory that they were angry at Kendra.

But I couldn't believe any of it about my sister. Didn't want to believe it.

"Did Klaus take photos that show anyone in my family around the Kevs? Do you know?"

"If he did, seems like he would have told the police."

"Could I look through his photos? Do you know where they are?"

"I don't. I'd need to ask him."

"Could you do that? And ask him if he'll talk to me? He may know something he doesn't realize he knows."

She said she'd think about it and let me know. Before I said good-bye, I asked if Klaus ever worked for Ted or Gail Kev or was partners with either. She said no, but confirmed Klaus was a computer programmer before he went to prison.

After typing my notes about the call, I studied the framed photos in the guest room. None featured Kendra. A younger version of my mother posed outside a red brick school with Q.C. Today my mother still weighed about the same and wore her hair in the same style as then. Aside from the silver hairs mixed with the blond, it was as if she'd frozen in time after Q.C.'s death.

My dad was recognizable, but only because I knew it was him. When he played with his bluegrass band, he was leaner and clean cut. Clean shaven, a full head of black hair cropped close to his head.

Something nagged at me about my father relating to Klaus's theory that he covered for Kendra. I scrolled through my chart of notes, skimming each one about my father.

The last note included him handing me the luggage tracking tag. Handing it to me. I never saw it in my car. He told me that's where it came from.

In law school and in practice I learned to never assume what came between points A and C. Usually the answer was B. But once in a while there was a detour that made all the difference. My dad might have found the tag on the car mat. Or he might have had it with him and given it to me to make me think someone else was tracking me. Someone else who was the murderer.

I closed the iPad cover. I'd keep it in mind. But it was something else I didn't believe.

I glanced at the clock on my laptop screen. Lauren should be here any minute so we could go visit Vanessa's aunt and uncle.

34

MR. AND MRS. SMITH

I HADN'T SEEN a house or any building in miles. The road devolved from asphalt to broken asphalt to dirt and was threatening to become open field. On either side of the road were acres of ridged dirt — corn fields waiting to be planted when no more frosts were on the horizon.

"Really glad you came along," I said to Lauren. "When Therese told me they wanted to talk on their home turf, I didn't realize it was in such an isolated area."

"No kidding." Lauren glanced out the window.

On the phone, Therese had agreed easily enough to my bringing a friend who sometimes helped with my investigations along. But she didn't quite understand why I needed to since she and her husband were good people. She also told me her daughter Kimberly said they shouldn't meet with me.

When I texted Kimberly to ask why, she said she'd been using reverse psychology. I wondered.

Now that they'd agreed to talk, the Smiths went all out with their hospitality. A platter of shrimp on ice sat next to a crystal bowl of spicy cocktail sauce on their glass-topped coffee table. Therese poured us each a glass of fresh squeezed lemonade.

Rows of whole wheat crackers were arranged in a square tray around cream cheese and chive dip.

I asked if they remembered Klaus Erickson.

"Klaus. Sweet man." Therese brushed long strawberry blond hair behind her ear. Five years older than her sister Gail, her face and figure were rounder and her body language more relaxed. Like Gail, though, she wore a designer suit. Hers had pants, not a skirt, and was beige. "Loved taking photographs."

"Was he a partner in Ted Kev's business?" I put a few shrimp on my plate.

"Partner?" James Smith Senior sat, legs crossed, in a wide-backed armchair. A head taller than his wife, he looked much older. His hair was completely white and flared out from his head. His flannel patterned pants might serve as pajamas in a pinch. A few tufts of gray chest hair poked over the stretched V neck of his pullover. "Where'd you hear that?"

"I've been digging into old corporate records."

Those records showed nothing about Klaus Erickson, but James didn't need to know that. Though I wasn't sure Kimberly was on my side, I wanted to keep quiet about my conversation with her. I might need her again.

"Can't imagine why that's in there," James said. "He did some programming for Ted, that's all. And his real love was photography. He was nominated for a Pulitzer Prize for it."

The nomination hadn't come up in my research on Klaus. I made a note to look for it. And to think about why Gail Kev denied Klaus had worked for Ted while James thought he did.

Next to me, Lauren's fingers flew over her phone.

"Was Klaus Ted's employee?" I said.

James frowned. "No. A consultant."

If Klaus developed some of Ted Kev's products and got no credit, that gave him a motive to hurt Kev. And a motive for Gail to deny the connection.

I asked if they knew where Ted and Gail Kev kept their

computers when they started their software business or where Klaus did his programming. Anyplace large enough to keep computer equipment might very well have been a perfect place to hide kidnapped children.

But they didn't know. Therese thought Ted and Gail might have used her company's computer after hours.

I doubted that. Unless the laws had been very different back then, using the company equipment could give Gail's employer a claim to the code Ted developed. I didn't find any lawsuits against him about that. Considering how much he made on it, I had to think the employer would have sued if it had any chance to get the profits.

"You've opened a few businesses," I said to James. "Did you ever partner with Ted?"

Therese's laugh sounded natural and musical. "Ted's only partner is my sister. Business or otherwise. But Ted invested in some of James's companies."

Her phrasing made me wonder if she and her husband kept their funds separate. Therese's name wasn't on any of the formal companies James founded. And she had her own company in the sense that she'd been selling Mary Kay cosmetics for decades and was a manager.

"Mostly he gave me advice," James said.

The advice might not have been that good. According to the State of Illinois, of the dozen or so businesses James started the longest lasted three years. The others closed anywhere from three to nineteen months in.

"No capital?" Lauren said.

"Small amounts," James said.

Therese patted her husband's knee. "Which we appreciate. We never felt Ted owed us."

If the amounts were very small, James might resent his far more successful brother-in-law. But motive, as I'd told Dylan, didn't mean a whole lot. In my experience, all killers believe they're entitled to do what they do. But their reasons don't always make sense to the rest of us.

Lauren passed me her phone and said to James, "It's hard to get a business off the ground without help. My parents paid for my broker's license. And gave me my first big commission. It made a world of difference."

Lauren wasn't exaggerating. Her parents also supported her while she got the license and during her single year of law school, which was where she and I met. They weren't thrilled when she dropped out, but they encouraged her real estate career. And sent her multiple real estate clients.

It puts Lauren a bit out of touch with what life is like for the rest of us. But she's not clueless as to the big boost she got. She gives her parents a lot of credit.

James gestured toward Lauren. "Exactly. An infusion of capital is key. Without it, it's hard to get through that first year no matter how much advice you have."

"Sounds like Ted could have done more for you," I said.

I glanced down at Lauren's phone. She had it open to a webpage that said anyone could nominate themselves for a Pulitzer Prize.

"Can't complain about Ted." James's chin drew back as if he were a turtle pulling into his shell. "Not his fault his Midas touch never wore off on me. Though I sure wish it had. His first year in business he made more than Steve Jobs and Bill Gates combined at the same point in their careers."

Lauren glanced at Therese. "Your family didn't help out?"

Therese smiled. "That's a very personal question. But I guess it's no secret my parents believe people need to build their own businesses from the ground up."

I turned to James. "Did you ever go into business with Klaus?"

James said he didn't. I asked if they stayed in touch with Klaus over the years.

"We lost track after Nessa's death," Therese said. "Lost track of a lot of people, really. The family just sort of closed in on itself."

I wanted to ask if they knew about Klaus's later arrest and conviction. But Therese's comment gave the perfect segue into her son.

"Sounds like you were a close family. Can you put me in touch with your son?"

"Don't see how he can help," James said.

"Vanessa's dance teacher said he and Vanessa were close. He might have noticed someone around who shouldn't have been."

"He didn't. The police asked him," James said.

Lauren spooned some cocktail sauce onto her plate. "But he was close with Vanessa?"

"Very," Therese said. "Sometimes I think it was hardest on him. That's why he struggled so."

"Struggled with what?" I said.

"Life. College. Everything."

They told me James Junior, or Jimmy, went away to school not long after Vanessa's death. Their story fit Kimberly's, including that he refused to return phone calls and never came home again.

"Did you argue a lot?" Lauren said. "I totally needed my own space when I went away to school. My parents and I fought all the time. It was a way to separate."

Lauren and her mother talked every day of her life. She was the only person I knew without any real issues with her parents.

But the lie worked. Therese nodded eagerly. "That was a lot of it. I told James that. Jimmy needed his space."

"It must be sad for you that he's stayed away for so long," I said.

"His choice," James said. "Always was trouble."

"What kind of trouble?" I said.

"Fights at school," James said.

Therese glanced at her husband. "Which weren't his fault."

James huffed. "Still sticking up for him. Not his fault. He goaded the other kids."

"Goaded them how?" I said. It seemed like a curious word choice.

"Never a team player. Fast runner, great high jumper, but would he join the basketball team? No. Only sport he liked was archery. What was he going to do with that?"

I doubted that caused physical fights. But I never attended high school. I glanced at Lauren.

"I seriously can't see anyone fighting him over that," Lauren said. "But maybe it's different for boys."

"He was a bit of a loner," Therese said. "One of those boys the others gang up on."

The loner part fit my trouble finding any of Jimmy's friends. I contacted a few classmates Kimberly told me about, but two didn't remember Jimmy at all. One said he kept to himself and rarely talked in class.

"He never fought back," James said. "That's why they picked on him."

"So he started fights? Or didn't fight enough?" I said.

James stood. "I don't have time for this." He stalked out of the room.

"Sorry," I said to Therese. "I didn't mean to upset either of you."

She waved a hand. "Oh, it's not you. It's a touchy subject. He and Jimmy, their personalities just never meshed. Jimmy and Ted got along much better."

Therese confirmed that Jimmy had been at the Kevs the night before Nessa was taken and became ill the next day. The police found that suspicious, though Gail confirmed she saw

Jimmy vomit. He'd eaten a lot of cherries the night before from a tree in the Kevs' back yard.

That raised questions. If Ted or Gail wanted Jimmy out of the way the day of the recital, they could easily have slipped something into his food to make him sick.

Therese also confirmed that James and Ted went to the fishing cabin the weekend Vanessa was taken, and Kimberly went with Therese to a Mary Kay weekend conference. She told me after Vanessa and Q.C. were found together in one grave, Jimmy dropped off the suspect list. He was home with Therese the whole day Q.C. disappeared.

That didn't rule him out in my mind. Therese Smith wouldn't be the first or last mother to give her son an alibi.

Therese didn't know how long Jimmy stayed in college or whether he graduated.

"Gail and Ted hired a private investigator to try to find him for us. But no luck. I should say for me. I didn't tell James until later. He was furious. Said if Jimmy wanted to see us, he would. Why should we chase after him?" She stared down at her hands. Her fingernails were polished in pale pink with white tips. "He had a point. Jimmy told me he never wanted to see or hear from us again."

"Did he say why?" I said.

"He said we stifled him. Not just us, but living here. Too small town."

"Did you talk to his friends?"

"We didn't know any. He never invited anyone to the house. When he was younger, he played with the neighbors across the street. But they moved before Jimmy started high school."

I got the neighbors' names.

I asked Therese more about the fishing cabin. Only the men used it. Neither Therese nor Gail liked fishing or felt the need for a country weekend. But the men still went there, though not as often. Every few months.

"Going back to Klaus," I said, "did Gail tell you he was arrested in the early nineties?"

She clutched her glass of lemonade. "What? What for?"

I told her about the charges.

"Oh, no. Oh no." Therese shook her head. "My daughter. She tried to tell us something was off about Klaus. Oh, my Lord."

"Did she tell the police about her concerns?"

"No, us. She told us. James didn't want to cause Klaus trouble by telling the police. And I agreed. Klaus seemed like such a kind man. Thoughtful. Personable."

"Sure he's personable," Lauren said as she got into the driver's seat for the trip back to my parents' house. "Like any Pulitzer pervert psychopath. How long you think it'll take his ex to get back to you?"

"No idea. I just hope she does get back to me and I don't have to hound her. As my mother would say." I scrolled through my email. "But one of the Kevs' former employees finally agreed to talk to me. A secretary, and she didn't sign an NDA."

"Fabulous. Another field trip?"

"I'm hoping I can convince you to research while I'm talking to her."

"Oh, sure. Give me the glamorous jobs." Lauren sighed. "What do you need me to do?"

"It's not terrible," I said. "You'll like it. Lots of schmoozing."

35

ANOTHER EX

LAUREN and I started the research together the next day at the Madison County Archival Library. A huge thermos of Earl Grey at my side helped stave off exhaustion. I'd been up until nearly midnight, very late for me, reviewing my client's bookkeeping records to be sure there were no attorney-client notes before I sent a copy to the other side.

Now I paged through yearbooks for Jimmy Smith's and Kimberly Smith's grade school and high school classes. I sent my paralegal the names of anyone in a photo with either Smith, as well as the names of the neighbors Therese told us about. The paralegal searched people finder databases while Lauren and I looked through old phone books.

I dropped Lauren at my parents' house around noon. Her task was to call everyone whose phone number we had to ask about Kimberly, Jimmy, and Vanessa. I drove on to the Garden Café, a small coffee and tea shop owned by two local musicians in Webster Groves, a suburb of St. Louis.

The café was small, with a handful of tables draped with colorful tablecloths. Ruthann Sellars, now retired, waited at one of them. She'd worked for TG Kev Computer Solutions for nearly ten years. Her hair flipped away from her face in a style popular in the 1970s and she wore a silver ring with a translucent oval stone that reminded me of the old mood rings. As if she had found her look in high school and frozen it.

After we introduced ourselves, I ordered an Earl Grey latte, which the owner told me was made with rich vanilla syrup and lavender. I ought to eat lunch instead. But I wanted to focus on Ruthann, not eating.

I took out my notepad and pen. "July 1980 to January 1990 with the same company. Something must have been going right."

"I can see where you'd think that," Ruthann Sellars said. "But in my time people stayed for decades at one company. Maybe retired from it."

"But it was a startup in 1980. Were you counting on it being around for decades?"

"Not counting on it. I was only twenty. But as it grew, I started thinking it might go the distance. And it did. Just not with me there."

Ruthann began as a typist soon after Gail Kev left the company to have Vanessa.

"I kept wishing I'd met her. Everyone said she was the idea person," Ruthann said. "The other women were typists, like me. A woman who helped launch a company — that was exciting."

"She's the CFO now. Is that what she did then? Mainly business and finance?"

"She had multiple roles. The company was small, so everyone at the top did. Officially, she managed human resources and marketing."

"The company website doesn't give any background on her."

"When she left the company, they stopped including her in the PR. Didn't want it to look like half the founding team was gone, I guess. Maybe they never quite caught up when she came back."

"Did she always plan to return to work?"

The bell over the door jangled as a couple with a black and white Labrador entered.

Ruthann glanced at the dog and back at me. "I heard she might come back. When Vanessa started school maybe. But no one knew for sure. And there was a lot of talk of taking the company public eventually. Everybody thought about that all the time."

"You said she was an idea person. What sorts of ideas did Gail contribute?"

"The way I heard it, the whole company plan. Gail had a degree in business and marketing. She worked at a big accounting firm in the HR department. That's mostly where women with business degrees got hired back then. If they got hired. The story went that she kept telling Ted about HR things that could be automated. They both loved computers. They started playing around and came up with the original program."

"She helped write the code?"

"Not sure on that. But they pitched it to her company together. Gail knew exactly what to say. At least, that's what her old secretary told me. The company had just invested in this computer but didn't know what all it could do. Ted and Gail told them. And they were thrilled."

"So without her, TG Kev Computer Solutions might not exist?"

"Sounded like that to me."

"Do you know if her family invested in the company?" I said. "Or loaned them startup money?"

If Gail's parents helped her business but not Therese's or Jim's that might cause ill feelings.

"Never heard that. But they bought Ted and Gail their first house."

"How do you know?"

"Gail's old secretary. She talked about Gail all the time."

I'd tried to reach the woman myself and learned she died of ovarian cancer five years ago. She would have been a rich source of information.

"Did Gail being gone hurt the company?"

If so, Ted Kev might have been unhappy about his wife's absence. And resented his new daughter.

"Her secretary said yes. The guy they hired knew marketing, but nothing about programming. Or HR. We called him the Interloper. They hired a woman to head HR. They needed two people to replace Gail."

Ruthann said while Gail was gone the company grew, but really took off on Gail's return.

"Why was that?" I said.

"Improved advertising and marketing probably. They fired the Interloper right away. Or laid him off I guess."

I asked for the Interloper's name and Ruthann gave it to me. I wrote his name down so she'd feel she'd been helpful. But he was one of the people who'd ignored my repeated emails.

"Couldn't Ted Kev have found someone better to fill in for Gail?"

"Maybe. The buzz was that he was too into the technical side. Didn't get what Gail brought to the company. So he bought the Interloper's big talk."

Or Ted on some level was saving a place for his wife.

Ruthann stayed at the company for five years after Gail returned, then left to take care of her aging mother.

"I tried going back to work at TG Kev after that. Couldn't get the hang of word processors. I told them I'm a crackerjack typist. Just let me use an old IBM Selectric. Loved those typewriters."

"Wasn't word processing easier?"

"Not then. It wasn't like now where you click a button with a B on it for bold. You had to use function keys to turn codes on and off. If you did it wrong you could mess up your whole document. Girls who loved techy things did well. Probably would have been programmers if they were men. Not for me."

I turned to a new page on my pad. "Anyone at the company who didn't like Gail or Ted?"

"Well, the Interloper wasn't a fan of Gail's. And nobody knew Ted well except the programmers. They worked in this back room. I called them Tappers. When you walked by there all you heard was them tapping on their keyboards."

"Did Ted work there, too?"

"No. He liked complete silence to think. His office was way in the back behind the storage rooms. But he stopped in to talk to the programmers, bounce ideas off them."

"Who replaced Gail in HR?" I said.

"Smiley Lady."

"Who?"

"Sorry. Just what I call her. Tacked up kitten posters and added smileys to every memo. But if you needed real help, forget it."

I asked if the company used a lot of consultants in the early days. Ruthann told me it did. It was safer to pay people by the hour as needed rather than hire someone who might need to be laid off if things didn't go well. But she didn't remember Klaus Erickson. She also never heard of Ted having a business partner other than Gail in the early days.

I asked what people at the company said when Vanessa Kev was kidnapped.

"We were shocked. All of us. Some wondered if someone did it to get back at Ted in business. Or throw off his concentration." Ruthann glanced at the tables around us, half of them filled, as if checking for anyone listening. "Since there was no ransom demand."

"Someone? Like a competitor?"

She nodded. "But I guess the police looked into that. Then when her body was found it was horrible. Just horrible."

Ruthann told me Ted Kev came to work every day other than the day Vanessa's body was found and the day of the funeral.

"His secretary made the rounds when Vanessa was taken. Told us all not to ask him about it. It was too upsetting. So we never did, other than to say how sorry we were at the memorial service."

"Did you see him at all at work?"

"Once. He sort of glided through the kitchen like a ghost. Looked like he'd lost a ton of weight. Sunken cheeks and eye sockets."

The police never questioned Ruthann, but she thought they talked to a few programmers. They also asked Ted's secretary mostly routine questions. When Gail returned to work a year after Vanessa's death, the employees followed the same approach of not speaking to her about it.

"Don't think anyone told us that. But she didn't put any photos of Vanessa in her office, and she never mentioned her. I feel like for both of them work was what kids call a safe space now. Where they could put aside their heartache. Or not put aside, but focus on something else."

I showed Ruthann photos of everyone on the Davis side of the investigation and of Klaus Erickson. She didn't recognize anyone. After asking her more questions about the Kevs and the company I thanked her, paid the bill, and headed out.

My phone was off during our talk. Now it showed plenty of emails and one voicemail to deal with for my law practice. Nothing from Klaus's ex-wife, Eva. That suggested to me she hadn't decided yet whether to talk to Klaus. If I wanted her to trust me, an in-person meeting might help.

I called Lauren. Her long day of phone calls didn't result in any new information, so she was more than willing to drive to southern Indiana the next day with me. After talking it through, we decided on a surprise visit. It'd be harder for Eva to refuse to talk after we drove all that way.

"And if she's got Klaus's photos, maybe she'll actually show them to you to get rid of you," Lauren said.

But that didn't happen. The following afternoon when we turned the corner onto Eva's street, a police car sat in the middle of the block.

36

SUSPICION

YELLOW CRIME SCENE tape anchored by sticks in the grass enclosed the front yard of a raised brick ranch. Red police tape crisscrossed the front door.

Lauren pulled to the curb behind the squad car. "Is that...?"

I double-checked the Directions app. "Eva Erickson's house."

A uniformed officer got out of his car at the same time I exited ours.

"Can I help you ladies?"

"We're here to see Eva Erickson." I shoved my hands, which felt like ice, into the pockets of my leather jacket.

Eva had answered my questions three days ago about her ex. Now she might be dead. I've known people who were murdered before. But I never suspected it was my fault.

"How well did you know Mrs. Erickson?"

Mrs. I needed to check the divorce records. Surely, the divorce from Klaus became final long ago.

"Miss?" the officer said.

"Not well," I said.

"She was expecting you today?"

"No. I talked with her recently and decided to stop by."

"I'm sorry to tell you that she passed away yesterday."

He refused to say more, though he was polite about it. After taking down my information, he gave me a card for the detective handling the matter.

She worked for the county. The town must be too small to have a detective of its own. To my surprise, she answered her phone on the third ring. After I gave her a short rundown of why I was there, she told me to meet her at a local diner.

Lauren put the car in gear. "Who knew you called Eva?"

"Besides you? Klaus. If she contacted him. And whoever Eva or Klaus told. My parents if either of them overheard me talking to her."

The diner was a mile away. Lauren ordered herbal tea for both of us. I wrapped my still freezing hands around my mug. We debated how much to tell the detective. Trusting police doesn't come easily to me. There's a Chicago police Detective Sergeant I've become friends with. But that took time and effort. On both sides.

This detective was a pale, fifty-something woman in dark pants and a tweed blazer. She asked for IDs right away.

Lauren handed over her driver's license. I rummaged at the bottom of my shoulder bag for what felt like twenty minutes and finally fished out my wallet. After rifling through credit cards, my Walgreens shopper ID, and my insurance cards I found my driver's license and Circuit Court of Cook County photo ID.

The detective looked over both. "Hm. Lawyer. But not a private investigator."

"No," I said. "But I've worked with police before. Looking into crimes."

I answered all her questions, including whether I owned a gun, which I don't. It took nearly forty-five minutes. We covered my family, Q.C., the Kev murder, and my conversations with

Eva. I left out anything I learned about my side of the family. I told her about Kimberly's statements about Klaus but made it sound like I learned that from her parents.

As I spoke, I pressed my knees together to keep them from shaking. But with each sentence I felt more focused. And calmer. It was like arguing a legal case. Not about things I couldn't change or control.

At the end, I texted the detective the name and phone number of the FBI agent who was responsible for the Q.C. and Vanessa Kev murders. I had to back up and retype characters twice because my hands still trembled, but I did it.

"He refused to talk to me," I said. "But maybe he'll coordinate with you."

"If I get that far. Looks like a break and enter gone wrong."

"What about everything I just told you?" I said.

She closed the tablet she'd been using to take notes. "You can play Agatha Christie or Veronica Mars as much as you want. Doesn't turn a simple burglary into a murder."

I wasn't sure what to make of her odd mix of pop culture references. But it was clear she didn't think much of my efforts. I longed for the Detective Sergeant in Chicago. He trusted my instincts.

"But you'll talk to Klaus?" I said.

"It's procedure to talk to an ex-spouse when a person dies in suspicious circumstances."

"Can you tell us who found her?" I said.

The detective crossed her arms and frowned. "Why would I do that?"

"Small town," I said. "People talk. I'm sure I can find out by knocking on a few doors. Why not save her neighbors from my questions?"

I planned to knock on doors anyway, but she didn't need to know that.

She sighed. "You're not wrong about people talking. All

right. A neighbor stopped by yesterday morning for coffee. Got no answer and raised the alarm."

She slid one arm through her olive green peacoat, ready to leave.

"Wait," I said. "At least tell me if you've ruled Klaus out already. If not, if there's a chance he did this, it raises the odds he also killed my sister and Vanessa Kev."

"How so?"

Lauren and I exchanged a glance. Like me, she must be wondering if the detective was playing dumb or really didn't follow my logic.

"Eva gave him alibis for Vanessa Kev's and my sister's disappearances. Klaus refused to talk to me. I asked her to try to change his mind about that. If she's dead and he's the main suspect, the simplest answer is he killed her because he feared she'd recant the alibis."

"That'd be foolish. Motive's too obvious. Also, this looks like a robbery. Drawers emptied, cabinets ransacked, electronics missing. Front door lock picked."

Eva hadn't let the intruder in, then. Or the person picked the lock after to make it look like a robbery.

"Including her computer?" I said.

"Laptop, according to the neighbor."

"Defensive wounds?"

The detective studied me for a moment, then rested her arms on the table. "It'll be on the news soon enough. Bullet in the forehead. Looks like she surprised the thief."

"Is there a lot of violent crime here?" Lauren said.

"No more or less than neighboring counties. But everyone's got a gun these days. Bar fights turn into shootings. Burglary becomes murder."

"Klaus could have staged it to look like a robbery. Or someone else could have," I said.

She stood. "You've given me good information, and I appreciate it. If you learn anything else that sheds light on Mrs. Erickson's murder, be sure to call me."

I promised I would. "Just one other thing. You keep referring to her as Mrs. Erickson. Were they still married?"

If Eva and Klaus had an on-going relationship despite everything, it made it more likely she might have been willing to alibi him decades ago. But then why talk to me?

"No."

"Why the Mrs.?"

"Her name of record is still Erickson."

Despite women detectives, Ms. apparently hadn't made it into common usage in this town.

"Was she seeing anyone new?" I said.

"You used up your one more question, Columbo." With that last pop culture nod, the detective pulled on her gloves. "And don't go bothering Mrs. Erickson's neighbors or you'll be brought in for obstructing an investigation."

There was no way that was the law. But I had too much to do to waste time in a county jail. And I was too far from home to have anyone bail Lauren or me out.

Better to return when the police tape, and the officer, were gone.

37

NOT WHO YOU THINK

My feet sunk into the mud in front of the house where my parents lived when I was born. Paint peeled on the wood railings of the wide, wraparound front porch. Two round dormer windows cut into the attic.

Dylan Sabatini stepped out of the brick building on the corner and waved. The day before, maybe moved by the story of Eva's death, my mother finally told Reverend Sabatini to talk to me. I hadn't brought Lauren with. It had been hard enough to get my mother to agree that I could talk to the reverend alone.

I was more and more convinced Klaus had been the killer and Eva alibied him. But I needed to follow every lead.

Dylan joined me on the sidewalk and gestured toward the swing set between the aging garage and the house. The unfenced yard stretched all the way to a line of trees. "The creek's not far into the woods."

"The one they dredged looking for Q.C."

"Yep." He pointed to a towering oak with thick branches that split into a Y shape. "Used to have a treehouse. Your dad built it. Q.C. loved it. Scrambled up the ladder the second she got out of the house."

"Kendra, too?"

"We all hung out in there."

"The police must have searched the woods."

"They did. That evening. Kendra stayed at our house."

"Did she say what she thought happened to Q.C.?"

"We all thought she was lost."

Kendra had told me months ago that my grandmother — not Gram but my mom's mother — told her Q.C. got lost, something our grandmother confirmed when I talked to her on the phone. Kendra stole a map of the city at the library so she would always be able to find her way back home. That didn't sound like someone who knew her sister was dead. Or even injured.

After the outdoor tour, Dylan introduced me to his father and left for school.

I half-expected Reverend Arturo Sabatini to have used car salesman bleached teeth, perfectly styled hair, and a smooth, unlined face, perhaps aided by cosmetic surgery. Instead, he looked ordinary. Unlike his son's, his eyes were an unremarkable brown. His mustache was neatly trimmed and his hairline receded so far I thought at first glance he was bald.

"Quille. Good to see you." When he clasped my hand to shake, his grip felt warm and almost comforting. The right amount of pressure to convey strength without crushing my fingers. He met my eyes long enough to feel he'd really seen me.

After he got me some Earl Grey tea and himself a cup of black coffee, we sat in padded leather armchairs in the corner of his office.

Everything he told me about Q.C. fit what I already knew. I asked if he'd spent much time with Kendra.

"Oh, yes," he said. "The two of them were in and out of here all the time. And my boys spent half their time in your parents' yard. Or the treehouse. Though I believe there was a brief No Boys Allowed phase on that."

"Did Kendra and Q.C. get along?"

"My wife would have known. I wasn't home as much. But Kendra seemed devoted to Q.C."

"Did they fight?"

"Not compared to Dylan and his brother. We separated those two ten times a day."

"Then almost anything would seem mild in comparison."

He smiled. "They weren't having brawls. Just the usual sibling rivalry. You have some concern about Kendra?"

He promised never to tell Kendra what I said in the unlikely event he ran into her.

"Someone I talked to thought Kendra might have killed Q.C. and my dad covered it up."

Rev burst into laughter. "Ridiculous. Your sisters fought over a toy now and then. Who got to jump in the wading pool first. But truly, Quille, nothing I saw suggested that type of rage. Or dysfunction."

"What about an accident?" I said. "And my dad came across them in the parking lot, panicked, and took Q.C. away to hide it?"

"And counted on a seven-year-old to say nothing to anyone ever? Your father has a level head. Panicked or not, he'd know he was only making Kendra look guilty. If it was an accident, it'd be a tragedy. But there'd be no reason to hide it."

My shoulders dropped in relief. Until Dylan's voice echoed in my mind. Reverend Sabatini knew how to say what you wanted to hear.

"Did you and my mom spend time together? Just the two of you?"

"We talked," he said. "But I imagine you're asking about more than that."

"Yes."

He tilted his head sideways, reminding me of his son. But no half-smile. "Your mother tells me I can speak freely with you."

"Would you not have otherwise?"

"I wouldn't have. Your parents trusted me. I saw my role as that of counselor. Without their consent I'd never share anything they said."

"Did they come to you for counseling?"

"Not formally."

"But you told the police they did."

"I told the police I couldn't share what anyone who came to me for spiritual guidance told me. And that included your parents."

"Both of them?" I said.

"Yes."

"Together?"

"Separately."

"What did they tell you?"

"Quite a few things. But first, how are you? This is a lot for you to take on."

"I've investigated crimes before."

"So Brenda said. She's proud of you."

My mother never told anyone she was proud of me that I knew of, including me. Once she came to see a play I was in and told me I did a good job. The only other two times she attended a performance she pointed out the flaws in my technique.

"It's kind of you to say that. But I'm sure she didn't."

Rev smiled. "Not in those words. But she told me about the other crimes you solved."

"I doubt that."

Whenever I mentioned my work, law or detective, my mother changed the subject. I tried not to take it personally.

She rarely talked with anyone about anything other than herself. But it felt personal.

The reverend waved toward a framed photo of Dylan with his mother. Dylan had gotten his looks almost entirely from her. She had the same pale blue eyes ringed with heavy black lashes and the same high cheekbones.

"My son's made you question me. Your mother may not ask the details of your life —"

"My mother doesn't ask anything about my life," I said.

"I'm sorry if that's true. But she loves you. A mother's love knows no bounds."

"I've heard that."

I wasn't trying to be difficult. My mother probably loved me. But nothing she did or said, at least until she told me she moved to be near my Gram for me, left me feeling that might be true.

"I wish you knew your mother before Q.C.'s kidnapping."

"She was different?"

"Not completely. Let's just say she never took a laid-back approach to life. But she did take joy in it. Did her best for her students. Attended all her children's events. Put their drawings on the refrigerator and told everyone about their grades and gold stars and choir concerts."

"For Kendra, too, not just Q.C.?"

"Not just Q.C."

"But my parents' marriage was in trouble."

It was time to get back on track.

"I wouldn't say in trouble. But they spoke to me about it."

"Both of them did? Isn't that a conflict of interest?"

"If I were providing marriage counseling, yes, but I wasn't. And they both knew the other spoke to me."

"What did they say?"

Reverend Sabatini cocked his head and studied me. "You're sure you want to know? It had nothing to do with Q.C.'s death."

“People always think things have nothing to do with what I’m investigating. Sometimes they’re right. Usually they’re wrong. So yes.”

He sighed. “All right. Your mother never had an affair with anyone that I know of. But your father did.”

38

UNFINISHED STORIES

FIVE BLOCKS FROM THE SABATINIS' house I pulled to the curb across from a deserted children's play park. The reverend hadn't shared details about my dad's affair. He learned about it from my father after it ended, which was a year and a half before Q.C. disappeared. My dad didn't tell my mother, though, until Q.C. was kidnapped.

I took out my phone. It was late afternoon in Dubai. Ty answered right away.

"Hey, was about to text," he said. "To see if you could talk later."

I stared through my windshield. Alongside the road bare tree branches swayed in the wind. "How about now?"

"Give me a sec." A long-legged spider skittered across the dashboard. I opened the window and did my best to shoo it away. It fell to the floor mat. Ty came back before I could do anything about that. "What's wrong? Where are you?"

"Side of the road. Sharing the car with a spider I might need to kill."

"Don't let me stop you. But why the side of the road?"

I told him everything.

"You're sure this Rev is telling the truth?"

"My parents didn't want me to talk to him. This must be why."

"So both your parents, rather than tell you about your dad's affair, let you find out from a stranger."

"I insisted on talking to him."

"Because they asked you to look into the murder. That's an awful way to find out. Can't imagine my parents letting that happen to me."

"Because your parents are wonderful people."

I shut my eyes and rested my forehead on the steering wheel. Despite the challenges of emigrating from another country and moving into an almost entirely white neighborhood in Minnesota Ty's parents built successful careers and somehow put their kids first at the same time. It probably wasn't fair to compare my parents to them, but I did it all the time.

"I won the parent lottery no doubt," Ty said. "But they're not perfect. And your dad's affair doesn't make him an awful person."

"It doesn't make him a great person."

"It makes him a human who made a mistake. And maybe I'd avoid hard conversations, too, if I lived through what your parents did."

"You're so reasonable."

"I can fly home and yell at them for you if you want. I'll stop by and kill that spider first."

I laughed and lifted my head from the steering wheel. "Please. You'd capture it and put it out the window. And make my mom tea and shower her with compliments until she opened up to you."

"Is that bad?"

"No. In fact, I wish you were here. Because I miss you. And

because you could talk to them and I could hide in the bedroom."

"Send Lauren after them. She won't hold back."

I found the lever and shoved the seat away from the steering wheel. "I started wanting to clear my parents' names. Find justice for them. All I've learned is the Kevs are grieving parents, too. Like mine except uberwealthy. I found a trail, but it got Eva killed. And I see no chance of her ex, the main suspect, talking to me."

"You didn't get Eva killed. Whoever killed her got her killed. It's awful, but you did not do that."

"It's not a coincidence. I set off the chain that led to it. And the chain that led to me learning this — thing — about my dad I don't want to know."

"Sometimes ignorance is better."

"And I still can't stop."

"Can't you? Not saying you should. But you can. You don't owe your parents."

The spider appeared from nowhere and crawled along the steering wheel.

"Ugh." I opened the car door and swatted it onto the street.

"Quille?"

"Got rid of the spider." I headed to the swing set and sat on one of the old-fashioned plank swings. "I can't stop when I've uncovered motives I never dreamed of for my parents. And my sister. I'm not leaving all that hanging so I can wonder about it forever."

"Your sister — sorry, so sorry, hold on."

The wood swing felt cold through my jeans. I pushed off with my feet and swayed as I waited for him to return.

"Back," Ty said.

"You've got to be somewhere, don't you? We'll talk later."

"Antsy client. But it's fine."

My antsy clients pay me a modest amount by the hour. Ty's

can sway billion dollar deals. Not that he gets the billion dollars. But I didn't want to keep him from it.

"I need to head to the music store anyway. Talk to my dad."

We set a time to talk later. I retrieved my iPad from the car. Perched on a picnic bench under a tree to block the sun's glare, I scrolled through my notes on the case. I didn't want to ask anyone else to talk to Klaus for me. But I wasn't leaving any other stone unturned.

Somehow, somewhere there was a connection between Q.C. and Vanessa. I meant to find it.

39

WHAT HE SAID

THE MUSIC STORE is on Main Street between a bakery and an old-time theater converted to an event space. The box office, which is bright red, still stands in front of the theater.

As soon as I stepped into the store, I smelled the familiar mix of steel strings, old wood, and oil soap. Rows of acoustic guitars hung on the far wall, banjos, fiddles, and other stringed instruments on the one near me. Reed and wind instruments filled the center aisle. My dad sat on a stool playing bass runs on a large-bodied Gibson guitar. A skinny customer with a bandana around his head watched my dad's fingers fly.

Dad saw me and handed the Gibson to the customer. "Try it." Then he joined me near the sheet music. "Rev told you."

"Yes," I said.

"Take a walk?"

Neither of us spoke until we crossed the cracked asphalt parking lot, cut through the alley, and emerged onto a quiet tree-lined street.

"I never wanted you or Kendra to know," my dad said.

"What about the police? You didn't think it mattered?" I knew I should study my dad's face and body language. But I kept my eyes on the sidewalk instead. If I looked at him, I'd think too much about how much he'd disappointed me and not enough about the investigation.

"It ended a year and a half before Q.C. disappeared. But the police were looking for reasons to target us."

I doubted the task force, had they known, would have seen an affair that ended only eighteen months before as unimportant.

"Target you, you mean." I wound long strands of my hair around my fingers.

"Your mother, too. If they thought she knew about the affair, they'd paint her as the angry, jealous wife. Willing to hurt our daughter to spite me. Or acting out of rage."

It fit the revenge-against-spouse motive for killing a child. Except that from all I'd learned, Dad didn't spend much time with my sisters. My mother would have been hurting herself more than him.

"But Mom was at the party. She couldn't have taken Q.C., not alone."

"She could if she made it a game. Told Q.C. to go somewhere and hide and wait for her."

"You, I — you think Mom might have done that?"

First Eva suggested Kendra did it, now my father suggested my mother. Both theories never crossed my mind. Either I was too close to this case to think clearly or other people were grasping at straws.

"I was afraid that's what the police would think."

"You had to think of it yourself to worry about it."

I'd never seen that theory about my mother in print. And Chief Highbottom never mentioned it.

"Rev pointed that out. To convince me we needed a criminal defense lawyer."

I was glad someone convinced them. They ought to have gotten one right away, not weeks into the investigation. My parents, before Q.C., trusted authorities. All the same, Rev was way more involved in my parents' lives than felt normal.

"Why was he so full of advice?"

"He counseled people before who dealt with police," my dad said. "Knew how they thought."

"Q.C. was five. You couldn't think she'd stay hidden for what, two or three hours, even as a game."

As I said it, Rev's comment about Kendra taking care of Q.C. came to mind. If Q.C.'s big sister told her it was game...but Kendra had been in the pizza place, too.

"It's far-fetched. But we couldn't afford to give the police ammunition. We needed them to focus on finding Q.C., not pinning it on us."

"When did you tell Mom?"

"The day after Q.C. was taken. I knew it might come out. I didn't want her blindsided. Or to think I hid it because it related to the kidnapping. I told her if she wanted me to, if she thought it mattered, I'd tell the police."

I stopped and looked him in the face for the first time. "You put that on her?"

I couldn't imagine my mother learning, while her daughter was missing, that her husband cheated on her. On top of that, he wanted her to decide if they should tell the police.

"I didn't put it on her. I told her and we decided together."

"If it was over, why hadn't you told Mom already?"

"Because it was over. And it was a mistake. Telling her might ease my conscience. But how would it help your mother?"

"She'd have all the information. To decide if she wanted to stay."

"Or she'd go through all that pain for nothing. You probably think all your mother's problems started with Q.C. —"

"Because everyone's always told me that. Q.C. and post-partum from me."

"No. Grief over Q.C., post-partum, deepened what was already there. Brenda got depressed before that. And anxious."

That didn't fit Rev's view. But my mother might have shown him another side of herself. Or Rev was as disingenuous as Dylan claimed.

"Maybe she was anxious because she was raising two kids almost on her own," I said. "And had a husband who was cheating on her. Whether she knew it or not."

"I wasn't a great husband, Quille. I wasn't a good one. But the way your Mom is right now on the current medication? That's pretty much how she was before it all happened. If you had to decide today between telling her something that might send her over the edge or holding back, what would you do?"

40

WHO IT WAS

"NOT HAVE an affair in the first place?" I said.

"If I could have gone back in time and changed that, I would've. But I couldn't."

We turned down a side street with three-story Queen Anne houses mixed in between raised ranches.

"Who was it?" I said.

"You really want to know?"

I nodded.

Dad stopped and veered to a high curb to sit. "The fiddle player. In the band. Alice."

I remained standing, one foot in the gutter, one in the street. "I don't remember anyone named Alice."

My dad had given me the names of the band members so I could call and ask what they remembered about Q.C.'s death. They'd all answered my questions. None offered anything I didn't already know. And none was named Alice.

"She wasn't in the band by the time Q.C. was taken."

"So you didn't give me her information? How do you expect me to solve this if you don't tell me what I need to know?"

"Honestly, Quille, I don't know how anyone could solve it.

It's almost forty years later. But your mother insisted she wanted you to look into it. You seemed to need to look into it."

Apparently no one thought I could do this. But that didn't matter to me now.

"How did it start? The affair."

"You need to understand. For years your mother and I had two modes. When I wasn't home, and when we argued. Alice's marriage was falling apart. For different reasons, but we started joking about how bleak things looked for both of us."

"And jokes turned into sex?" I glared down at him.

"It was four decades ago, Quille. It's hard to remember how exactly it started. But for the first time in years, I had fun. Relaxed. Felt —"

"Irresponsible?" I said.

"Like a person."

A silver sedan sped around the corner and, startled, I leapt onto the parkway. It didn't come that close to me, but I stumbled when my foot hit the curb. My dad stood and steadied me.

"Guy should've been watching," he said.

"I shouldn't've been in the street." I sat on the curb, too, but a few feet from my dad.

"I was a lot like you, Quille," he said. "Started playing guitar at eleven. By the time I was fourteen, I joined a family bluegrass band. Replaced the youngest brother who decided music wasn't for him. Three years down the road, with all new members but me, we were getting regular paying jobs. Traveling. Cutting albums. Never looked back. It's part of why I wasn't as excited as your mom about you acting so young."

"Mom? Excited?"

I didn't remember that. She noticed me when I started singing and acting, but I couldn't recall her being excited about anything I did.

"In her way. But I didn't want her to push you."

"Because you worked too hard too young."

"Nothing wrong with hard work. But it's so tough to make a living in this business that when you find yourself doing it, people tell you how lucky you are. And I was. Plenty of bands were just as good and worked just as hard and didn't get where we were. But it doesn't leave much room for thinking you might be happier at something else. That's why your Gram encouraged you to pursue theater but look beyond it, too."

"She did the same for you, though, didn't she? You went to college."

"Your Gram and grandfather insisted. And paid. They paid for some of your mom's school too, when her parents refused after they found out she was pregnant. But I was going through the motions, doing the minimum to check the box and get the degree. Especially after your mom and I had Kendra."

"And this relates to the affair how?"

"I put my feet on a path young and stuck to it. Somewhere along the line it started feeling like a treadmill I couldn't get off. By the time Alice and I met, I didn't want to do it anymore. But I didn't know how else I could earn a living. When Alice and I were together, it felt magic. Like another world. Off the treadmill."

"While Mom was still on her treadmill at home."

"I didn't say what I did was right. But I didn't do it to hurt your mom or Kendra."

My father told me the affair went on for about six months.

"Who ended it?"

"She did. Quit the band. After I told her I'd never leave your mother."

"She wanted you to?"

My hands curled into fists at my sides. My dad made it all sound so passive. The affair just happened. Alice just left.

When it came to the murder investigations, that might be a good thing. Someone who went with the flow was unlikely to plan to kidnap and murder two little girls without ever getting caught. But it also spoke to someone who couldn't take responsibility for his actions. Who might do terrible things and act like it wasn't his fault or didn't relate to him.

"Alice said so. But I don't think she really did. Diving into another marriage wouldn't solve anything for either of us."

Alice must have been angry at him and probably my mom, too. I wasn't sure that gave her a motive to kidnap and kill Q.C. eighteen months later. But I had only my dad's word for when the affair ended. Or that it ended.

And for the first time in my life, I didn't know if I trusted his word.

"You didn't think the police needed to know?"

"They questioned her. And everyone who'd been in the band when I was in it."

At least the police talked to Alice. But not knowing Alice's history with my dad, my guess was they didn't grill her.

I told my dad I needed to talk to my mother. Instead, I drove with no purpose, ending at the St. Louis Arch. In the nearby parking garage, twice I started to dial my Gram's number but stopped. If she didn't know about Dad's affair, I wasn't sure I ought to tell her. And if she did know, I didn't want to put her in the spot of trying to explain it to me. She was the one person who was always there for me. Why make her life harder?

Finally, I bought a ticket and wandered through the natural history museum in the base of the Arch, gazing at exhibits without really seeing them.

I couldn't imagine my father as a killer. He was the man who took Kendra and me for ice cream. Ordered pizza every Saturday night and played games with us. Explained my mother was ill, not mad at us, when she closed herself in the bedroom.

But some people who did terrible things had families they loved. They must.

I wandered over to a presentation on Wild West markswoman Annie Oakley.

Terrible things, yes. But serial murder? That wasn't, as Ty more or less pointed out, the same thing as having an affair. Cheating on my mother didn't put my dad in the same category as Ted Bundy or John Wayne Gacy.

In college my therapist pointed out how much I talked about my mother while giving my dad a pass. I felt she was unfair. I saw my dad as the good guy and my mother as the difficult one.

My mother was difficult, no question. But maybe there were no good guys.

41

CHOICES

I DELAYED TALKING to my mother long enough that I needed to eat lunch and call Ty. At Sacred Grounds Café, an independent coffee house on Main Street, I had a sundried tomato and squash panini. It tasted fresh and full of flavor, maybe due to the locally grown produce. At one-thirty in the afternoon my time, which was a half hour before midnight in Dubai, I popped in earbuds and called Ty on FaceTime. I used my phone because my iPad battery was drained.

He was in his hotel room. "How'd it go with your parents?"

I told him briefly about my dad. Ty listened but seemed distracted. I shifted my chair so I was wedged between a large empty table and a shelf featuring a chess board and an antique volume of War and Peace. It gave me the illusion of privacy.

"Is there something you wanted to talk about?" I said.

"It can wait."

"Did they ask you to stay on in Dubai?"

He blinked. "No. But there are some hints they might. Strong hints. How did you —"

"Lauren said that might happen. Or something like it."

"Nothing's for sure."

I rested my elbow on the table to prop up my arm, which suddenly felt shaky as I gripped the phone. "If it were, are you talking about being away a long time?"

"Longer than four months, but we're not talking years." He looked directly into the camera. It felt as if his eyes were meeting mine. "It's a possibility I need to think about."

I swallowed hard. "And you're thinking...?"

"That's why I wanted to talk to you."

My mother was in the garden pulling weeds before spring planting season. I inhaled the rich scent of wet dirt. My desire to avoid thinking about my talk with Ty finally got me to confront her.

"Why didn't you just tell me Dad had an affair?"

"He had it. If he couldn't bring himself to tell you, I didn't think I had to." She gave me a handful of wet, tangled weeds. I took them to the compost pile on the side of the garage.

When I returned to the edge of the flower bed, I asked why she agreed not to tell the police.

"All I could think about was getting Q.C. back. If we told the police, they'd focus on him — or me — instead of looking for the real kidnapper." On her knees in the dirt, she yanked at a stubborn weed. "Shows you what I knew. They did that anyway."

"You were sure Dad had nothing to do with Q.C.?"

She shifted to the next flower bed. "I was sure."

"Did you believe him that the affair was over?"

"I knew it was."

"How?"

She sat back on her heels and looked up at me. "Because I knew. I'm not an idiot, Quille. Your father's busy, busy, busy but he stops arguing with me over everything. Starts singing songs around the house. Six months down the road, the only female band member quits. Your father spends more time at home. But he argues about everything again. And when he's not doing that, he mopes."

"You put it together."

"And asked one of the other wives. We were friends."

"When did you ask her?"

My mother shrugged. "A few weeks after that woman quit."

Nearly a year and a half before Q.C. was taken. "But you didn't confront Dad?"

"I had two girls, one barely into preschool. Sometimes I felt like a single mom. But I knew from watching your Aunt Cathy that really being one was a hundred times harder." My mother stood and stripped off her cotton gloves. "Better a tenth of a husband than none."

I felt less sure about tenths of husbands, but I only needed to take care of myself. No one depended on me.

"What about the woman he had the affair with? She could've taken Q.C. out of spite."

My mother sat on the bottom step. "That long later?"

I'd still been grieving the death of Marco, my former boyfriend, a year and a half down the road. I pointed that out.

"But she remarried," my mother said. "Six months after she left the band. Happily, I heard. Started some degree program in St. Louis."

"You kept tabs on her?"

"The bluegrass world is small. My friend's husband saw her in a local band. Talked to her after."

I joined my mother on the stair. "Did you tell Dad?"

"Fill your father in on his girlfriend? No, I did not."

A bunny hopped to the center of the yard and froze when it noticed me watching. I looked away. From the corner of my eye, I watched it finish its trek and disappear into the bushes that divided my parents' yard from the neighbor's.

A happy Alice had less motive to hurt my mother or father.

"Did you ever go to Rev — or anyone — for couples counseling? Deal with how you felt about the affair?" I said.

"You mean did we spend hours or days analyzing it? Go to therapy to yell and shout? No. Your dad's been a good partner over the years. Actions mean more than talk."

"Having an affair is an action."

"One in a nearly fifty-year marriage."

"But —"

My mother put her hand on my arm. "Quille, if you're mad at your father, deal with it. Go back to talk therapy if you need to. Yell at your father. Better yet, find that fiddle player and rant at her. But I don't need any of that."

She shook the last clumps of dirt off her gloves and headed into the house.

I didn't want to rant. Or maybe I did. And I definitely wanted answers to whether the affair held any clues to Q.C.'s death.

First, though, I wanted a drink.

42

WHISKEY TALKS

"YOUR DAD? SERIOUSLY?" Lauren said.

"Yeah. Not something I needed to know."

Lauren had researched property records all day for me. I'd texted her to meet me at Recess Brewing, the same bar Dylan took me to the week before, after checking to see there was no live music scheduled. It was within a mile of my parents' house. I'd walked there and gotten a table near the brick fireplace.

Before we ordered I spilled out everything about my parents. And nothing about Ty. I wanted to sort out how I felt before hearing Lauren's views.

Now Lauren pushed a stack of pages from the clerk's office across the table. "All I could find on the Smiths' neighbors from way back when. And Eva Erickson's neighbors now. Oh, and I looked online through every rent by owner site and finally found the fishing cabin. If you want to check it out, it's available."

"I don't think there's any real evidence there after all this time."

"But the Smiths still own it. So who knows? And, big plus, we stay somewhere other than your parents' house for a night."

"You can head home, you know. Really."

"Not until I have to. Besides, I already got us a reservation. In a friend's name so no one knows it's us."

I put Lauren's pages into my shoulder bag to look over tomorrow and started to open Facebook on my iPad. I was pretty sure I'd found the fiddle player.

Before I could show Lauren, Dylan came in the front door. Lauren raised her eyebrows to ask if I invited him. I shook my head.

He dropped into the chair on the long side of the table and shrugged off his leather jacket. "Thought I might find you here."

"Because?" I said.

"You didn't answer your phone. And Dad said you seemed upset when you left. I assumed there must be something that called for whiskey what with all the permission-getting before he could talk to you."

Lauren turned sideways in her chair. "Be totally honest. Any chance your dad and Quille's mom had an affair?"

"Quille's mother?" Dylan said.

"Your dad said they didn't," I said.

"But it's seriously possible," Lauren said. "Maybe he spilled the beans about your dad's affair to keep you from looking at him and your mom."

"Then why wouldn't my dad say so?" I said.

"Protecting your mom. Or completely clueless."

I glanced at Dylan. "You're oddly silent."

"First, processing that your dad had an affair." His lips pursed. "Second, obviously I'm not my father's biggest fan. But I never got that vibe about your mom."

"Would you?" Lauren said. "You were, what, seven?"

"I meant when I came back to town. My mother knew my dad 'broke his vows,' as she so quaintly put it. But she never said anything about Quille's mother."

"Did she say anything about other women?" I asked.

"Oh, yes. Mentioned quite a few 'lady friends' by name. Also her words."

"You didn't tell me that," I said.

He shrugged. "Mom didn't want me to talk about Dad's extracurricular activities. Perfect preacher's wife, remember? Never make the pastor look bad. Did you ask your mother?"

"If she had an affair? But we're getting along so well." I fished out my Advil bottle and shook out three. "I suppose I need to."

"Is it worth it?" he said.

"Asking her?"

"The whole investigation. If all it gets you is migraines. Literally."

"You must've been talking to my boyfriend." I downed two pills together, then the third by itself. "I don't know if it's worth it. But it's the only way I can find the truth. If there's any chance, I can't walk away."

"Will your mother ever thank you?" he said.

"Doubtful. But I'll get some peace of mind."

Unless someone in my family was a murderer.

Lauren tapped her fingers on the table in front of Dylan. "Where were your parents when Q.C. was taken?"

I knew what other people told me. But I waited to see what Dylan would say.

"Washington, DC. Whole weekend. Religious convention. That's why they weren't at Q.C.'s party. My brother and I stayed with our cousins."

Lauren shifted her gaze to me. "Can you check that?"

"This long later? No. But it's what my mom, my aunt, and Rev all told me."

"They brought us back little models of the Supreme Court," Dylan said.

They might have been able to get those without visiting the

Court, though it had been the 1980s. It wasn't as if you could hop on the Internet, search Supreme Court models, and order them shipped to you.

The server brought our drinks.

Dylan stood. "I'll leave you ladies to your drinks." He gave me that half smile. "Just wanted to be sure you were all right."

After he left, I said to Lauren, "You think he's checking up on me for his father? Playing some game?"

"I think he likes you. But you're investigating two murders, and one witness already got killed."

I looked after Dylan. "I didn't tell him I was talking to Eva Erickson."

"Still, you should seriously watch your back. And I'll watch it, too," Lauren said. "Now let's see what we can find out about your father's girlfriend."

43

THE OLD DAYS

ACCORDING to Facebook and other social media sites, Alice Roberts was a professor in a music therapy program. She also played fiddle, though it was listed as violin on her university biography.

My dad's band cut five albums — real albums on vinyl — while he was with them. The three covers I located online didn't show a woman in the band. But an old flyer for sale on eBay did. It dated from when they played at a festival at the Tennessee fairgrounds.

YouTube yielded only a few songs playing behind static album covers. Wikipedia wasn't interested.

It was time to try some old-school research.

LAUREN and I found an old VCR in the unfinished part of my parents' attic along with a trove of videotapes. The band's name appeared on the labels for four of them.

"Surprised there aren't more," Lauren said as we made our way out, ducking our heads where the roof slanted.

"Harder to video anything back then. And it's not like there was somewhere to post it."

We set the VCR and tapes on the floor at the foot of the bed.

After dusting off her hands, Lauren opened the bag of chips we'd brought upstairs with us. "Think your dad's been so ridiculously attentive to your mom all these years out of guilt?"

"It's not ridiculous to do a lot for a spouse who's clinically depressed."

"I get it way back when she could barely get out of bed. But why didn't she take antidepressants sooner? Or try therapy? If you have bad vision and refuse to wear glasses, does your family have to spend forever leading you around to make sure you don't bump into things?"

"That's Gram's view," I said. Gram had little patience for my mother. She often warned me not to wallow in my feelings and become like her. "But Mom had intense anxiety, too. The early meds helped one thing and made another worse. She got discouraged."

"At least she could treat you better. It can't be that hard to not say mean, critical things."

"She's nicer than she used to be." I fast forwarded through the early part of the first video. It contained old episodes of *Cheers*. I hoped no one taped over the band footage. "We had a pretty good talk about the affair thing. Almost like normal people."

What looked like a stage full of musicians flipped past on the screen. I hit Stop, then rewound. Five band members played on a wide stage. A tobacco company banner hung behind them. The men wore cowboy hats, blue blazers over red checked collared shirts, dark jeans, white neck kerchiefs, and red lizard skin boots. Sweat dripped down their faces.

The fiddle player dressed almost the same way other than wearing a denim skirt rather than jeans and a red hairband rather than a cowboy hat.

My dad did most of the talking between songs.

Lauren hit Pause. "What's with that southern drawl? Thought your dad grew up near Chicago, like you?"

"Yeah. In an apartment a few blocks from the one Gram later bought with my grandfather. But Dad and his sister moved to Edwardsville for college."

"And this performance — how long later?"

"Few years. The drawl is probably a mix of spending a lot of time traveling in the South and stage craft."

It made me uneasy, though. The man on the tape didn't sound like my dad. And while I saw my dad in suits when he worked as a copier repairman when I was growing up, I'd never seen him in lizard skin boots or a cowboy hat. Or with his hair cut so short it looked like he was in the military.

"You, Danielle, and Joe sound like yourselves when you talk on stage," Lauren said. "You look like yourselves."

"I wear more makeup," I said. "And we're not trying to earn a living. This look must be the band's brand. Red, white, and blue. Conservative. Country."

I compared Alice Roberts' university photo to the fiddle player in the frozen video. Alice's face looked wider and her pale skin smoother. She wore a dark blazer over a pale rose turtleneck. Nothing about her suggested a country look. But she resembled the fiddle player far more than my dad did his former self.

Lauren handed me my phone. "Might as well call her now."

"I could email."

"So she can ignore you and then dodge your calls?"

"It's after seven. She's probably not in."

"Leave a message."

"And say what? 'Hi, you had an affair with my dad and I need to talk to you about my sister's murder?'"

Lauren shrugged. "Works for me. You want to keep this investigation moving."

I dialed, fumbling one digit at the end twice before the call went through. A woman with a low voice and a syrupy southern accent answered.

"Hello. My name is Quille C. Davis. Cliff Davis's daughter."

"Who?"

"Quille C. Davis. You played in a band with my dad?"

"I don't know where you got my number, but if you think this is funny —"

"No, I — no. This is not — did you not know my parents had another child? After Q.C.'s death? I'm Quille Catherine Davis the second."

"Quille C.... My Lord, they named you the same thing? That's — I don't, well —" She cleared her throat. "I apologize. Very unprofessional of me. What can I do for you?"

My grip on the phone loosened. Her surprise at my name suggested that she and my dad hadn't kept in touch.

"I'm an attorney. And I look into crimes. My parents asked me to see if I could find anything about Q.C.'s death."

"Tall order after all this time."

"I'm looking for any connection between the two families. Mine and the Kevs. No matter how small."

The phone buzzed with some sort of alert, but I ignored it.

"Doubt I can help with that," Alice said. "Never heard of that other poor girl before she was found with Q.C."

"She went missing a few weeks before that. It was in the local news."

"I was starting a masters' program then, playing in a band, and working a side job. Didn't watch news. Or TV. I only heard about your sister because the bass player called and told me."

College and law school had been like that for me, so I didn't find her claim strange. But that didn't mean she was telling the truth.

"There might be a connection you aren't aware of. I'd like to meet with you. Show you some photos, ask a few questions."

I could email her the photos, but I wanted to meet this woman.

"Oh, I'm so sorry. My schedule's jammed. Finals to grade. And a charity event to play at."

"My dad told me about you. About your relationship."

There was a long silence. "That's got nothing to do with Q.C."

"But I have questions. Such as why you never told the police."

More silence. Finally, a shuffling sound came through the phone, as if Alice were flipping through pages. "Honestly, the only time I've got free is on my break during a fundraiser next Tuesday night. It's in Clayton —"

"Send me the info. I'll be there."

I had trouble sitting still as Lauren and I watched the rest of the tape. I couldn't believe I'd soon be meeting my father's ex-girlfriend.

Lauren paused the video multiple times so we could study the crowds. I thought someone from the Kev side of the case might have seen my dad's band play. But no one looked familiar, except the one time my mom, Kendra, and Q.C. appeared in the audience. All blond, fair-skinned, and smiling.

"You seriously are the only one who looks like your dad," Lauren said.

"Yeah, Mom didn't get the Q.C. clone she wanted."

"Maybe it's not about that," Lauren said. "Maybe she wasn't thrilled you resembled your dad. She still had to be majorly mad at him."

"Never thought of that." Seeing her on video reminded me that I wanted to visit Kendra. I took out my phone.

Before I could text her, the phone buzzed again, reminding me I hadn't looked at the alert. It was a ping from a search I set up to watch for anything relating to Eva Erickson's death.

"What?" Lauren said.

"How do you feel about crashing a wake?"

44

WHAT THE NEIGHBOR KNEW

YELLOW CRIME SCENE tape fluttered in front of Eva's door, one end loose. Bare sticks stuck in the grass without any tape. The police car was gone. Through the front picture window, I saw a carpeted living room with a large flat screen TV. A matching leather sofa and recliner faced it.

I knocked in case Eva's sister, who I hoped was in town for the wake, might be staying there. No answer.

Lauren walked around the side of the house. "Shed in the back. No windows."

I'd called several neighbors the evening before. None answered or returned my calls. Now we rang the bell of the neighbor who found Eva. She answered but shut the door before I finished my first sentence. Lauren and I split the remaining houses and started knocking.

A white-haired woman was dragging a ladder out her front door as I approached the fifth house. She wore boots and a down vest but no coat.

I hurried up the stairs. "Can I help?"

"Oh, dear, I don't know. I need to change the lightbulb. But last time I had a devil of a time getting that shade off."

She gestured toward a plain round glass shade that covered the overhead porch light.

"I can try. If you don't mind holding the ladder."

I did my best to keep my balance on the third rung from the top as I gripped the shade. On the third try it loosened a bit. Dirt fell into my eyes. I blinked it away and tried again. I almost lost my balance when the shade came loose.

"Careful, careful," the woman said.

I backed down a few rungs and she handed me a bulb. After I screwed it in, I carried the ladder to her garage and introduced myself on the way.

"Oh, dear, I got your voicemail but forgot to call you back. You're police?"

"No. An investigator. I'm looking into two other murders that might be related to Eva Erickson's."

I suggested that she step inside her back door so she could be warmer. I'd stay on the patio and talk to her through the screen.

She held the door open. "Oh, no, no. Please come in. And I hope you don't mind if I ask you to put in the smoke alarm battery. My son took the old one out but hasn't been around since I got a new one. And it's so hard to reach."

I thought I might need the ladder again. But she had a step stool that was high enough. The challenge was that the smoke detector was wedged at an odd angle above her refrigerator. As I stretched and twisted, I gave her the shortest version I could of Q.C.'s and Vanessa's stories.

The woman told me she used to work with Eva. She wasn't going to the wake because she'd recently finished chemo and felt too fatigued by the late afternoon to go out.

"But you were going to climb the ladder?"

"I get tired of not doing for myself. So I try. That's not so bad, but it gets a bit lonely not being able to go out much."

I closed the alarm and pressed the button to check it. It gave a quick beep. "Anything else I can do while we talk?"

She said no, but when I asked again pointed me toward the guest bathroom.

I texted Lauren to let her know I might be a while. Then I replaced two more bulbs on the bathroom vanity and took down a box of extra shampoo and bar soap from an upper cabinet. The neighbor told me she hadn't heard anything during the night or early morning before Eva Erickson was killed.

"Did you know her ex-husband? Klaus?"

"Never met him. But saw him stop by a few times in the last couple years. You probably know he was in prison before that."

I nodded. "Did Eva tell you what for?"

"Some type of fraud."

That must be Eva's way of avoiding the problems in her earlier neighborhood.

"Did they get along?"

"She never said much about him. But he fixed her porch railing last summer. And the other times came by to run the snow blower. Did her neighbor's walks on either side with it, too."

My phone buzzed with a text from Lauren. She'd had no luck with other neighbors and was waiting in the car.

"But he lives pretty far away, doesn't he?" I said.

"No idea. She never said."

"Did he stay with her those times you saw him?"

"There was an extra SUV out front for a day or two. One of those smaller ones." She glanced at the floor. "I noticed because I worried about it getting towed. You're supposed to park on one side when the plows come."

"We have that in Chicago, too. How often did you and Eva talk? Or visit?"

Klaus staying over, if he had, didn't quite fit how Eva depicted the relationship. I'd been left with the impression the two spoke when they needed to but weren't close. But she hadn't exactly been testifying under oath. She might have had any number of reasons to shade the truth.

"Mostly just if we happened to leave the house at the same time. But I got her the job she has — had. Recommended her for it when I retired. Before that she worked as a checkout clerk."

The job was at a doctor's office as a receptionist and billing clerk.

The neighbor didn't know Eva's sister. I asked if she could think of anything else about Eva or Klaus. "Even if you're guessing. You never know what might help."

As a lawyer, I warn my clients never to guess when they testify, but I try to get the other side's witnesses to do it. Guesses can lead somewhere interesting.

"Hmm. Well, Eva had a bit more money than it seemed like she could. Working as a checkout clerk and then a receptionist."

"How much is a bit more?"

"She let slip once her house was all paid for. And she bought all that nice furniture."

I'd confirmed through online court records that the Ericksons' divorce was final, but the file wasn't available. I didn't know if Klaus paid alimony. Child support was likely about twenty-five percent of his income. But given eight years in prison, it was hard to imagine he paid Eva large sums.

"Family money?" I said.

The neighbor didn't think so. Eva's parents had come from Poland in the 1940s and struggled most of their lives.

"Did you see her with a lot of cash?"

"Once. We went to an appliance store together. I needed a dishwasher. She needed a dishwasher, refrigerator, stove. And she paid cash. Not something most anyone around here can do."

Some people prefer paying cash. It helps them keep a grip on their finances. And sometimes get better deals. Other people spend cash because they don't qualify for credit cards.

Still others earned the cash legally but didn't report it to the IRS. Or they earned it illegally. If Klaus Erickson not only used drugs and bought them for his sister-in-law but sold them, he might have accumulated extra cash. But I doubted he socked away enough that Eva had extra money years after he went to prison.

The neighbor couldn't think of anything else. I showed her photos on my iPad of everyone I'd interviewed on my side and the Kevs' side.

"The police showed me these. Never seen any of these people."

I'd sent the photos to Detective Ferrell, the county detective on Eva's case. I felt pleased. Despite calling me by various fictional detective names with more than a little scorn, she'd paid attention to what I told her.

After asking a few more questions to be sure there was nothing else, I thanked the neighbor.

"If you find out who killed her, you let me know, will you?"

"I will," I said.

It was time to visit the funeral home.

45

ANGRY SISTER

GOLD LEAF LINED the edges of the guest book in the funeral home lobby. My hand sweated, making the pen I held slippery. I hadn't been to a wake since Marco's. Sometimes I felt like he'd died forever ago. Other times, like now, it seemed like yesterday.

I handed Lauren the pen. "Sign in for us."

Beyond the arched doorway, mourners gathered in small groups. A closed casket stood at the far end, a sofa and a few armchairs facing it. People gathered in the rows of folding chairs behind them and stood on the sides of the parlor.

My hands shook as I folded two twenties, all the cash I had with me, into a donation envelope with my business card. I felt wrong coming to a funeral to ask questions. But I didn't see a better way.

Before leaving that morning, I'd reviewed all the photos I could find online of the family members. I didn't see Klaus or anyone from his family. But Nadia — Eva's younger sister whom Klaus had photographed — stood near one side of the coffin. Eva's two children stood in the opposite corner.

Nadia's angular face and fair skin made her look so like her sister that it must hurt the hearts of everyone who loved Eva. She spun a series of colorful bracelets around on her wrist as she spoke to each person who approached.

Lauren, on a mission, drifted to the videos and photo collages along the back wall. I got in Nadia's line. Thanks to two talkative cousins ahead of me, I learned Klaus wasn't expected today. The children, who hadn't seen him since before he went to prison, didn't want him there.

When I got closer to Nadia, I saw how cracked and dry her lips looked. On my turn, I expressed my sorrow and told her my name. She didn't react.

"My card's here with a donation." I handed her the envelope. "I talked to your sister a couple days before her death."

She thanked me, but her eyes shifted to the man behind me.

I inched sideways to stay in her line of sight. "I'd like to talk more with you soon if you're up to it. Detective Ferrell might have told you about me. I called Eva about her ex-husband."

As if speaking her name conjured her, the detective slipped in through the archway. She stalked the room's perimeter.

Nadia's eyes narrowed. "You know Klaus?"

"I don't. I'm looking into two crimes he might know about. That's why I contacted Eva."

"You. You got her in touch with him again." The buzz of voices around us hushed. "Now she's dead. And you have the nerve to bring that here."

"I'm so sorry." I wasn't sure exactly what "that" meant, but I felt terrible for upsetting her more. I stepped back and bumped the person behind me. I murmured an apology but kept my eyes on Nadia. "I didn't come to cause problems. My card's in the envelope. If I can help —"

"If you can help?" Nadia laughed. It sounded high pitched, almost like a scream. "You helped enough."

"I'm sorry."

Detective Ferrell darted toward us and blocked my path to Eva's children. "Time to go."

"But Klaus's children —"

"Know nothing." The detective gripped my arm and steered me toward the lobby. "Already talked to them."

Lauren followed us out onto the wide sidewalk in front of the funeral parlor.

"Heard from Chief Highbottom," the detective said. I'd asked Highbottom if he could call and explain what I was doing. "He vouched for you. But that doesn't mean I'll let you badger people at a wake."

"I wasn't trying to badger. But the deaths must be related."

"Klaus Erickson didn't kill Eva. He lives three states away. And he was at work all night when Eva was killed. I confirmed it with his coworkers."

Gravel crunched as an SUV pulled into the parking lot.

"He could've paid someone to kill her," I said.

"In theory. But he spent eight of the last ten years in prison. And stocks shelves in the midnight shift at a discount store. Doesn't sound like someone who can afford murder for hire."

"He's also a computer programmer," I said. "Or he was. Could be doing side jobs for good money. How did he react when he heard about Eva's death?"

The detective sighed. "Sounded shocked. And numb. I told him over the phone. Didn't see his face, so no real sense if it was genuine."

"You didn't send a patrol officer in his town to talk to him?"

"I asked the sheriff to check on him after my call. But I wanted to hear his voice when I told him."

At least the detective took my Klaus theory seriously. She told me, though, that the FBI didn't, though she wouldn't say why. I got the feeling the FBI agent refused to tell her.

"And Eva's and Klaus's children?"

"Haven't seen their dad since before he went to prison. Definitely not fans of his. They didn't know anything about your call to Eva or about her being in touch with him."

"You're sure."

"Can't see why they'd lie."

After cautioning me not to do anything to get in her way and reminding me to keep her informed, the detective walked us to the car. "Watch your back. If this all relates to your cold cases, you're a target, too."

After she left, Lauren put her arm around my shoulders. "You had to talk to Nadia. And at least now you know Eva did call Klaus."

I nodded.

"I learned a few things, too," Lauren said.

46

GOSSIP

LAUREN TOOK the keys from me. "When Klaus went to prison, Eva stored his things. Including his cameras and dark room equipment. In that storage shed in back."

I got in the passenger side. "How'd you find out?"

"Listened and lurked. Someone said that's where the older photos in the montages came from."

Feeling queasy, I rolled down the window. Cold air hit my face. "He preyed on her sister, tried to blackmail her, and basically forced Eva to move. And she stores things for him."

"Yeah. Seriously odd. Sure, he's her kids' father, but why not sell his stuff? Or junk it or make him find his own storage? She did other favors, too."

I glanced at her. "Like what? And what did you do, grill all the family members?"

"Pretended to be a real estate agent who met Eva once at an open house. And I didn't need to grill. People gossip at wakes as much as anywhere else."

She told me Eva managed Klaus's money, what there was of it, while he served his time. She also let him use her home as his mailing address after he was released. "And then he repays her by paying someone to kill her. Maybe."

"The more I think about it, the more paying someone to kill her doesn't make sense," I said. "If he didn't trust her to stay firm on her alibi, and he could afford to pay someone, why not do it sooner?"

"Like during the eight years he was in jail and had an airtight alibi?"

"Right." I glanced in the side view mirror as I buzzed the window up again. "Was that silver car behind us since the funeral home?"

Lauren glanced in the rear-view mirror. "Maybe. Didn't notice."

"A silver sedan like it drove past my dad and me yesterday." The sedan changed lanes and passed us. I caught the first few characters on an Indiana license plate as it did. AG7.

"Seriously lot of cars just like that around," Lauren said.

I typed the partial plate number into a note on my phone anyway. "Wish we could get ahold of Klaus's old photos. We might see someone who links the Kev family to mine. Or someone who could lead us to Jimmy Smith, who I still can't find a thing about."

Vanessa's missing cousin was a huge loose end. He was the only person who disappeared after Vanessa's death. Made me think he knew something. Or might have gotten into some sort of trouble himself.

Lauren turned onto the road leading to the expressway. "The padlock on the back shed didn't look too sturdy. But I've got another idea."

"Good. Because breaking and entering is a great way to get my law license revoked."

"Look at my phone."

Her Internet browser was open to a website called Nadia Speaks. The About section included a photo of Eva's sister.

Nadia offered to help people heal their psyches through divining tools and charts. Shamanism, tarot cards, astrology, numerology, and other ologies I didn't recognize were covered. But she listed no last name, which was why it didn't come up in my searches.

"Heard one of her friends talking about it." Lauren merged onto the expressway. "Speaks is her stage name. Or pseudonym. Whatever. Cute, huh?"

I scrolled through the site. Nadia gave readings by email, social media, phone, or video conference.

"She started two years after her creepy brother-in-law assaulted her," Lauren said. "Could be she dived into all the woo-woo to help get past it."

The contact information included e-mail, a chat box, and a telephone number. I clicked Chat, which recognized me as Lauren. I asked if research studies existed about energy healing. "Can't imagine I'll get an answer from her personally. But I want to see how it works."

"Thanks for doing it as me," Lauren said. "Now I'm going to get email about my chakras or energy healing or some such."

What looked like a canned answer popped up.

Quantum physics shows why energy healing works. Would you like a free consultation?

I exited. Ambushing Nadia in a business consult after doing it at the funeral home wasn't going to win me any points. But during the drive I wrote and rewrote an email to her. In between typing I kept an eye out for the silver sedan. But I didn't see it again.

I also texted back and forth with Kendra and set a time to visit her.

Dear Nadia,

I am so very sorry I upset you at the funeral home. I'm no friend to Klaus. All I want is to find peace and justice for my family. Decades ago, Klaus knew a little girl, Vanessa Kev. Her body was found along with my sister's. Eva alibied Klaus. She told me he knew the other girl's family well. I wanted to talk to him because I hoped he might tell me more about them. If you could speak with me, it might help me free my parents from at least a small amount of the pain they've lived with for decades. The pain of not knowing what happened to my sister. Please think about it.

I included my phone number and email at the end.

She called me two days later.

47

FAVORS

LAUREN and I were on my way to visit my sister. I put the phone on speaker so Lauren could hear.

Nadia's voice sounded quiet, and there was a lot of background noise. I had to strain to hear her. She was calling from the airport.

"Klaus had jarring, dark energy. None of us wanted that when we were honoring Eva at the wake. But after the funeral lunch I brought leftover cake to a few neighbors. One of them went on and on about how kind you were. I decided I should at least call you."

I explained how I thought Klaus fit with Q.C.'s and Vanessa's cases. And asked about the charges against Klaus.

"Does it matter?" Nadia said.

"Anything could matter. The more I know about Klaus the more I can sort out if he was involved."

"Well, short story is he got more and more into drugs. Started sharing them with me. Mostly pot."

She said that was in the early nineties. After Q.C.'s and Nessa's deaths.

"Did he sell pot to you?"

"No. I paid him back when he got it for me. Like how your older brother buys beer for your high school party."

I don't have brothers and dislike beer. But I got what she meant.

"Anything other than pot?" I said.

"We celebrated my seventeenth birthday a day early. He gave me Ecstasy. That was my gift. That's when we first had sex. And he took the photos of me. He was as wasted as I was."

Her mild tone amazed me. "Klaus was over fifteen years older than you," I said. "He did so many terrible things. Yet you don't sound angry."

"I was. But I recognized later I drew his energy to me. Whatever I was putting out there in the world that got me in that space is my responsibility."

It sounded like something a member of Seminar, a self-help corporation I came across in an earlier investigation, might say.

Nadia agreed Klaus broke the law and should have gone to prison. But she didn't want to feel like a victim, so she didn't think about him very much. She had no idea why Eva agreed to store Klaus's things or did him favors.

"She was madder at him than I was at first."

"Did Klaus pay her alimony?" I said, thinking of the extra money the neighbor talked about.

"Doubt it. Even before he was in jail, he was always quitting one job for another. Starting all over at the bottom."

"Computer programmers were probably in demand back then. He didn't quit to move up?"

"No. Just got restless and left. A couple of his ex-bosses tried to get him to come back but he never wanted to."

Nadia didn't know anything about Klaus ever working for or with the Kevs or James Smith. She didn't remember anything about when Vanessa's body was found.

"I need to ask you something else about Klaus and your sister," I said. "It will probably sound insensitive."

"Will it help find who killed her?"

Lauren changed lanes to pass a slow-moving SUV.

"I can't promise that," I said. "But I'm pulling on all these strings. If I could find the right one, everything might unravel."

"Go ahead."

"Is it possible Klaus sold drugs? Maybe not to you, but to other people."

"He never said so. But it wouldn't surprise me."

"If he did, is there a chance Eva had some role, however small, in his business? Maybe helped him find ways to account for the cash? Stored inventory? Acted as a contact person?"

It had occurred to me that if Klaus and Eva worked together, she might have continued dealing drugs after he went to jail.

"You're asking me if my sister laundered money or sold drugs?"

"I told you it was insensitive."

There was a long silence.

"Nadia?"

"It'd explain why they stayed on sort of good terms despite everything. There's the kids, too, but she didn't need to do Klaus favors."

"Was it hard for you? That she didn't cut him out of her life?"

"Well, she did divorce him. But at the time, at least once I got sober, yeah, I wasn't happy she kept talking to him."

"So the answer to my question?"

Nadia sighed. "Honestly? The way we grew up — won't bore you with it, but Klaus is not the worst guy in our lives. And Eva's main goal in life was making a better life for her kids. If a drug business helped her do that, she might think it was worth it. But I don't know for sure if either of them sold drugs."

"Say Eva knew Klaus was out doing a drug deal or meeting

a contact and later police asked where he was. Would she lie for him?"

"Well, not after she found out about me. But before that? I mean, maybe. Probably. She wouldn't want him getting arrested."

That earned Klaus a spot near the top of the suspect list.

I asked if I could look through Klaus's photos from the 1980s. The good news was that he left well-organized files in Eva's shed. The bad news was that Nadia was about to board a plane to Santa Fe, New Mexico. And no matter what I said, she didn't feel comfortable letting me go through any of Eva's things on my own.

But she agreed that when she came back the following week to go through Eva's things, she'd send the 1980s photos to a service, at my expense, to have them scanned for me.

During the last part of the drive to my sister's, I called Chief Highbottom. He'd told me twice before that he was busy with his grandchildren now that he was back from Florida. While he was willing to talk again by Zoom, he was less excited about meeting in person. Which was what I wanted so I could get a better sense of him as a person. And as a cop.

I had at last figured out the right lure. He agreed to meet later in the week.

Lauren dropped me off in Normal, Illinois, to visit Kendra alone. Lauren was touring open houses and meeting a local real estate agent in Bloomington, the city next door. She had no interest in moving away from Chicago herself. But with more and more clients considering less pricy areas she wanted to understand the competition.

And I wanted to talk to my sister. Or, to be more accurate, I needed to.

48

CHILDHOOD

"I THINK I MET HER." Kendra paced between the faux leather recliner and the half-wall that split the living room from the townhome's narrow entryway. "He actually introduced us to her."

"Us who?" I said.

"Mom, Q.C., and me. When we saw Dad's band. Q.C. kept saying she wanted to be a 'girl fiddler,' too, when she grew up. Did not make Mom happy."

"How old was Q.C.?"

"Four."

"You're sure?"

"She'd just been singing at her fourth birthday party. And not *Twinkle Twinkle*. Some song Dad taught her. She kept forgetting the words on the verses, but she sounded good."

"A bluegrass song?"

"Definitely not. Slow tempo. And about wine. Red wine. Not pigs in pokes or cabin homes or moonshine."

"Hmm." My a cappella trio mainly sings songs with great harmonies from the fifties, sixties, and seventies. But sometimes we branch out, and we all listen to a lot of types of music.

I searched my app and played the beginning of *Red Red Wine*.

Kendra nodded. "That's it. The adults thought it was hilarious. This tiny girl in pigtails singing about wine."

The eighties were a different time for sure. But I was less interested in the alcohol imagery than the lyrics, which I only vaguely remembered. I found them online. "These are about a guy who can't forget someone he loves unless he drinks a lot of wine."

Kendra held out her hand for the phone. She winced as she read. "Think Mom knew about the affair by then?"

"Probably."

"Must be hard for you." She dropped onto the couch. "Daddy's girl finding out he was a fraud."

"I got along with Dad better than Mom. But I wasn't a Daddy's girl."

"I'm probably not being fair. You were a baby. Everyone had to take care of you. Especially with what Mom did."

I sat next to Kendra. "I don't think she chose to be depressed."

"No, not that. Look, there's something I remember. Everyone thinks I don't, but I do." Kendra took my hand.

It was so unlike her that my whole body tensed. "What is it?"

"You said on the phone anything could matter for the investigation. This is the real reason we moved to live with Gram."

I waited.

"Dad came home one day and found Mom standing at the top of the stairs, holding you. About to throw herself down them and take you with."

"She couldn't just have been standing there?"

"No. Because she told me what she was going to do."

I stared at my sister. "What exactly did she say?"

"Not to worry. That Daddy would be home soon to take care

of me. And she'd be better off where she was going and so would you." Kendra squeezed my fingers.

I gripped the edge of the couch cushion with my free hand. My head started throbbing. The reasons parents kill children ran through my mind. One was termed altruism. Believing you were saving a child from a too harsh world. If she was willing to do that to me...but she'd been at Q.C.'s birthday party the whole time.

"She told Dad life was too terrible for a baby. Or for her." Kendra grimaced. "Not too terrible to leave him and me in it I guess."

The throbbing in my head turned to pain needles, but I kept holding my sister's hand. "Tell me you're not jealous Mom didn't want to throw you down the steps, too."

The needles turned to jackhammers as Kendra spoke more. She hadn't been jealous exactly, but she felt ignored her whole life. By my mother, who couldn't do much to care for us, and my dad who often worked late. And by Gram, who managed my acting career.

Kendra agreed Gram tried to do more for her, too, but Kendra was so angry at my parents and so upset over Q.C.'s death she pushed Gram away.

I excused myself before the pain took over entirely. In the powder room, I fumbled out four Advil and swallowed them with cold water from the sink. My stomach twisted and a sour acid taste filled my mouth as the tablets threatened to come right back up. I staggered backwards until I hit the door, then sank to the floor.

Head cradled in my hands, I focused on deep breaths. I know better than to take that much Ibuprofen on an empty stomach. But it only works if I take it early. And it was worth the risk to avoid pickaxes jabbing my brain from now until tomorrow morning. Or longer. I gulped more cold water.

The sourness lessened. Moving carefully so as not to jar my

head, I searched for washcloths. None. I ran cold water on a corner of a hand towel and pressed it to my forehead.

Older siblings often feel jealous of new babies. I reminded myself of that, and of all the reasons seven-year-old Kendra couldn't and wouldn't have killed Q.C. But every time I talked more to my family members, I found new motives for them.

And then there was my mother.

I massaged my neck muscles, which felt like rocks, and struggled not to grit my teeth against the viselike pain in my head. Clenching my jaw only makes it worse.

In my head, I knew my mother planning to throw infant me down the stairs wasn't about me as a person. It stemmed from her deep post-partum depression. And it explained why she said we moved to Gram's apartment for me, not Kendra.

But it made me feel horrible for both of us. I couldn't imagine how dark the world must have felt to my mother. And in my heart, no matter how much I told myself otherwise, I felt sure it showed my mother never loved me.

I ran the water until it felt icy, rinsed the towel, and put it at the base of my skull, imagining it absorbing the throbbing. Normal, Illinois, was halfway between my home and my parents' house. Lauren and I could drive north to Chicago instead of south to Edwardsville. I could sit in Café des Livres tonight by the fire with a hot cocoa and talk with my friend Carole, who was kind and supportive, before going home to sleep in my own condo.

And let my parents' problems be theirs alone.

49

REVELATIONS

SOMEONE KNOCKED on the bathroom door about ten minutes later. "Auntie Q? You okay?"

It was my niece. The pain was down to a dull pounding. I came out to hug her and my nephew, who'd also just gotten home. They both attended high school a mile away. While my niece ran to get Settlers of Cataan, one of our favorite games, and my nephew raided the cabinet for Doritos, Kendra took me aside and put her arm around my shoulders.

"I'm sorry. I shouldn't have told you that. And I should have told you I appreciate what you're doing. I wasn't very supportive before. But Q.C.'s death keeps hanging over us. No matter what you find, or don't, maybe we'll be able to put it behind us."

I nodded and rubbed my hands together. They felt freezing. Kendra made a mug of hot tea for me.

The four of us played Settlers for over an hour. After, I helped Kendra with laundry while they put the game away.

"I really want you to keep going with this," she said as she loaded the washer near the small TV room in the basement. "And to help. Ask me anything. I'll answer."

"You won't love my only other question."

It'd be a good test, though, to see if she truly wanted me to continue. If she did, maybe I would. At least it'd weigh on that side.

I told her about Klaus's guess, based on the JonBenét Ramsay case, that Kendra was jealous and killed Q.C., possibly by accident, then one or both of our parents covered it up.

Kendra measured out some powder detergent. She didn't look angry, just bemused. Her forehead crinkled. "I was jealous, sure. But not homicidal. And if I did it by accident, who would prosecute a kid for that? It would've been awful. But Mom and Dad would have told the police and dealt with it."

As she loaded the clothes, Kendra admitted to being jealous of Q.C. and sometimes shutting her out of the treehouse, but it all sounded like normal sister rivalry.

"What about anything unusual the months before the party?" I said. "Whoever grabbed Q.C. must have known a lot about her. About our family. You remember anyone who was around a lot? Or anyone following you?"

Kendra shut the washer lid and it began to churn. "No. But who knows if I would have noticed. What about someone at Q.C.'s concerts?"

In my month of phone interviews from my office, I'd had no luck with that line of inquiry. I talked with Q.C.'s former choir director, teachers, old neighbors. No one recalled anything unusual.

I asked about Dylan and all the Sabatinis. Kendra remembered hanging out with the boys, and my mother spending time with the parents, but nothing more. She agreed to talk to Dylan. If the two reminisced, one might think of something out of the ordinary that happened before Q.C.'s party.

My brother-in-law never made an appearance that day. He drove for two rideshare companies to chip in for the family expenses. Something he'd rarely done before. His bad luck, as he called it, with finances was why the family now rented a townhome rather than living in their own house.

I declined staying for dinner. My niece and nephew had other plans. And Lauren was eager to stop in Bloomington at Alexander's, a restaurant she loved. Patrons cook their own steaks there on a large grill. I'm not quite the meat eater Lauren is, but I enjoyed the smell of sizzling butter and meat and the fun of cooking.

Over dinner, Lauren listened to the story of my mother's attempt to send me to the Great Beyond. When the server brought our check, Lauren offered to drive the rest of the way home so I could unwind a little. She knows I'm a fan of walking or public transportation, not driving. It's a big part of why I love living near downtown Chicago.

"And cheer up," Lauren said. "I bet tomorrow will be exciting."

"You mean firing a gun? Or meeting my dad's girlfriend?"

Lauren finished the last bite of her dessert – flourless chocolate cake with cinnamon ice cream. "If you're lucky, both."

50

RUNNING IN CIRCLES

When I stepped outside at seven the next morning for a jog, my dad stood on the porch waiting for me. He wore sweatpants and a thick long-sleeved fleece. It was the first time I'd seen him since our conversation in the street.

"I know you hate running," he said. "Thought some company might help."

"Okay."

For the last nine months I'd been training with a retired police academy instructor to improve my fitness and learn self-defense. He and I had negotiated a routine of four miles of slow jogging that bordered on fast walking. I interspersed short sprints once every mile. My dad kept up with me, though he got a bit breathless on the first short sprint.

"You keep looking around," Dad said. "Not much street crime in this neighborhood."

"Habit," I said.

My instructor had drilled into me a rhyme for when I walked anywhere, but especially after dark in Chicago: *Know who's ahead of you/Know who's behind you/Know what's beside you/Know where to run to.*

At one of the intersections, Dad pointed left to a path leading to a trail that ran beneath Main Street. It was pretty there, and I made a mental note to try it again. But I didn't thank him. I wasn't ready to talk.

He sensed it and stayed quiet as we jogged. But when we parted ways at the house again, he said, "Be careful today."

I didn't ask if he meant at the shooting range or when meeting Alice.

"THANKS AGAIN FOR DOING THIS." I loaded Highbottom's revolver. "My instructor's been after me to learn to shoot."

Though unwilling to miss time with his grandkids just to talk more about my investigation, Highbottom had been thrilled when I asked if he'd take me to a shooting range.

"Happy to help." Highbottom reeled a paper target down to the far end of the shooting lane. "You getting a Concealed Carry?"

Illinois is one of many states that allow people to carry guns hidden on their person. But you need to attend training sessions to qualify, then apply for a Concealed Carry permit.

"No. But my instructor thinks I should know how to handle one. Just in case."

"Smart man."

I lay the gun pointed down range on the waist-high ledge. Highbottom stressed how important that was during the safety lesson he gave me before we stepped into the range. I adjusted my earmuffs.

"Two hands," Highbottom reminded me. "And hang on when you fire. Kickback surprises people. Sometimes they drop the gun. And if it's an automatic, it can fire when it hits the ground. This one shouldn't, but you want to practice good habits."

I gripped the gun carefully, keeping the barrel pointed down range. He'd told me those same things in the car on the way over and in our safety lesson. But I didn't mind a third time. There's no such thing as being too careful.

I aimed at the target, which had a print in the shape of a person. The revolver was old and had a stiff trigger. It took a lot of effort to pull it.

I felt the kickback in my shoulders when I fired, but I didn't let go. After reloading three times, my arms ached, and my jaw felt tense from clenching it. But all six of my last bullets hit the inner rings, though none got the bullseye.

Highbottom reeled in the target and looked it over. "Not bad for a first time. You'd qualify to carry. If you wanted."

"I don't," I said.

He sent out a new target for himself. One of his bullets hit dead center. The others gathered near it.

It was too loud to talk much in the range, especially once the other lanes were filled. But I'd offered to buy him lunch after to thank him. And so I could ask him more questions.

On the way out, Highbottom asked what I had against guns.

"My instructor says if you don't practice a lot, not just shooting but handling one under stress, the most likely thing that'll happen if you're attacked is the other person takes it away. Then you're in more danger, not less."

Highbottom opened the door to the parking lot. "Correct. And if you do hang onto it, it's still not always helpful. You saw how hard it is to hit a paper target. Now imagine someone running at you and moving while you try to aim."

At lunch, Highbottom confirmed the Sabatinis' alibis based on his street file. It was what both he and Danielle called a detective's or officer's personal handwritten notes that later got typed into the official record. These days police enter reports right into a computer. But it hadn't been like that in the eighties.

I asked a few more questions about my dad and Kendra before I asked him about members of my dad's band. It was the real reason I wanted to meet with him, though I hoped it wasn't obvious. He told me police interviewed all current and former band members. All had alibis, though he didn't have detailed notes on them. He said nothing that made me think he knew about Alice.

"What about on the Kev side?" I said. As long as I had him here, I might as well see if he could help me find Vanessa's elusive cousin.

Highbottom was surprised I thought Jimmy Smith, at seventeen, was a suspect.

"Why not?" I said. "He's the only person in Vanessa Kev's life who left town within months of when she was killed. He was alone, no one to vouch for him, when she disappeared. She was attached to him. Easily would have gone somewhere with him. And he was good with kids. Probably wouldn't have seemed threatening to Q.C. though he was a stranger."

"I'm sure someone on the task force checked his alibi."

"But no one on your team ever asked where he was when Q.C. was taken?"

"We weren't involved by the time anyone talked to him."

In my parents' guestroom later, I added notes about our conversation. Then, a large mug of Earl Grey at my side to keep me going, I turned to two legal cases I'd fallen behind on.

I had one email left to write when a message came in from the copy service that scanned Klaus Erickson's photos. I paid the bill so I could open the zip file, ignoring the high price and refusing to think about whether I had enough money coming in this month to cover my expenses.

The first photo I saw showed a teenage Kimberly Smith Byerly, hot dog in one hand and can of Pepsi in another. Next to her stood her brother, Jimmy Smith.

51

PHOTOGRAPHS AND MEMORIES

THE HUNDREDS of photos were all from the 1980s. None showed anyone in my family, dashing my hopes of finding an overlap between the Kevs and the Davises. Lots of them featured Vanessa, usually in her dance outfits. A smiling little girl with curly brown hair and apple cheeks much like Q.C.'s.

One group of photos showed people sitting in wood folding chairs at a lawn party. Michelle O'Brien talked with Gail Kev in one of them. In the background, two young girls played with a bright pink hula hoop.

I pinched to enlarge the photo of Kimberly and Jimmy Smith. The resemblance was obvious. Both tall and skinny, with narrow faces.

The only photo of Klaus showed him talking with Therese and James Smith Senior. All had red plastic cups in their hands. Probably beer, based on the keg near the barbecue pit.

I texted multiple photos to the dance instructor, Michelle O'Brien, to see if she could identify anyone. I sent the same photos to Kimberly. But she didn't remember any of the other kids or any adults beyond those I recognized.

My laptop dinged with a client email about document

requests from the other side in my largest case. The client needed to visit the company warehouse. Old file cabinets full of paper reports about a merger two decades ago were stored there.

I dropped my head on the desk. The warehouse was in Naperville, about forty-five minutes west of Chicago on a good day. The last thing I wanted to do was fly or drive back and forth an extra time.

Before I could answer the client, Lauren knocked on the guest room door. It was time to talk to my father's girlfriend.

ALICE'S FIDDLE playing wove in and out of the electric guitar, drums, and bass. Without thinking, I tapped my foot to the music, a mix of country, bluegrass, and rock.

Lauren leaned close to whisper in my ear. "Just shoot me. Now."

"You can take off. I'll get a Lyft back."

She shook her head and sighed. "It's for a good cause."

The band was the opening act at the fundraiser. Our twenty-five dollar donations were sent to a non-profit in South Africa to help women start microbusinesses. The venue, called The Alley, was a long, narrow building in Clayton, Missouri, literally built into a wide alley between a coffee shop and a bar. All thirty or so rows of folding chairs were packed with people.

Lauren's my perfect partner in crime. She loves a room full of people she doesn't know. During the break, she disappeared into the crowd. I felt sure Alice, when she appeared, would be more open without an audience.

In the meantime, I bid in the silent auction on a set of signed Nickel Creek CDs for my dad, who still had a fondness for old technology. A moment later, Alice emerged from backstage.

"Quille?"

"Yes." I shook her hand. "Thanks for meeting with me."

She looked a little older than her university bio photo, with a single striking streak of white hair framing her face on the right. The rest of her hair hung straight and dark down her back. Nearly forty years older than in the video, she looked relaxed in dark jeans, an emerald green long-sleeved T-shirt, and plain black heeled boots. Her dark eyes stood out against her pale skin.

"Had a feeling you'd hound me if I didn't." She gestured toward two metal folding chairs near the sound board. A wide stone pillar blocked us from the crowd. We sat across from each other.

I took my notepad and pen from my shoulder bag and flipped to a new page as I asked if she ever met Q.C.

Alice told me only once, and her story fit Kendra's. And my dad's, as she said the affair ended more than a year before Q.C. was taken.

"How did it start? Between you and my dad." I twirled my pen between my fingers.

"I don't quite see how that matters."

The question might not relate to Q.C. in the slightest. But I wanted to know. "If the police knew about the affair, or guessed, that might be why they're so sure my dad did it."

Her head reared back. "The police blame Cliff?"

"You didn't know?"

"No." She adjusted her shirt, which had slipped at the shoulder to show a turquoise bra strap. "That's awful. He's a good man. Can't believe anybody thinks that."

"Well, the police don't know him personally. They just know his daughter was taken and nobody can give him an alibi."

The cake shop owner and the pharmacy where he got the

balloons verified when my dad stopped in. But that only covered a fraction of the time he was gone.

"I suppose...if you think — look, I never planned on getting involved with your dad."

"But?"

"But being on the road — I was happy. When Cliff and I talked or sang together, or sorted out a new set, I felt this connection. Completely unlike my marriage."

"My dad said you were struggling."

"I was twenty-two when I got married. Not so young as your parents, but young. And my husband, he'd had a tough family life. Seemed like he couldn't get a break."

"At what?"

"Anything. Life. Career. Took me a while to see the pattern. Every job, people were unfair to him. He worked the hardest but never got the promotion. Every co-worker, every friend turned on him sooner or later."

"So all his problems were other people's fault."

"Every last one. When he got fired from the fourth job in three years, I said maybe he ought to change his approach to work. And just like that, I became one more person who disappointed him."

"And that's when you started seeing my dad?"

"No. For a year or so I kept trying to make it work. The marriage. It was exhausting. Downplaying my success so my husband didn't feel bad."

I nodded without meaning to. She was describing my first boyfriend, an actor who resented anything I achieved. At the time I didn't see it. But years later it was obvious and I wondered why I stayed with him as long as I did.

"Cliff was the opposite," Alice said. "The band didn't officially have a leader, but he was it. He built relationships with festival promoters. Inspired us to do our best. Made you want to work harder because he knew you were amazing and you wanted to prove him right."

This picture did and didn't sound like my dad. He always told me what I did well when I acted or sang on stage. But I couldn't see him taking charge of a group. Or being the point person with festival promoters. Though maybe they found his low-key approach a refreshing change from the swagger some performers adopt.

"You knew he was married," I said.

"I did. But being around him, I felt like myself again. For the first time in forever. A happy girl who loved playing fiddle. It was like I'd been living in this black and white world and someone turned on the color. Cliff said it was the same for him. He glowed when I told him what a skilled musician he was and how good he did running the band. All true. But your mother, sorry to say anything bad about her to you, all she did was tear him down. Just like the way my husband treated me. But your Dad didn't see it."

52

MY FATHER'S GIRL

THE FEATURED BAND took the stage and launched into their version of *Blue Moon of Kentucky*. Lauren slipped into a seat and shot me a look for bringing her here.

I inched my chair closer to Alice so we could hear each other better. "What didn't my dad see?"

"Let me think how to put it." Alice's knee bounced in rhythm with the song. "Here's an example. Your dad got so discouraged once after a visit home. Your mother had told him she read an article about this other bluegrass band, one that was pretty new on the scene. She said they were featured all five days of Bill Monroe's Bean Blossom — the biggest bluegrass festival of all."

"So my mom shouldn't have mentioned them?"

"She shouldn't have made up things. Our bass player knew someone in the band. They weren't 'featured' at Bean Blossom, and the article didn't say they were. They ran an informal song circle at their campsite. The same year we opened for Bill Monroe And His Bluegrass Boys on the main stage, by the way. There were lots of things like that."

It reminded me of how my mother told me Q.C. soloed in

all these children's choirs and was a child model. When I learned the truth about the couple things she'd done, I was shocked that I'd felt dwarfed by her. But I wasn't going to tell Alice I agreed with her take on my mother.

The band, much louder than Alice's had been, leaned heavily on the steel-topped guitar and banjo as it launched into *Foggy Mountain Breakdown*. Alice suggested we talk outside. We stood under one of The Alley's black and white striped awnings. I breathed in the damp air and felt my shoulders relax in the sudden quiet.

Alice took out a pack of cigarettes. "You mind? I let myself smoke one a week. Down from a pack a day."

I shrugged. She lit it and inhaled deeply.

"Nothing you've said makes an affair okay."

"No," Alice said. "But I started seeing your dad as someone like me. Who needed to get out of a bad marriage."

"He ever say that?"

"No. But I'm not sure I was wrong."

"You wanted him to leave my mom."

"I thought I did. He shut that right down. Said he had to stay."

Had to stay wasn't the same as wanted to. It was a bit far-fetched, but if the task force heard him say he felt trapped they might see it as a motive for killing Q.C. as a way to lessen the burden so he only needed to care for one child, not two.

"Is that why you quit the band?" I said.

"It was too hard to see him. I felt horrible. But it didn't take that long to see I was better off away from him. I didn't want to start a life with someone by upending his children's world."

I noticed she didn't worry about upending my mother's life. "Did you think my dad might leave my mom with two little girls? Did he seem like someone who would do that?"

I meant it as a real question. I never dreamed my dad had an affair. The guitar player on the videotape looked and sounded very little like my dad. Maybe he was a completely different person than the one I knew.

"Abandon his family? No." She dropped her cigarette butt and ground it into the sidewalk with her heel. "Keep supporting them after getting divorced so everyone could be happier? Maybe. But I was wrong."

Everything else she told me fit with my dad's story. After leaving the band she played in a bluegrass band that didn't travel, and in a country rock band a lot like the one I'd just seen.

Alice lit a second cigarette despite her claim to one a week. "About a year later I started the Masters in music therapy. Kept playing on the side."

She told me the police talked to her only once. It was a day after Q.C. was kidnapped. She said nothing about the affair. She felt it was up to my dad to share that or not. When Q.C. was taken, Alice was visiting her ex-in-laws, whom she still got along with. The police, according to her, talked to them to verify her story. Vanessa Kev hadn't been kidnapped yet, so there were no questions about her.

I didn't expect I'd have any luck, but I took out my iPad and showed her photos of people on the Kev side.

Alice immediately tapped one of the photos. "Him. I know him."

I bent closer to the screen. She was pointing to James Smith Senior.

53

INTO THE WOODS

AFTER SHE QUIT the band a friend of Alice's, a waitress and songwriter, told her about a weekly gig at a bar in Kirkwood, Missouri, about fifteen miles outside the St. Louis city limits. Alice couldn't remember the name of it, but she recognized James Smith Senior as the manager or owner.

Alice played there for about nine months. Then the bar sold to a new owner. It reopened under a different name as a sports bar. No more music. She hadn't, though, spoken to my dad during that time.

She also couldn't remember talking much with James. "He tended bar now and again. Or dropped in and sat in the back. But didn't talk much."

None of the names on Highbottom's list of where my dad's band played or my list of businesses James Smith Senior owned rang a bell with Alice. If he ran the bar as a sole proprietor, though, or only managed it, the business might not appear in any corporate database searches. Not only that, information about short-lived businesses from the eighties likely never found its way into the online world.

"Did anyone at that bar know you'd been involved with my dad?" I said.

"My friend. I used to drink whiskey sours and cry on her shoulder about it toward the end of the night."

"Whiskey sours?"

"Cliff got me hooked on them. Though I switched to straight whiskey for a while there. Which I don't recommend."

It shouldn't surprise me that my dad liked that drink all along. But I felt somehow betrayed that the drink we so often made for each other was one he enjoyed with his girlfriend.

Alice didn't remember anything else about James Senior. But she agreed to find the latest phone number and email for her friend and send them to me.

LAUREN and I had the fishing cabin reserved for the following night. But after Eva Erickson's murder, neither of us wanted to stay after dark in a wooded area hours from the closest police station. We agreed to drive there early the next day and skip the overnight.

We parked behind an empty cabin about a half mile from the Smiths' property. That way if anyone drove by, they'd be less likely to see my rental car. Between the tracker and suspecting someone might be following me in that silver sedan, I wanted to stay under the radar.

Lauren got the key out of the lockbox and let us in. "Definitely rustic." She set her purse on the butcher block counter. The knotty pine walls and kitchen cabinets looked more worn than in the photos.

It took less than twenty minutes to go through the entire place. There was no basement or second floor. The living room, which flowed into the open kitchen, had a stone fireplace and smelled of burnt wood. A Queen-sized bed and pine chest of drawers filled the master bedroom.

The closet was shallow.

"Couldn't keep a living child hidden in here for very long," Lauren said.

"No." I shivered and pulled the sleeves of my sweater over my wrists.

Two sets of bunk beds sat opposite one another in the second bedroom. The third featured a brown leather pull out sofa, a TV, and an armchair. The plaid carpet looked clean, if old. But it smelled like peaches over dust and stale, acrid smoke.

Lauren sniffed. "Fatally heavy on the Febreeze."

I nodded and glanced at email on my phone. Michelle O'Brien, true to her promise to help, had gone through her old photos and school records and compared them to the photos I sent. She recognized a girl in two photos, one of the few people of color in any of them. She wasn't one of Michelle's students. But Michelle felt sure she was a dancer. She'd contacted another instructor and gotten the girl's name for me.

I sent a quick thank you and followed Lauren in a circuit around the outside of the house. The wood stairs to the front and back decks sagged in spots that made me worry for guests who weren't surefooted.

"Liability traps," I said.

"No wonder Ted Kev quit claimed it to his brother-in-law."

The owner information was part of what Lauren learned by digging through property records. Ted gave the cabin to James Smith Senior in the early 1990s, around the time TG Kev Computer Solutions really took off.

We ended in the utility room. Two bows with brittle strings that looked ready to snap from age were propped between the dryer and the wall.

"Jimmy Smith's?" Lauren said. "Didn't his dad say he liked archery?"

"Yes. He might've come to the cabin sometimes." I looked behind the bows but didn't find arrows. "Or this is where his parents store his things."

A corner closet held cleaning supplies, a vacuum cleaner, and propane tanks for the grill out back.

I glanced through the window. The back yard turned quickly into woods. "Ready to hike?"

Lauren rolled her eyes. "Words I never ever wanted to hear."

But she'd worn her gym shoes. I wanted to see if there was anywhere — a cave, a shack, a set of oddly grouped trees — where a killer could keep a child hidden for a few days or weeks.

54

PLAYING THE ODDS

MY ODDS of finding anything that mattered were low. According to Highbottom the task force searched the area and the cabin thoroughly after Vanessa was taken. But the No Stone Unturned approach meant exploring whether I felt hope or not.

Two and a half hours later, we'd covered the entire area that belonged to the Smiths plus the land of three of the neighbors. If Ted Kev or James Smith Senior kept first Q.C. and then Vanessa on the property, evidence of it was long gone.

Lauren fell behind me as the path narrowed near a shallow stream. "What's up with Ty? He's not asking you to move to Dubai, is he? You've been strangely silent."

"No." A pebble got into my gym shoe. I knelt to fish it out but it slipped under the arch of my foot. "He doesn't have a firm offer. Or any offer. Yet."

"But he might get one. And ask you to move?"

I stood and balanced on one foot as I worked off the gym shoe. "He knows I can't. It's hard enough to practice law in a different state. Another country, forget it." Holding Lauren's arm to stay steady, I shook the shoe. If the pebble fell, I didn't see it.

"Then what?" she said. "He couldn't have proposed. You totally would have told me that."

"He asked what I see for the future." I felt around inside the shoe, which was sweaty from the walk despite the cool morning air. No pebbles. I slipped it back on.

"No more live in the moment, huh?"

Ty and I met less than a year after my boyfriend Marco's death. I'd still been wearing the ring Marco bought for me on my left hand. And Ty was struggling to get over a bad ending to his last relationship. Neither of us felt ready for a serious relationship.

"Nope," I said. "Which I understand. Before he turns down a great opportunity, he wants a sense of whether we have a future."

Lauren and I paused at the edge of a wide pond. "And do you see one with him?"

"He's fun. Sexy. Kind. My parents love him."

"He absolutely ticks all the boxes on the boyfriend shopping list. But you were ready to move in with Marco after a few months. And you're not sure about Ty after almost a year."

"Because Marco needed to move out of his place. The question was out there early. With Ty, I thought we had all this time."

"Are you spooked because of what happened to Marco? The night before he was supposed to move in you found him dead in his apartment. Not a great association with making a commitment."

I hadn't thought about that. "Maybe." The sun was fading. "We should head back."

Lauren gestured to the pond. "They dredged this?"

I nodded. "A day after Vanessa was taken. Nothing."

We started up an incline toward a grove of trees, but had to stop after a few feet. That pebble was still there, and it dug into my heel.

IT TOOK me until ten that night, but I traced the girl Michelle O'Brien identified, now a fifty-five-year-old woman. She taught dance at a studio in Chicago's West Loop neighborhood.

After talking with Lauren, we decided to get the earliest flight home. She had a new client to meet with. And I had a warehouse in Naperville and cases to catch up on. I hoped that somewhere in there, I'd finally meet someone outside his family who remembered Jimmy Smith.

55

CHICAGO AGAIN

I SPENT my first half day in Chicago in my office and my first evening at Café des Livres with my laptop getting my bookkeeping and billing done.

The next day I took a Metra train to Naperville. It took over an hour, but it felt like a luxury. No driving. No missing turns when the GPS wasn't quite clear about a hard or soft right, no aching shoulders from gripping the steering wheel for hours. Instead, I worked or looked out at the suburbs flying past the train window.

My jogging routine had improved my walking pace. The six blocks to my client's office took me less than ten minutes. The client drove from there to the warehouse. I didn't mind sorting through old documents all day. It felt better than an investigation where I learned nothing but awful things about my family.

While waiting for the train home, I got a call back from Bonita Taylor who had once played in a yard with Jimmy Smith. She was responding to my email and voicemail. She suggested we meet the next night in the West Loop at Bar Siena.

It's one of many restaurants on Randolph Street. But it's

distinctive. A tree grows in the center of the restaurant. Both floors are built around it. Tiny white lights twinkle in its branches.

The host took me to the second floor, which was beautiful. And loud. The music was turned up high and the voices of the diners around us bounced off all the hard surfaces.

"Sorry," Bonita said after we were seated. She wore her black hair in cornrows and had a dancer's lithe, muscled physique. "Always wanted to try this place. Didn't know it'd be so crowded on a Wednesday night."

"I used to be an actor," I said. "I know how to project."

"Good thing." She glanced over the menu. "I heard the spinach and artichoke dip is fantastic. If you want to split it, I won't say no."

"Sure. I'll call it my vegetables for the day."

I'd covered who I was and why I was asking questions first by email and then by phone. Michelle O'Brien's name helped, as Bonita remembered her. As soon as our drinks were served, I asked about Jimmy Smith.

"Sweet boy. Most of the time."

"And the rest of the time?"

Bonita wiped the salt off the rim of the margarita glass with a napkin. "Always forget to tell them to leave it off. Sure you don't want one?"

"I'll get one for dessert. So Jimmy was mostly sweet?"

Ice shavings spilled onto the table when Bonita sipped her drink. She wiped them away, then called to the waiter for extra napkins. After he disappeared, she drew the straw out of the glass and lay it across the napkins.

"Can't use straws. I get TMJ. You know, when your jaw tightens up? My dentist told me straws are bad."

I said nothing.

"It's hard for me to bring myself to say things I don't know for sure are true." She gestured to the diners around us. "Or shout them I should say."

"Then why not start with what you know is true?"

She sighed. "All right. This you may already know. Jimmy got picked on. A lot. What they call bullying these days."

"Did you see that?"

"Saw it. And he told me. I was a year or so behind him in school. And knew him from the dance competitions. He always came to see Nessa dance."

"Why did the kids bully him?"

"Same reason his daddy did." She glanced around the restaurant as if looking for anyone who might know Jimmy.

I stowed my iPad, thinking she might be more comfortable if she didn't worry her words were being taken down or recorded. "Would you rather talk somewhere else?"

She scanned the room again. "No, no. It's not like anyone can hear us above the din. And no one cares about these things these days. At least, not here they don't."

"What things?"

"Jimmy's dad used to call him a sissy. And worse. Tell him to man up."

"The kids at school called him names like that too?"

"Yes. All the slur words they used back then for gay. Jimmy got beat up twice the first month of his freshman year. That's when he started fighting back."

James Smith said Jimmy didn't fight back. But the stories matched well enough.

"You said his dad bullied him, too. Physically?"

"Not that I saw. Or that Jimmy said. But his dad blamed him for getting beat up. Told him not to be so girlie. Except he used a meaner word than that. Told Jimmy he deserved it."

I was getting an idea why Jimmy left home and didn't look back. "And his mother? Therese?"

"She had sympathy. But from what Jimmy told me, she believed in the father as head of the household."

"Meaning?"

Head of household is a tax term, but I rarely thought of it in a personal sense. Growing up, life with my parents revolved around caring for my mother. But my Gram made the decisions.

"In sixth grade, Jimmy wore a pink T-shirt to school. And went home with a black eye. His mom felt bad for him. But she didn't say anything when his dad grounded him. James said Jimmy shouldn't have worn the shirt."

"Didn't his parents buy it for him?"

"Hm. Never asked. Maybe he borrowed it. Either way, he felt like no one was on his side."

"What about his sister? Kimberly?"

"Went back and forth. But as we got older, it felt like she was embarrassed by Jimmy."

"Did he identify as gay?"

"I don't think anyone in our school did. Jimmy just told me he felt wrong. Different."

"Why did he talk to you?"

"Vanessa liked me. And my parents liked Jimmy. My mama used to tell me to bring him home for dinner any time if he had a rough day and didn't want to go home."

"Did she think he was gay?"

"It's hard to explain to someone your age. But we didn't think anyone we knew was gay. That was for artists. Or actors in Hollywood or New York. Not regular people in Missouri."

If Jimmy was gay, it must have been lonely. And dangerous and scary.

After we placed our order, I asked Bonita how often Jimmy was suspended for fighting.

"Often enough that they talked about sending him to one of

those behavioral schools. He was petrified. Said he'd never survive. From what I know now, I think he was right."

"And the teachers, the principal, they didn't look into why Jimmy got bullied?"

"It wasn't like now. If boys fought, they fought. If a teacher saw it or anyone tattled, to use an old word, everyone in the fight got in trouble."

"Did his father get mad at him for anything else?"

"Not mad exactly. But he didn't love that Jimmy loved ballet. Or spent so much time with his little cousin."

"That was bad?"

"It was girlie. Boys weren't supposed to like babysitting or be good with kids."

"But your parents didn't think that."

"In theory, probably they did. I'm sure they would have said homosexuality was a sin. Our pastor said so. But my parents followed what the Bible says about not judging. And about loving your neighbor."

"I heard Jimmy got along well with the Kevs. Vanessa's parents."

"Oh, he did. Jimmy liked computers — his dad approved of that at least — and Ted Kev talked to Jimmy about them. And he and Gail appreciated Jimmy's help with Vanessa."

"Help? Did they need help with her?"

"Maybe help's the wrong way to put it. But my mama said Gail planned to go back to work full time when Vanessa turned three. But Nessa was so good at dancing by then, and loved it so much, Gail delayed. Spent a lot of time getting her to rehearsals, getting her costumes, extra lessons, that sort of thing."

"And Jimmy helped how?"

"Took her to rehearsals if Gail was busy. Gail was on a couple boards, too, lots going on. And Vanessa loved it when

Jimmy painted her nails or styled her hair. Or picked out makeup for her to wear to her recitals."

"Gail didn't do those things?"

"Usually, it was Jimmy. Gail worked with her more on her dancing."

I set my glass of soda aside. I felt grateful to live in a time and a city where people were more open to any gender liking makeup and hair styling. And the last thing I wanted was to buy into myths about people posing more harm to children simply because they were gay.

At the same time, I couldn't ignore a key fact. Vanessa was found with her hair dyed and styled to match Q.C.'s.

56

SWEET BOY

BONITA and I talked about other things for a few minutes as we enjoyed the spinach and artichoke dip on unsalted chips. But I didn't want to waste too much time.

"You said earlier Jimmy was a sweet boy — most of the time," I said. "What about the rest of the time?"

"Didn't mean to say it that way. He was always sweet. He just got — frustrated."

"Frustrated how?"

She rolled her napkin under her fingers. "During a Kev family cookout, he threw a bat through an upstairs window. He was mad because he struck out and he just flung it. Another time he stomped all over his mother's roses."

"What prompted that?"

"He was trying to help in the garden. His mama kept changing her mind about what he needed to do. And he got frustrated."

It turned out Bonita knew Kimberly pretty well, too. Yet Kimberly had claimed not to recognize Bonita. I found that especially hard to believe because Bonita appeared to be the only person of color in the photo. Kimberly might not remember the name, but I felt sure she'd recall the one Black dancer.

"Were you surprised Jimmy left for college and never returned?"

"Not for a second. I hoped things would be better for him away at school. So why come back? His family didn't give him any reason to."

"What about friends in the St. Louis area?"

"Not sure he had any. Other than me and his sister."

"You didn't hear from him?"

"Couple letters early on. Then nothing. But I went away the year after he did. Missed him, but I'm afraid I didn't think much about him. Lots of people lose touch around then. Make new friends."

Over the main courses — baked salmon for her and a wagyu burger for me — I asked about Vanessa's death. Bonita said Jimmy was heart-broken over it. She thought that might be another reason he never returned. It could be easier for him to live somewhere his cousin never did.

Bonita had no guesses as to where Jimmy might be now. She was sure he attended Boston University, not Boston College as Kimberly told me. When social media became more widely used, Bonita looked for Jimmy.

"Found plenty of Jimmy Smiths and James Smiths. Too many. But never him."

Bonita remembered Klaus the photographer, though not his last name or anything else about him. She didn't share Kimberly's uneasy feelings about him. But she couldn't remember ever talking with him. I asked if she recalled anything else about James, Therese, or Kimberly Smith.

"Oh, my Poppa called Mr. Smith — James — Mr. Can't Complain. Not to his face, of course. Just to us."

"Meaning?"

"When you asked how he was, James always said he couldn't complain. Then made a bunch of complaints."

That fit my conversation with Therese and James. James claimed he wasn't complaining about Ted Kev's failure to invest money in James's businesses. Then launched into complaints and later stalked off.

Bonita didn't recognize anyone from my side of the cases when I showed her photos. But she did have questions for me.

Over coffee for her and herbal tea for me she delved into why I was investigating. I answered everything I could without sharing anything private I learned from other witnesses.

After I paid the bill, she took out a card and wrote something on it. "Such a sad story. Vanessa's. Your sister's. I hope you find answers. This might help. I found a Facebook profile for this name oh, maybe ten years ago? Sent a Friend request. The next day, the profile disappeared. It's the closest I got. Not positive it's him."

I glanced at the name written in rounded, even cursive. "Collie Smith?"

"Jimmy's mama's middle name is Colleen," Bonita said.

"Thank you." We put on our coats and headed for the stairs. "Why not tell me this earlier?"

"Wanted to get to know you. See if you were trying to pin anything on poor Jimmy. Or Collie if that's the same person. Some people, if someone is different, they think it must be bad. Makes them an easy target."

At the bottom of the steps we layered on our gloves and hats. The temperature was in the twenties, much colder than in Edwardsville or St. Louis.

"And I know people here," she said. "In the legal community. They said good things about you. And I know Jimmy would never hurt Nessa. But I want you to promise me one thing."

"What?"

"Must be a reason Jimmy doesn't want to be found. If you do locate him, please be careful about sharing anything you learn. Protect him."

"I'll do my best," I said.

I also meant to find a way to talk to James Smith Senior, again. Whether he wanted to talk to me or not.

57

GOING BACK

OVER THE NEXT two days and the weekend I did my best to track down Collie Smith and get a solid grip on all my cases. I returned to my parents' house on Monday morning.

James and Therese Smith were ignoring my calls. So were Ted and Gail Kev. Gail texted to say she didn't want to talk more, it was too upsetting. Kimberly, though, filled me in on a few of her father's usual activities. And his favorite stores, including a hardware chain with a large plant section he visited every Wednesday and Friday.

For a couple days I lurked in his favorite places. I wore workout clothes, put my hair in a ponytail, and pulled the bill of my cap low over my forehead. I spotted James once, and he didn't seem to notice me.

I researched the bar, too. Alice had sent not only her friend's contact information but the bar's name. Ted Kev appeared nowhere on any of the paperwork. James Smith Senior rented the space from a private landlord.

Unfortunately, Alice's friend, now a resort manager, didn't live anywhere near St. Louis. Or Illinois. She lived in Honolulu.

It was one thing to go home to Chicago or drive to Bloomington or southern Indiana. It was another to fly to Honolulu. All the flights from St. Louis required at least one stop and cost over seven hundred dollars for coach. Worse, eleven hours was the shortest travel time one way. I could get to Europe faster and for the same price.

At least Alice's friend was willing to talk to me on Zoom, though it had to be late at night to fit both our schedules. By ten-thirty Tuesday night I was exhausted and still needed to stay up another half hour. I spent it writing and rewriting an email to Ty. Then I deleted it.

I couldn't imagine Ty not being in my life. But he hadn't asked me to marry him or to move in together. We'd never talked about either, both content with spending a lot of time together but still having our own places. At least, I'd thought we were. And I wasn't sure yet if that changed for him or if circumstances forced the change.

On Zoom, Alice's friend Sherlese wore a flowered halter top. The open glass doors behind her showed a few palm trees, a busy city street, and an apartment building against a gold and orange lit sky. It was just after sunset there.

"No ocean view," she said. "Nice having a balcony, though. Didn't have that in St. Louis. And no winter. Big plus."

"You're happy you moved there?"

She'd moved twenty years before when she married a man who taught school there.

"It was an adjustment." Sherlese's voice had a warm, throaty sound. "Our place is a third of the size we could have in St. Louis. And I had trouble getting a job at first. But I'm good now."

"Do you remember working at the Idle Hour Inn?"

"Oh, yeah. Fun place. I don't play guitar or sing very well, but I write songs. Love bluegrass, country, rock, all of it. I got to hear so much free there."

"And Alice told you why I'm interested?"

"Yeah, so sorry. I remember when those girls were taken. It was all over the news."

"Both stories?"

"Both. Saw more about your sister after Vanessa Kev was taken. That's when it became a big story. Reporters talking about patterns and serial killers."

"Did you know Vanessa Kev was James Smith's niece?"

She nodded. "Never talked to him about it, though. The police came once or twice to question employees, but none of us ever met Vanessa or knew anything."

Sherlese thought James Smith owned the bar, but said he could have been the manager. She didn't keep in touch with him after the bar closed.

"Did you stay in the area for very long after?"

"Moved to Nashville. I'd been thinking about it for a while. Fabulous place for country music. I hoped I'd sell some of my songs. When the bar closed, I took it as the Good Lord telling me it was time to go."

I bit my lip to keep from responding to her last comment. It drives me crazy when people say an all-powerful deity found them a job or made their favorite sports team win. But if true, it explains a lot. The ruler of the universe is too busy on things like that to stop killers of five-year-old children. Or to get rid of crime all around.

Either that or Sherlese's deity just really liked country music.

She was looking at me with raised eyebrows. I asked if she sold any songs to buy myself time to reorganize my thoughts.

"Did sell a couple. Never became hits, but earned a little in royalties. Met my husband on vacation a year later. He's a singer on the side. Does some of my material now."

I asked if she talked much with James Smith at the bar.

"Hello and good-bye. He didn't talk much. But he hung about."

"Hung about?"

"Liked to sit at the end of the bar. Or near the exit. Kind of staring into space. It got so you didn't notice him at all, he was so quiet. He called it absorbing the atmosphere."

A perfect way for him to eavesdrop on patrons or employees. Including, maybe, Alice telling Sherlese about my dad.

58

THE WRONG PATH

THE BAR, according to Sherlese, was always crowded. The daytime manager told her James liked to sit and listen to understand what customers liked and didn't. I asked if James could have overheard Alice talking about my dad. If my idea was right about Q.C. being killed first as practice for Vanessa perhaps James, if he did it, decided my dad deserved the pain of losing a child.

"Sure could've," Sherlese said. "Got so you forgot he was there, he was so quiet. And Alice was awful upset at first. Be surprising if he didn't hear."

"Would she have said my dad's name?"

"Hmm. Can't say for sure, but I'd think so. His first name at least."

A first name would be enough. If Alice talked about Cliff and the band she was in, it'd be easy enough for James Smith to find out the band's name and then my dad's last name.

Sherlese never met James's kids, Ted or Vanessa Kev, or Klaus Erickson. The only person she recognized from the photos I emailed her was James Smith.

It was after midnight by the time I finished filling in my

notes about the conversation. I put my phone in Silent mode and was so tired I dropped into bed without brushing my teeth. But then I lay awake, thoughts racing. Every half hour my parents' cuckoo clock downstairs cuckooed. I crept downstairs to close and lock the tiny door so the bird couldn't emerge.

As I did, something rustled in the back yard. I stood in the dark in the sun room. I couldn't make out much of the yard, but my parents' motion detector lights hadn't come on. After a few minutes, hearing nothing else, I brushed my teeth and went back to bed.

I DRAGGED myself into the shower at six-thirty the next morning. When it comes to exercise, especially the hated jogging, if I don't do it first thing I don't do it. And I had too much else on my plate to sleep late, including a video conference to try to settle a case.

I ran to the trail my dad showed me. But I covered only a half mile or so before turning back. Today wasn't going to be one for a long run. I exited where I'd gone in. Despite being worn out, I jogged in place at a Stop sign as I waited for the traffic to clear, looking left and right. When I glanced over my shoulder, I saw someone running about five hundred yards behind me. The person wore sweats and a red hoodie. The hood hung low, half covering their face.

No one had been there a moment before.

I pulled the small nightstick I carry out of my side pocket. There were houses to my right, one with lights on. I pivoted to cross the street.

But as I stepped into the crosswalk, a silver sedan raced toward me from nowhere. I leapt back, then spun to cross the other way and avoid the car and the runner. But the stranger barreled toward me, arm cocked back, and flung something at me.

I jerked away. Brakes squealed. Someone yelled my name.

My foot caught in a giant pothole and my ankle twisted. Then the street itself seemed to spin, rise up, and smack into me. Everything went dark.

59

UNREMARKABLE

My head ached. Grass tickled one of my arms. Eyes too heavy to open, I grappled with where I was and why. No grass grows on the block where I live. There are sidewalks and skinny trees growing out of grates but no grass. I smelled leather.

"Where's that ambulance?"

I didn't recognize the voice. But Ty squeezed my hand. His fingers felt warmer than usual. His body runs cool, mine warm. We balance one another. Maybe living in Dubai changed that for him. He shouldn't be home. But I squeezed back. The warmth felt comforting.

"Quille? Try not to move." Same voice. Familiar. But not Ty's.

Sirens wailed.

"They should be here in a few minutes." A woman's voice this time.

My lower back throbbed. As I shifted to try to ease it, I opened my eyes. Squinted against the glaring sun. Trees and houses surrounded me. A leather jacket lay across my stomach and chest.

Dylan Sabatini knelt next to me. The wind rippled the sleeves of his crisp maroon collared shirt. "You awake?"

The sirens grew louder.

"Head." I lay mostly on lumpy, grassy ground, but under my head felt hard and pebbly. Like concrete. "Hurts."

A woman appeared above me, clutching a phone at her chest, and said something I couldn't hear over the wailing siren.

It cut off.

Dylan's pale blue eyes, contrasted by the dark ring around his irises and his black lashes, looked more striking this close. My brain must be working fine if it could notice details. I hoped.

The moments before I hit the ground filtered into my consciousness. I stiffened and pulled my hand from Dylan's. Had he attacked me?

The woman, now kneeling too, brushed my hair from my eyes. "It's all right. Safe. They're gone."

"Jogger?" I said. "Car?"

Dylan nodded. "Couldn't tell if the car was aiming for you or just wrong place, wrong time."

"Jogger definitely was," the woman said.

They moved aside for the paramedics. When one felt the back of my head, I winced. My right elbow and low back on the same side felt bruised. My ankle twinged. But I sprained it once before and this wasn't nearly as bad. I answered questions about who and where I was.

When I guessed the time within five minutes, they let me sit and cleaned the wounds on the back of my head. It stung.

I still wore Dylan's jacket around my shoulders and felt too chilled to give it back. He had one sleeve rolled up and a second paramedic cleaned the scrapes and cuts along his bare arm.

"You're hurt, too," I said to him. Despite being oriented times three, my brain hadn't moved much beyond stating the obvious.

"He tackled that man," the woman said. "Saw it from my front window."

"Teacher, musician, and superhero?" I said.

"Just a teacher who also coaches the wrestling team." He gave that half-smile but still looked worried. "And not much of a superhero. The guy got away."

"It was a guy, though," I said.

Dylan nodded and rolled down his shirtsleeve. "It was a guy. Little shorter and stockier than me. Wore a ski mask under his hood. Covered his whole face."

Because I'd been unconscious, the paramedics insisted on taking me to the closest Emergency Room, which was in Maryville. The police wanted to talk to Dylan and the neighbor. Dylan promised to call my dad and tell him what happened.

Two officers interviewed me in the emergency room bay while I waited for my CAT scan results.

I told them everything I remembered. I added that I'd seen a sedan twice before and the second time caught the start of the license plate – AG.

They weren't too impressed given how common silver sedans are. And that I admitted I couldn't tell one model from another and didn't notice the hood ornaments or logos on any of them.

"Your friend thought the driver aimed for you," the female officer said. "But the neighbor said it looked to her more like he wasn't paying attention, took the corner too fast. Unfortunately, neither got a good look at him beyond probably male, possibly white. Who knows you run in the morning?"

"My parents. Anyone who saw me running, so maybe the neighbors."

I wondered how Dylan knew where to find me.

"You take the same route every day?" the male officer asked.

"Maybe half the time."

Internally, I kicked myself. My instructor had impressed on

me the importance of not following a routine. Three days out of six gave an attacker pretty good odds of guessing where I'd run.

The male officer sat on the chair near the heavy curtain between the corridor and my bay. "Anyone know you were taking it today?"

"My dad. I text him which way I'm going each morning just so someone knows."

I explained about my Q.C. and Vanessa Kev investigation. And Eva Kev's death.

"This had to be related," I said. "The jogger, the car."

"Jogger maybe," the female cop said. "It's almost fifty degrees. Little hot for a ski mask. The car could go either way. Lots of drivers are distracted. Staring at their phones. No idea where they're going or who's in the road."

I shifted on the examining table to take the pressure off my right hip, which had started to ache. "But they took off."

"Might be driving on a suspended," she said. "Or have alcohol or drugs in their system."

"Did you find whatever the guy threw at me?"

"There was a large rock a few feet from you," the male officer said. "Your boyfriend thought that was it. We bagged it, but it could have been there before."

Like the luggage tracker it seemed weirdly low tech and ineffective.

I read through the statement on the female officer's iPad and signed it.

"We'll pursue every lead." She snapped her book shut. "Call if you have questions. Or remember anything else."

My CAT scan showed no issues. I declined any medication, figuring a single Advil would probably cost me twenty or thirty dollars and I had a bottle of it in my shoulder bag.

My legs shook as I made my way to the waiting area. Dylan rose from the chairs. "Sorry. They wouldn't let me back there. Got you these." He held out a bottled water and a power bar.

"Thanks."

"And this." He pulled my nightstick from his soft leather briefcase.

I sat next to him and took a long drink. Then I devoured the power bar in three bites and took three Advil. By the time I finished I felt less shaky. "That helps."

"Yeah, emergency rooms. Not great on basic needs. Ironically. How's your brain?"

"Officially unremarkable."

"Good. Though it doesn't bode well for your crime solving efforts."

"How'd you know where to find me this morning?"

He told me he'd called the house when I didn't answer my cell phone. Knowing I was a morning person, he decided to stop by on his way to the school. My dad told him I'd just left to go running and that I liked that trail. Dylan parked near the house and headed out to try to intercept me.

When I felt steady enough we left out the emergency entrance. "What did you want to talk to me about?"

"Your sister called me last night. Said it was your idea to try to help her remember anything unusual in the months before Q.C. was taken."

"And did she?"

"No. But I did."

60

NOT PONG

Dylan drove a restored Dodge Charger from the 1970s, back when cars had recognizable body styles.

"My grandfather owned a car like this," I said. "Gram kept it another decade after he died."

"Got it when I first came home. Mom loved cars. I knew it was near the end when she didn't get out to the garage anymore to see my progress." He saw me shivering and turned on the heat full blast. "Your parents' house? Guessing they want to see that you're in one piece."

I nodded, then winced as it jarred my head. "What did you remember about Q.C.?"

"The year she was kidnapped, I'm pretty sure it was the same year our grade school got its first personal computer. Big clunky IBM with green text on a screen."

"What did they use it for?" The view out the window was soothing. All trees, shrubs, and grass on the verge of turning green.

"Compared to today? Next to nothing. But it was a huge deal. Cutting edge in education. My dad thinks some sort of community grant funded part of it. May be a stretch, but Ted Kev being this big software guy —"

"Might've written the software."

"Or his company funded the grant."

I thought about the timeframe. "Q.C. wasn't in school yet."

"No." Dylan changed lanes to pass a semi-truck. "But the school did a dog and pony show about it. To show parents — and taxpayers — it was worth the money. Mom took us to the assembly."

"You remember it? Sounds a little boring for a seven-year-old." The Advil was finally working. My head felt less achy though the bump in the back throbbed when I rested my head for a moment on the headrest.

"Not at all. It was very sci fi. The computer displayed on a big screen in the auditorium. After the talk, people went up to try it themselves."

"But you said it didn't do much."

"They typed in words and you saw them on screen. That was exciting in the age of typewriters. And the guy at the computer gave one kid a simple code to type. Made the computer add two plus two. Or three plus two, I don't know. Everyone oohed and aahed. Plus it ran a few games."

Kimberly said her brother Jimmy liked computer games.

"Like Pong?"

"Like stories. Q and As where the next prompt you got depended on how you answered."

"Did Kendra remember any of that?"

The highway was becoming busier. I kept an eye on the traffic. No silver sedans.

"She thought it rang a bell, but wasn't sure. The kid things were mostly aimed at boys," Dylan said. "Early eighties, Edwardsville, not the vanguard of gender equity."

"Meaning my mom might not have taken Kendra and Q.C.

Though she taught there, she probably would have wanted to see the computer."

"Or your sisters might have tagged along with us."

"If Q.C. was there, she might think the computer guy was a teacher."

"Yep. And if he turned up at her party, she might think he was invited." Dylan pulled to the curb in front of my parents' house. "One of my friends is in admin at the grade school. I'll see if she can find old records about the computer."

"Fantastic. Speaking of school, aren't you supposed to be there?"

He shrugged. "Took a personal day. Might have played up my injuries a bit for sympathy."

I felt bad that I hadn't asked about him yet. "Are you okay?"

"Nothing some alcohol and a few band-aids couldn't fix." He smiled. "They gave me ones with Tweety Birds on them."

My dad invited Dylan in for a late breakfast. He'd closed the store for the day. The smell of his trademark banana chocolate chip pancakes and frying bacon brought my mom down to the kitchen. She wore sweats and a rumpled T-shirt. But her hair was combed and she'd washed her face.

Dylan answered questions about what happened so I didn't have to. My hand shook a little when I poured myself orange juice and some spilled on the counter.

He grabbed a paper towel to clean the counter. "You okay?"

"Delayed shock, I think."

"Maybe take the morning off from sleuthing."

"I'm only planning to go to the library."

"Now who's pretending to be a superhero?"

As we ate, I asked my mother about the computer assembly.

She turned her fork over and over for a few seconds, studying the tines. "There were a couple assemblies about the computer. But it didn't do anything with music."

"You saw the demo?" I drank more of my orange juice. The tangy taste made me feel more alert.

Her blond hair caught the sunlight as she shook her head. "No. But we were at the school one of the nights. Kendra wanted to see the gymnastics meet. And Rev's wife was there. She warned me about letting Kendra join the team. One of her friend's daughters broke her back on the vaulting horse."

"Was Q.C. with you, Mrs. Davis?" Dylan asked.

"If I brought Kendra, I brought her." My mom tilted her head sideways and shut her eyes. "I don't think we went into the auditorium."

"But could Q.C. have? With Dylan's family?" I said.

"Could've. She had a little crush on Dylan's brother."

"You think Ted Kev was the computer person?" Dad said.

I ate a last bite of bacon. "That's not the kind of software he wrote. But could be. Also could've been Klaus Erickson."

Dylan insisted on going with me to the public library. "If you pass out, someone needs to call 911."

"The librarian can."

"The librarian won't notice if you start spouting nonsense or show other signs of a concussion. I will." He smiled. "I teach high schoolers. I quickly recognize nonsense."

My dad told me if Dylan didn't go with me, he would. I still didn't want to spend time with my dad, so I agreed. But I insisted Dylan do his own work rather than help me. He admitted to being behind in his lesson plans. We stopped first at the Sabatinis' house so he could get his laptop.

The *Edwardsville Intelligencer*, a local newspaper, began publishing in the late 1800s and still had a storefront on Main Street. The library had digitized copies for the 1980s with some gaps in coverage. The library was undergoing renovation, so I searched the database on a computer at a low table downstairs in the children's library. American Girl dolls that kids could borrow sat on a shelf across from me.

I found two articles that fit Dylan's and my mom's memories. About six months before Q.C. was taken, a local bank awarded a grant so the school could buy an educational computer. So much for Ted Kev's company giving out the grant.

The second article described an IBM 5150 the school bought and included photos of it. The first personal computer IBM made, it used floppy disks for storage and looked clunky by today's standards. An online search told me many schools bought 5150s in the early eighties. Other companies copied them, making what became known as IBM clones.

A Wikipedia article confirmed that early PCs couldn't do much of anything unless you knew how to program. Most people didn't. Software companies, though, raced to develop and sell programs and games for them.

I signed onto one of the corporate databases I use. After upgrading to a premium account and cross-referencing multiple search terms I discovered Klaus Erickson ran a software company in the 1980s. It made educational software and games called interactive novels. I clicked through all the information I could find about the company, looking for Ted Kev's name. It appeared nowhere.

But James Smith Senior's name did.

61

NOT QUITE LEADS

I FOUND DYLAN IN A CORNER, his back to shelves of old cassette tapes and DVD audiobooks.

"Thanks anyway," he said into his phone.

I touched his elbow. "You hiding?"

He turned around and put the phone in his back jeans pocket. "Didn't want to disturb anyone. Bad news."

"Just what I need."

We headed for the stairs.

"My admin friend talked to a retired math teacher. The teacher remembers the computer assemblies." Dylan pushed open the door for me. "But nothing about who did the demo. The school's been scanning paper records, but only ones they think are vital."

I blinked in the bright sunlight, the glare making my head hurt.

"You okay?" Dylan said.

We paused outside the entrance beneath a sixteen-foot weathered marble monument. It depicted a woman on each of its four sides.

"Fine," I said. "I'm guessing 'vital' doesn't include purchase orders from the eighties."

"You guessed correctly. Ditto flyers about assemblies. If any still exist."

I thanked him for trying, but didn't tell him about the Klaus and James link. During the drive to my parents' house, I pulled photos from the 1980s into a folder on my iPad for him to look at. They included the few I'd been able to find of Klaus Erickson, James Smith Senior, and Ted Kev. Dylan had looked at them before. But after he parked the car, I asked him to try to recall if any of these people might have been at the school assembly.

He studied each one. "No idea. Way too long ago. And this guy's so generic he'd blend into any crowd. Other than those glaring white sneakers."

He pointed to Ted Kev.

Dylan was right. Ted Kev in his late twenties could have gone anywhere and been forgotten. Compared to his present-day striking silver hair and self-possessed way of carrying himself, in the old photos he faded into the background. Medium brown hair, combed straight down to form a center part. Eyes directed toward the floor, not the camera. And rather than a close fitting turtleneck and slimming jeans he wore bulky patterned sweaters that made him look heavy. Plus high-waisted baggy blue jeans and that decade's ubiquitous white sneakers.

I flipped to a current photo of Kev.

"Definitely found his look later in life," Dylan said.

I thanked him again for tackling my attacker and sticking with me all day.

"No problem. Listen. You look great for someone knocked unconscious this morning." His hand grazed the back of my lower arm. "But promise you'll stay in sight of someone all day today. In case you — you know, they missed something on that CAT scan."

I was planning to retreat to the attic guest room. But with Dylan's words in mind, I opened my laptop on the dining table. My mom read on the sun porch. She surprised me by checking on me every twenty minutes or so.

Over the weekend I'd researched Boston University, where Jimmy Smith supposedly attended college. I hoped to find information about Jimmy Smith through the school's yearbook, the Bostonian. But no digitized copies existed. If I wanted 1980s yearbooks, I needed to visit the City of Boston Archives. Another day, if I had all the time in the world, and all the money, flying to Boston sounded fun. I'd never been there.

But now it sounded exhausting. I called three docket services in that city to ask if they could research in the archives and copy whatever they found about Jimmy Smith. But two only did runs to courthouses to file paper documents or pull old paper records. The third referred me to a local law firm that, for a price, was willing to send a paralegal to do what I needed. For about the same cost as a flight because I wanted it expedited.

I ought to check with other lawyers. Someone likely knew of a smaller Boston firm that would charge me less. But my head, bruised back, and hip were throbbing again. I opted to pay.

After I emailed the information, I texted Klaus's sister-in-law, Nadia, and called the number I had for Klaus. No answer and no response. Then I texted my dad's former girlfriend and her friend the bar manager to ask if they told anyone we talked. Something triggered the attack on me. It might very well have been something one of them said.

NADIA ANSWERED my text as I was writing a motion asking the court to move a deadline in one of my cases. When we talked, Nadia confirmed that Klaus briefly had a side hustle writing software, including educational games. She thought it was during the eighties. She wasn't sure if Klaus owned the company alone or with someone else. After a few years, though, she was sure he sold out to a large corporation.

"I play tested some games," she said. "They were for little kids but sort of cool. Text adventures. Scale the mountain, fight the monsters, collect the gems."

"And the education part?"

"You needed math skills to trade gems. Or if you spelled words wrong when you typed your choice, you had to try again. That kind of thing."

If Klaus sold the company or the rights to the software, that could explain why he and Eva had more money than Eva's neighbor thought she ought to. That made me rethink my drug selling theory. On the other hand, Klaus might have two businesses. One legal, one illegal.

I asked if he ever spoke at schools.

"Pretty sure he did. I remember Eva saying standing on stage and talking made him nervous."

That didn't sound like he stayed behind the computer. But on stage might make more of an impression. He'd definitely seem like a teacher. Someone Q.C. could trust.

"Did anyone help him? Run a computer demonstration maybe?"

"Huh. You know, I think Yes. You'd need to show people how it worked. And if he were sitting there doing that part, he wouldn't have been nervous."

James Smith Senior or Ted Kev — or anyone else — might have helped Klaus. Or no one had. Which was the problem. Nadia's memory was too hazy.

I wished I could ask her to ask Klaus about it. But I couldn't. Not when Eva called Klaus for me and ended up dead.

An email marked Urgent popped into my In Box as I was thanking Nadia. I groaned when I opened it.

My mother shocked me by appearing in the doorway a second later. "What is it? Are you all right?"

"It's not my head. But it is another headache." I cleared my throat. It was almost worth dealing with the Temporary Restraining Order my opposing counsel wanted to discover my mother really was watching out for me. "I've got to get a flight to Chicago."

62

THE HUNT FOR COLLEEN

My iPad in hand, I peered through the glass door into Courtroom 2602. Four lawyers stood before the judge, one gesturing emphatically. The hearing on the request for a Temporary Restraining Order was set for eleven. Or whenever these four finished.

I returned to my client, who stood scowling near the floor-to-ceiling windows with the view of Lake Michigan. We ran through his testimony again. The law, the facts, and common sense were on his opponent's side. But we had a sliver of justification for his locking his brother out of their joint factory. I'd won on less with this judge. I'd also lost before him when everything was on my side, so it was more or less a coin toss.

There's a point where rehearsing too much hurts your witness. They start to sound too practiced. I left my client to stew. After checking to see the four lawyers still going at it, I perched on a hallway bench. The courtroom deputy knew me and knew I was there. She'd come find me when it was our turn.

I clicked open the first PDF attached to an email from the Boston research service and stared at James Smith Junior's photos from his freshman and sophomore years. A researcher note told me no later yearbooks referred to him. Access to individual student records was blocked, so I didn't know if Jimmy transferred to another school. A second attachment included a school newspaper article with bios of new students. Jimmy's said he was from St. Louis and planned to major in psychology.

The last PDF included the bill. I suppressed another groan as I eyed the total. Real legwork costs a lot more than running online searches.

On the upside, today's hearing and the prep time covered most of the cost. And this client, difficult as he was, paid quickly. I had a good chance of covering this month's bills without dipping into savings, something I hadn't needed to do since the first couple months of running my own law practice.

This time when I peered through the door the four lawyers were gathering their briefcases. I waved to my client, stowed my iPad in my shoulder bag, and entered the courtroom.

THE HEARING TOOK ONLY forty-five minutes. It wasn't a total loss. Though the judge ordered my client to turn over keys to the new locks on the factory, he expressed some sympathy for my client's views. That boded well for a motion I hoped to file down the road.

At my office, I ate a sandwich at my desk, caught up on other cases, and set out to see if Jimmy Smith ever filed a name change petition to become Colleen or Collie Smith.

Two hours later I'd barely scratched the surface. A patchwork of state laws governs name changes. And many of those laws changed since the 1980s, so I needed to look at different versions of them over time. Some required publishing notice of name changes, others didn't. Without knowing where Jimmy lived when he changed his name, if he did, it turned out to be impossible to track down.

In the late afternoon I headed down to Café des Livres, hoping the owner, my friend Carole, might be there. But she'd taken a day off. Someone else had my usual spot near the stone fireplace and bookshelves. At a table near the window, I ate a goat cheese salad and opened search results from Lauren. She had a quiet week and had been combing social media and running online searches for me.

About thirty Colleen or Collie Smiths were about the right age and listed psychology or a related field as a major. I didn't feel confident narrowing it down that way, though. Not that many people go into the field they chose as college freshmen. I decided to email everyone in the right age range.

A server I know dropped over with a complimentary mug of dark hot cocoa. I sipped it as I struggled to write an email that might prompt an answer if the right person got it. At the same time, I didn't want to reveal too much to all the other Colleen Smiths.

I contacted Bonita and Michelle to ask if I could include their contact information. After six drafts, and with a conference call in fifteen minutes, I finally called the email finished.

> Dear Collie,
>
> I hope I'm writing to the correct person. Bonita Taylor thought you might be able to help me. I also spoke to your cousin's dance instructor Michelle O'Brien (now Zamorski).
>
> Both will vouch for me if you need to know more before answering. Their current emails are below.
>
> I'm looking into the death of my sister, Quille Catherine (Q.C.) Davis I. You might know that her body was found with your cousin's. I don't want to interfere with your life. I'm only trying to find some peace for my parents and, I hope, for everyone who loved your cousin. Anything you remember or

know, however small, might help. All my contact information is below.

Call, text, or email any time. Please.

After one last look, I hit Send to the first five emails on my list, all blind copied. Then I copied the body of the email and sent it to the next five and every five after that. And I pasted the message into direct messages in every social media platform that allowed it.

It was all I could think to do.

63

IN TRANSIT

MY ROLLER BAG banged against my knees as the L train took a curve, brakes squealing. The Orange Line runs on an elevated track that circles downtown and shoots south to Midway Airport. I felt like a ping pong ball bouncing around the Midwest, ricocheting off one lead after another. But the main people I needed to talk to again other than Jimmy Smith were all in Edwardsville or St. Louis.

Kimberly Byerly, James Smith Senior, and Therese Smith. Ted and Gail Kev if I could ever persuade them. It was two days since I'd sent the Collie Smith emails. So far, no response.

My phone buzzed with a text from Bonita.

> Heard from someone who asked about you. Didn't share her name. Needed to know if you're really looking into Nessa's death. I told her yes and it was okay to talk to you. Good luck.

I sent a quick thank you. Then texted Michelle to ask if anyone contacted her. She answered right away, but no one had.

The train squealed to a stop ten minutes later. The escalator at the end of the L platform stood frozen. My thighs ached as I lugged my bag up the stairs. I needed to get back to my weight machine workouts.

The phone rang as I maneuvered my roller board under the exit turnstile. The smell of coffee and strawberry donut frosting filled my nostrils. I scooted to the side, pausing in front of the small Dunkin' counter.

Unknown number. I answered.

"Quille? Quille C. Davis?"

"Yes." I covered my open ear with my hand to block out the airport announcements and the voices buzzing around me.

"Ted Kev hired you?"

The voice might be a woman's, one with an alto voice. Or a male tenor. The pronunciation reminded me of a singer, actor, or news anchor. Every syllable and consonant sounded clearly and distinctly. I couldn't detect any specific accent.

"No. I spoke to Ted Kev, but only once. My parents asked me to do what I'm doing."

"And what are you doing? In this so-called investigation?"

"Studying police reports, researching online. Talking to everyone who might know anything."

"Hmm."

The wall clock over the list of airlines told me it was forty-five minutes to my flight. I gripped my rolling bag and strode toward the moving walkway. "I've solved crimes this way before. I can tell you about that, answer all your questions. But I'm about to catch a flight. Can I call you back?"

"This number won't be good. I'll try you."

"Wait. Please." I didn't know which email or message had gotten the response. "Can we set a specific time? Maybe talk in person?"

"I'm nowhere near the Midwest."

Too many people crowded onto the walkway. I veered around it so I could simply walk. "Zoom? Facetime?"

"Who have you talked to so far?"

If this wasn't Jimmy Smith or if Jimmy was the killer, I didn't know how wise it was to share details. But it wasn't as if my suspect list would surprise anyone.

I ran down the list as I wove in between passengers dragging luggage carts behind them or pushing strollers in front of them. The wheels on my suitcase caught on the escalator tread as I boarded. With my free hand I turned the bag sideways, struggling to keep my balance.

I righted myself. But dropped my phone.

64

FAMILY MATTERS

One hand on the moving banister, I squatted and scrambled for the phone. It was scuffed and smeared with dirt.

"Are you there?" I winced as I pressed the phone to my ear. I'm not exactly a germaphobe, but a lot of people tracked things I didn't want to think about onto those escalators.

"Still here. Anyone ask you about me?"

"They asked about Jimmy Smith. If that's you — or was you — they miss you."

"Doubt my father does."

It was the first clear confirmation of the caller's identity.

"I haven't talked to James Senior much. Yet." The escalator neared the bottom. "I need to go through security. Could we —"

"I'll call you."

The line went dead.

I wanted to talk to both Therese and James Senior, but not together. That made it too easy for them to avoid questions.

And each might know something they didn't want to share in front of the other.

The problem was, both were semi-retired and spent a lot of their days at home.

Based on the time spent following Therese on social media and James in person my best shot was the day James shopped and attended talks at the gardening center in a local home improvement store.

So the morning after I returned to Edwardsville, I rang the Smiths' doorbell a few minutes after ten in the morning.

Therese answered. Her caramel-colored turtleneck and rust colored corduroys gave her a dressed down yet businesslike look. But she held a round brush, and her hair was still damp on one side. Her face looked rounder and less defined and her eyes smaller. After a second, I realized it was because she wore only a light coat of foundation. No eyeliner, mascara, or blush to bring out her features.

She dropped the brush to her side. "Oh, hello. It's, uh —"

"Quille," I said. "Sorry to surprise you. But I need to talk to you about Jimmy."

65

NOTHING BUT RESPECT

THERESE RAN the box cutter along the center seam of a large cardboard box. "I knew about the pink shirt."

"You mean before the fight?" I buttoned the top button of my wool coat and put my gloves back on. It was about five degrees warmer here than at home, but still chilly for mid-March, and we were in the Smiths' unheated garage.

Therese unpacked and sorted products for her customers as we talked. Though she mainly managed other salespeople, she had loyal customers who still bought from her.

"It was my T-shirt." Therese took shiny cardboard boxes in various sizes out of a large cardboard box. "Jimmy borrowed it without asking."

"And that's why he got beat up?"

"That's what James told me." She stood straight, rubbed her back, and sighed. "Seems so ridiculous now when you've got men all over wearing makeup and pretending to be women."

I wasn't sure who she meant or why she thought they were pretending, but I didn't want to get distracted. "But wearing a pink shirt then — big deal?"

"Oh, yes. That's why James tried so hard to get Jimmy to

toughen up. James knew how harsh life can be for a man. But Jimmy wouldn't listen."

"Did James experience something similar in high school?"

"What?"

"You said James knew how harsh life could be."

"Oh." She stacked small rectangular boxes on a workbench under the windows. They provided a view of back yard trees with still-bare branches. "No, high school was good for him. But he's had a tough time professionally."

"Did he ever go into business with Klaus Erickson?"

I'd asked when I met Therese and James before. But it never hurts to ask again. Sometimes you get a different answer.

"They were friends. Much as I hate to admit it now that we know how awful a person he was. But business...not that I ever heard."

"Does James tell you about all his business ventures?"

She laughed. "Tell the truth, he probably does, but I don't remember all of them. There've been so many. Still, I'd recall if he went into business with Klaus because that's someone I knew, too."

Therese checked her phone before sorting lipstick boxes into piles.

"Could James have been a silent investor?" I said.

I expected her to say No. James seemed like someone who always needed investors, not one who put money into other people's businesses.

But Therese surprised me. "Possible, possible. He likes to hedge his bets by funding other people's ventures now and then."

I debated trying to prompt her memory by asking about a software group. Or asking if James or Klaus ever spoke at a school. But I wanted to surprise James with those questions. She might tip him off. Instead, I asked about the bar where Alice's band played.

She smiled. "His most successful business. He loved it, and it did so well."

"Why did it only last three years?"

Her jaw tightened as she explained that the landlord refused to renew James's lease. Once James moved out, the landlord opened his own bar.

"James couldn't find a good new location. Not one he could afford."

"Ted Kev was a partner in the bar, wasn't he?" It was a guess.

"Ted? No, no. His money in the eighties all went to his own company."

"And you and James were never angry at Ted? For not helping out more?"

Therese laughed. It sounded relaxed and genuine. "I understand why you need to ask these things, Quille, I do. You're looking for reasons for anyone to want to hurt Ted by hurting his daughter. But James had nothing but respect for Ted. And appreciation for whatever Ted could do for him."

That might be so. But as my hearing the day before showed, things are never simple when business and family mix.

I scrolled through my notes. "You said James knew life could be harsh for men. Harsh how?"

"Oh, there's no one thing. But men supposedly have these advantages. Yet the feminization of business started decades ago. And it's getting worse. All these hashtag Girlboss posts. What about man bosses? No one's hashtagging them unless it's to accuse them of something."

Last I'd checked, nearly ninety percent of Fortune 500 CEOs, all forty-six U.S. presidents, and sixty percent of federal judges were male. Not to mention I never heard of male supervisors being called "boy" bosses. They're just bosses.

I tried to think what to say that was honest and offered some sympathy.

"Sounds like your husband felt he needed to prepare Jimmy for real life. Which can be hard."

"Yes, yes. Exactly."

"And Jimmy didn't take that well?"

"It's probably why he never came home. He just didn't understand James was trying to help him."

"Could fear of the police have kept him away? If they hounded him about Vanessa's death?"

"They didn't hound him." Therese brushed dust off the workbench. "They asked questions. So did the FBI. And he answered. Same as everyone else in the family."

"Did Jimmy seem upset by the questions?"

"He was upset about Nessa. We all were. But he thought there ought to be more questions. Of everyone."

Before I left, Therese asked what I'd learned about Jimmy. I told her I talked with some of his friends but none remembered where to find him, which was true. I also said I was doing a lot of online research.

"If you could talk to him, what would you say?" I said.

"That I love him. And he should come home."

I promised to relay that message if ever I could.

66

YOUR SISTER MIGHT SEE YOU NOW

IT WAS A SMITH DAY. In between my talk with Therese and planning to catch James at the garden center, I met Kimberly at the St. Louis Zoo. Like the Lincoln Park Zoo in Chicago, it's free. But it's much larger. Kimberly volunteered there as a docent. I met her near the butterfly exhibit twenty minutes before her shift began.

I didn't plan to confront her about claiming she didn't know Bonita. That might make it too obvious Bonita helped me find Jimmy. I didn't know yet if Jimmy, or Collie, posed a danger to anyone. But I did tell Kimberly I made progress and had a few questions.

We sat on a bench just inside the exhibit, blocked from the wind.

"Did you know Jimmy got bullied at school? For being what kids saw as too feminine? And your dad was angry about that, too?"

"Bullied. Bullying." Kimberly waved her hand. "Everyone whines now. But my dad was right. You've got to stand up to bullies. Then they leave you alone."

I doubt that's always true. But as with Therese, I wasn't there to argue.

"You told me before you didn't know why Jimmy got into fights. Sounds like you did, though."

"It was embarrassing, all right? And it had nothing to do with finding him."

I took off my knit hat and stuffed it in the pocket of my long leather jacket. "Embarrassing for you?"

"You probably can't understand at your age. And living in Chicago where they had those Pride parades even way back. But I got made fun of all the time because of Jimmy. All the time." She poked her index finger in the air with each word.

Yet she didn't see bullying as a problem.

"Your mother said the police didn't focus on Jimmy. But I can't help thinking they might have targeted him just based on the attitudes at the time."

"They might have. They brought him in twice. Second time he came home shaking. Infuriated my dad."

"He was mad at the police?"

"At Jimmy. Stormed around the house saying real men stay cool. Thought it was Jimmy's fault the police suspected him. Because he was so, so — the way he was."

I asked if she remembered the bar her dad ran. She did, but she didn't know anything about the bands or employees there.

"Your dad ever mention working on educational software or games?"

"My dad? He knows zero about computers."

"Could whatever Klaus's side project was, the one he wanted you to do keyboarding for, have been about that type of software?"

"Could've. He never told me."

I asked if she knew where either Ted or Klaus did their programming work.

"Well, when Nessa was taken Uncle Ted and Aunt Gail

already had the warehouse property they're in now. They only used a small part of it. They rented out the rest."

The police must have searched that.

"And Klaus?"

"No idea."

"What about when Ted and Gail started? Before the warehouse?"

"Their garage?"

"You sound unsure. Do you remember that?"

Kimberly would have been a toddler when Ted and Gail started the company.

"Hmm." She wound her gold necklace around her finger. "Not sure. It just feels like something I know. And Uncle Ted didn't like to work at home. He couldn't stand noise, and Aunt Gail wanted the TV or radio on all the time."

Unlike some better-known computer pioneers, no stories about Ted Kev talked about him starting in a garage. I found no stories at all about how he began. The earliest article focused on how his software revolutionized human resources, not his company's origins. It fit with him being a very private person. Also, business-to-business software doesn't get the hype trendy apps consumers use do. I guessed that was the same in the seventies and eighties.

Kimberly needed to start her tour soon, leaving her little time to contact her dad before I could ambush him. I decided it was safe enough to tell her about the record showing James Senior partnered with Klaus Erickson in an educational software business.

"You said your dad knows nothing about computers. But could he have invested?"

Her face scrunched. "Doubt it. Love my dad, but he's not a great businessperson. Thinks he is, but he's not. Mom is. It's why she always handled the money for the house and the family."

"People who are bad businesspeople still invest. Some might say it's how brokers get rich."

"I suppose, hon. But truly, my dad barely keeps his own businesses going. And if he did invest in someone else's company, I don't know why he'd pick computers."

"Could Ted have advised him?"

"But why? If Uncle Ted thought it was a good company, he'd invest in it himself."

Ted might have done just that. His company was growing in the mid-eighties. He was almost certainly in a much higher tax bracket than James. If he gave James money to invest for him and it paid off, he could cover James's lower taxes on the profit and come out ahead. But that didn't make a lot of sense. Startups have a low success rate. Ted would be just as likely to show a loss from that type of investment, which could help him on taxes.

Kimberly didn't remember hearing about her dad, Ted, or Klaus giving demonstrations at any schools.

She pushed her jacket sleeve up to check her watch. "My shift's about to start. Let me know what else you learn about Jimmy?"

"If I get in touch, is there anything you want me to tell him?"

"Whatever's going on his life, whatever reason he stayed away, tell him I really want to see him."

67

RUNNING DOWN THE MAN

About ten minutes after I figured the gardening talk would end, James Smith exited the store with an armload of purchases. As he loaded his bags into the tail of his mini-SUV, I stepped between him and the path to his driver side door.

"Hi, James. Quille Davis. Could I buy you a cup of coffee?"

The week before James stopped for coffee after the garden center. I hoped it was part of his routine.

He rested one hand against the side of the vehicle as if steadying himself. "I know you talked to my wife this morning. I don't know anything she doesn't. And I'm not telling you about my family."

I raised my hands in a surrender gesture. "It's not about your family. I'm curious about your businesses. How you started them. What worked, what didn't. Maybe I can learn from you."

According to Kimberly, James thought he was a good businessperson. Most people respond if you ask them to help you with something they're good at.

"Learn what?" he said.

"How to start a business that can run without me." From Kendra, I knew that was the motive for my brother-in-law's serial tries at starting businesses. "Which my law office obviously can't."

James pocketed his car keys. "Suppose I have a few minutes."

I ordered a vanilla bean tea at the coffee shop at the end of the strip mall and bought James a black coffee. My gambit turned out to be a good one. A few questions sent him into a laundry list of successes and grievances. He told me about the landlord and the bar. His story matched Therese's.

"You had music there, didn't you?" I said.

He nodded. "Three weeknights and every weekend. The trick was hiring just one band to play the weeknights. Gave them a chance to develop a following and try new material in a safe place. We did PR and so did the band. Brought a lot of people in."

I asked how he figured out what his patrons liked best. He told me about listening to the audience members talk. But he claimed not to remember any details about the bands or musicians he hired, including their names.

"Music's a tough way to earn a living," I said. "No trouble with your regular bands showing up or staying together?"

"There was drama. One person left a band, another joined. But everyone liked being booked weekly. They made sure to be there."

I pushed but he said he didn't remember anything more. As he talked, his body language and speech didn't show any awkwardness. My best guess was that he didn't know about the connection to Q.C. and didn't remember Alice's complaints about my dad.

That cast some doubt on my theory that the killer learned about my father or Q.C. through James. But if James was the killer, he'd be cold enough to hide the truth. And if he wasn't, not remembering the conversations didn't rule out him telling someone else about them at the time.

When I asked about software businesses, James shook his head. "Not my thing. That's all my brother-in-law."

And Gail, but no one seemed to give her much credit.

"You never invested in anyone else's computer business?"

"Wish I had. Ted's. I'd be rich now, too."

"But you invested for Ted, didn't you? In an educational games and software company."

I figured it was worth guessing at what happened.

"What?" His eyes widened. "No. I don't know anything about that."

"I did some corporate records research. And learned Klaus created text adventure games with an educational spin. Ted invested. But through you."

"There's a record of that?"

"You'd be surprised at the paper trail now that so many bank and transaction records have been digitized."

I'd be surprised, too. I didn't find any such thing, and most bank records require a subpoena. But people who don't understand computers or law tend to think of them like magic. Hit a computer key or hire a lawyer and you can make anything happen.

He pressed his lips together. The door behind him swung open, letting in a blast of damp air. A group of three teenagers entered.

"Ted didn't want his name on it," James said. "He hoped to take his company public one day. Thought someone might see it as a conflict of interest."

I nodded, though that didn't make a lot of sense to me.

"The software sold to school districts, right?" I said.

"Right. Really took off. Wish I had put my own money in."

"Ted must have been a good marketer," I said. "Getting the schools to buy his programs."

"That was all Klaus, not Ted."

"What did Klaus do?" I said.

James scratched the side of his neck. "Gave computer demos to teachers and parents. I thought it was crazy. Why would teachers want kids playing games? Shows what I know. The teachers loved it. The students loved it. And the schools bought."

"Did Ted do the demos, too?"

"Might've. I never went with. Didn't see the point since I didn't think the company would get anywhere."

I asked a few more questions. But James either knew nothing more about the school demonstrations or knew better than to admit he took part in them. In that case, though, I couldn't see why he wouldn't have simply claimed he invested the money but knew no details at all.

"I heard a story about your brother-in-law. That he started in his garage, like Steve Jobs."

James frowned. "When he started, he and Gail had a house with a carport. No garage. Sometimes he went to the public library to work. He liked it quiet."

"Was there a computer there?"

"Not sure. I think he wrote some things longhand before typing them up." James took the lid off his paper cup and drained the last of his coffee. "And rented computer time somewhere."

James didn't remember where. Before I left, I told him I'd been trying to find Jimmy, which I figured Therese might have passed on anyway.

"If I do find him —"

"You won't. Ted's investigator looked for him on and off for decades."

"But on the off chance I did, anything you want me to tell him?"

"He chose to stay away. He's the one who should think of something to say to me."

As if asking the question three times today conjured the person, when I returned to the car and checked messages I found one from Collie Smith. It included a link to a video conference in two hours.

I had a conflicting phone conference with a client. I rescheduled it. If Collie wanted to talk, I wanted to listen.

68

THE PRODIGAL CHILD

Collie Smith, now fifty-something years old, had longer hair dyed a deep brown hue, but the same walnut-shaped eyes and narrow chin as the teenager in the photos of the Smith family.

We spoke on a video conference platform that was new to me. Collie chose it. It didn't transmit information about the conference participants' locations or allow recording.

We both appeared in front of blank blue backgrounds. Collie asked about my experience investigating crimes and my reasons for looking into this one. I did my best to answer quickly. I didn't want to use too much of the hour meeting time Collie set.

"Not sure you can be objective about this inquiry," Collie said. "You have every reason in the world to decide someone in my family is guilty."

"That's true. But I asked my family hard questions, too, and I'm not jumping to conclusions about yours. And no one else is looking at Q.C.'s and Nessa's cases. If I don't solve them, they'll stay open. Just like they've been for decades."

After a moment, she nodded. "Will you keep what I say

confidential? Unless you're certain you need to tell someone to find answers about Nessa."

"Agreed."

"I don't see how my history matters to Nessa's case, but let's get it out of the way. Jimmy to Collie: short version. Always knew I was female. My parents and sister hated that. Couldn't — wouldn't — accept it."

"I'm sorry."

"Or acknowledge it. It's She/Her/Hers by the way. Never heard of anyone who was a They when I transitioned. Never wanted to be a They. She."

"Does anyone in the family know?"

"Uncle Ted. He's the only one who understood. When I said how much I wished I could stay away from home, start over somewhere, he paid my college and living expenses. Plus my surgery later. And everything I needed to qualify for it."

"Qualify?"

"It was a long, expensive process. Talk therapy. Hormones. Psychiatric evaluations. Never could have afforded it at eighteen."

"You had surgery at eighteen?"

"Started the process at eighteen. Surgery at twenty-three."

"And Ted paid for all of it."

If Collie was telling the truth, Ted was in her corner all the way. Or he wanted her out of the way.

"His one condition was that I stay away from my family."

I drew in my breath. "Why?"

"He thought they were toxic. Except Aunt Gail. But he said she'd hate keeping secrets from her sister. And he was right. She and my mom are close. After all she and Ted went through, I didn't want to make her life harder."

I scribbled notes, my writing uneven on the page, my mind spinning. Ted could have many reasons for keeping Collie away, including the ones he told her. Or she might know something about the murders that pointed to him or someone he cared about.

It was also possible Collie was lying and stayed away because she committed the crimes.

"You believe Ted about why he wanted you to stay away?"

"You've met my family. Clearly toxic. Why go back?"

"Still, I'm sorry you had to make that choice," I said. "I can't imagine never talking to my Gram again. Or my sister or parents."

"Since you mentioned her first, sounds like your Gram's the one who matters most. For me that was Uncle Ted and Nessa. And Nessa was gone already."

I asked about the postcards.

"I wanted Kimberly to know I was alive. After Nessa, I couldn't leave her wondering. No matter how awful she was to me."

"Do you ever talk to Ted?"

Collie's dark hair swung side to side as she shook her head. "Only those first few years. After that, he said to call if I needed something. But he worried if we stayed in touch someone in the family could connect the dots."

It sounded paranoid. On the other hand, I read through private emails and text messages all the time in cases. The people who wrote them never dreamed a lawyer might one day rummage through their devices.

Collie didn't remember hearing about Q.C.'s disappearance until Vanessa's body was found along with Q.C.'s. Her actions on the day of Vanessa's kidnapping fit what everyone else had told me. She thought she got sick from eating too many cherries from the Smiths' tree the night before.

The police grilled her about whether she really got ill or stayed at Ted and Gail's all day.

"No neighbor saw me because I stayed in the house. I didn't

make any calls. It didn't help that I felt guilty. I'm sure it showed."

"Guilty about what?" I said.

"Not being there that day. I kept thinking if I had been, maybe whoever it was wouldn't have gotten to Vanessa."

Collie said she was at home with her mother the day Q.C. was taken, helping sort out orders to send to customers. The police pushed hard on that as well. Like me, they didn't see a mother's alibi as especially solid.

"Who do you think killed Vanessa?" I said. "If you had to pick someone you know. You must have a theory."

Collie grimaced. "I don't want to get into this. I want it to be a stranger. Someone from your family for whatever insane reason."

"But if you had to choose someone you know?"

"If I had to....Gail."

69

MOTIVES

I POINTED out that Gail was in a crowded room when Vanessa disappeared.

"I attended lots of those events," Collie said. "It was chaos. Kids running everywhere. Parents taking photos. And that dance teacher loved Gail. She'd want to remember Gail being there. Want to remember the best."

"But what's Gail's motive?"

"Exhaustion? Anger? She missed her job. She missed Ted. Once she had Nessa, Gail barely saw him. And she felt overwhelmed all the time."

"Was Nessa a difficult child?"

No one else had suggested that. But everyone sees a different side of the people they love.

"No. But Gail was angry all the time. At the limits being a mom placed on her. On having no time to herself. I remember her getting mad once when I stayed over because I took a long shower. It seemed so weird. And it finally hit me. She resented it. Because she could barely get five minutes to herself."

"Couldn't she and Ted hire help?"

"Gail didn't believe in it. She felt she ought to raise her daughter. Not a stranger."

"She told you that?"

"We talked a lot. Looking back, she must've been lonely to tell so much to a teenager."

A few of my acquaintances and clients had babies or toddlers. Everything Collie said rang true at least to some extent. Even from what Kendra had told me, despite that she tended to stick to a perfect mother persona.

"But a lot of parents go through times like that," I said. "Especially moms. It doesn't make them kill their children."

"And I don't think Gail did that. But you asked me who out of everyone I knew. If I had to pick someone, that's my only guess."

The guess gave me pause. I might have ruled Gail out too quickly. But Collie could be trying to deflect suspicion from herself. Or from Ted, who'd been much more of a father to her than her own dad.

"How was your aunt's and uncle's relationship?"

"Didn't see them together much. But when I did, they seemed more content than my parents."

"Yours weren't happy?"

She wiggled one hand back and forth. "They argued a lot. About me, about Dad's business flops, which Mom had to tiptoe around. She worked so much. Did everything around the house, too. All the women's work, as Dad called it."

"Your father didn't work much?"

"He worked. In theory. Didn't help that he smoked a lot of pot."

"You knew that?" I said.

If my parents ever indulged, I didn't know. Gram never would have stood for them using any illegal drug around me. I was twenty-five before she felt it was okay to pour me a glass of wine when I visited.

Collie rolled her eyes. "Couldn't miss it. He smoked every Friday afternoon in the basement TV room. Which was also his office. Kept the windows open. As if Mom wouldn't smell it."

"Did she say anything?"

"Ignored it. Like a lot of things."

I thought back to the heavy air freshener in the Smiths' home and the faint odor I hadn't been able to identify at the cabin. Had it been pot? I've smelled it outside on Chicago streets and at festivals, but I've never been inside somewhere where pot smoke got into the drapes or carpets. Neither Lauren nor I smoke it. Maybe neither of us recognized it.

I asked if Collie remembered Klaus.

"Sure. Used to buy my pot from him."

"You smoked too?"

"Not like my dad. And never in the house. I wanted to show my mom a little respect."

"Was Klaus your dad's source, too?"

"Probably. But Klaus never admitted that to me. He was quiet about it all. Wise choice back then."

"Because it was illegal."

"For sure."

I'd already guessed Eva might have given Klaus false alibis for the times of Q.C.'s and Vanessa's disappearances if she believed he was dealing drugs at the time. Now Ted might have alibied his brother-in-law for the same reason.

70

THE RIGHT ENVIRONMENT

A SECOND LATER, I discarded the idea of Ted covering for Klaus. I couldn't see him taking James's word that he was off buying drugs when Vanessa disappeared. He might like his brother-in-law, but with his daughter missing he'd tell the police the truth. Unless he, too, wasn't at the cabin that afternoon.

I asked if Collie knew where Ted and Gail Kev worked when they started the business. If Ted had a separate workspace and he was the killer, it could be where he hid Vanessa or Q.C. or both.

"Hmm. Not sure. They had a pretty small house when I was a kid."

"Did they own a computer?"

"Not when I was little. I think Ted went to some computer lab somewhere. Or maybe a university."

I told her about Klaus's software company.

"Educational gaming?" Collie said. "Uncle Ted might've gotten into that for fun. He worked or played on computers all the time. But not my dad."

Collie didn't recall anything about Ted, her dad, or Klaus

speaking at schools. She did remember the bar James Smith owned.

"He took over when the previous owner retired. Dad at least knew enough not to change anything. It did pretty well."

Interesting that when talking to me James took credit for the business model.

"I heard the landlord pulled the rug out from under him," I said.

"That's Dad's story. Who knows, though."

I glanced at the clock on my laptop. Not much of the hour was left. Collie might talk to me again, but I didn't think I could count on it. I asked if she ever went fishing with her dad and Ted.

"Went to the cabin once or twice. Never fished." Collie laughed. "Not sure they did either."

"What do you mean?"

"Pretty sure my dad used those weekends to kick back and smoke weed."

"And Ted?"

"Not him. He didn't even drink beer. But he liked the peace and quiet and the outdoors. Helped him recharge."

"How did your Aunt Gail feel about that? All the time your uncle spent at work, then he has a free weekend and spends it with your dad."

"They bought the cabin around when Vanessa started really getting into the dance thing. Gail was busy all the time, too."

"Did your dad ever pass out after smoking pot? Or while, I guess?"

If he did, Ted Kev could have left the cabin without James knowing it. On the other hand, the cabin was nearly an hour from the school. Ted would have had to spirit Nessa away, hide her somewhere, and return to the cabin before James became conscious.

"Not that I saw. He liked a steady, mellow buzz. Not to obliterate himself. You want to do that, there're better drugs out there."

I took Collie's word for it. I was definitely out of my area of expertise. Because of my mom's history of depression, and because more than one or two drinks can make me feel blue, I'm cautious with anything that affects mood.

With five minutes left, I told Collie what Kimberly and her mother said. "If you contacted them, I think they'd be happy to hear from you."

"They'd be happy to hear from Jimmy. Not me."

"You won't know if you don't give them a chance."

"I promised Uncle Ted. He's the only one who was there for me. And I've got my own life now."

Collie agreed to call me in a few days in case I had other questions. She refused to give me her phone number.

As soon as the meeting ended, I researched the ideal conditions for computers in the 1970s and 1980s. That turned out to be dust-free, low humidity, and cool. One article talked about people repurposing 1950s bomb shelters.

"I seriously question bomb shelters for those old computers," Lauren said when I called to get her thoughts. "Even ground level isn't dry unless you're somewhere like Arizona. Guess you could put in dehumidifiers."

"But you can seal a room to keep it dry and dust-free, can't you? Like a panic room. That could be done to a repurposed bomb shelter. I read that's why a lot of people use them for wine cellars."

"Maybe. But how would you get a computer down there? Unless there's a tunnel, which seems complicated. Anyway, none of Ted Kev's houses had a bomb shelter."

I hadn't thought enough about that. The early personal computers were still fairly large. You might be able to carry the components in separately, but Ted might have needed a midsized computer like the one Kimberly saw at her mother's company when she first met Klaus. Or a mainframe, which could fill an entire large room. Still, I wasn't ready to rule the idea out.

"Would a shelter show in the real estate or property listings?"

"It should. I'd list it. It's additional space. People use it for all kinds of things, like you said."

I ran my finger along the edge of my desk as I thought about it. "What about Kev's neighbors in the seventies? He could've rented a shelter or shed or something from one of them. Though you'd think Gail would have known that and told the police."

On the other hand, he might have told Gail and James that he was at the library working and been somewhere else.

"I'll start digging," Lauren said.

71

THE BIGGER FISH

IT TOOK forty-five minutes before I caught Danielle between court appearances. In the background, voices hummed as I told her what I learned. I was working on the sun porch again. I paced in front of the windows as I talked to her.

"You were a prosecutor before the marijuana laws changed," I said. "And a cop. Big deal if someone got arrested for possession?"

"If it bordered on enough to distribute — meaning the person could be a dealer — you could bring serious charges."

"Could, but did you?"

"For possession alone? I usually didn't. Some prosecutors did."

"Could someone go to jail for buying marijuana?"

"Could. Most charges got plea bargained down. Especially if the defendant gave information against a dealer. The bigger fish is who we really wanted."

I paused and wrote on my notepad: *Could Ted Kev be a bigger fish?* Klaus, James, and Ted seemed intertwined in other ways. Maybe Ted, though not imbibing himself, profited from Klaus's drug dealing.

"Would it be the same in downstate Illinois?" I said.

"State drug laws would be the same. Obviously. But small towns usually take a harder line. Still gets some college kids in trouble today. They grow up in the Chicago area and think it's nothing to have a gram of cocaine. Their parents expect them to get a slap on the wrist. Then they get arrested in Carbondale and go to prison for it."

"And Missouri?"

"Don't know the law there. Now or in the eighties. But marijuana was serious everywhere. The public saw it as a gateway drug. No prosecutor wanted to look away."

I filled her in on what I'd learned and my theories.

"It makes Klaus's alibies shaky," Danielle said. "Possibly James's if Ted Kev covered for his brother-in-law, thinking he's protecting him from a drug charge. But you really think Ted was dealing?"

"Probably not. More likely Klaus meets James to sell him drugs both when Nessa's taken and when Q.C.'s taken. Eva alibies Klaus. James asks Ted, who really did take each girl, to lie for him so he doesn't get arrested."

"And has no idea Ted wasn't at the cabin himself," Danielle said.

"Exactly. Plus Collie said her dad smoked a lot of pot at the cabin. Who knows how aware he was of time passing?"

"But you said Collie didn't go to the cabin much. She can't know for sure what her dad did every time."

"No." I sat on the wicker couch. "And she might not be telling the truth. For all I know, she's the one who's been following me around and attacking me."

"She big enough?"

"For sure. At seventeen Jimmy Smith was six feet tall and a hundred seventy pounds. On video, Collie looks about that weight. And all the attacker did was throw a rock."

"Dunno why she'd get in touch with you, though," Danielle

said. "Not likely you'd've found her if she didn't. But I've seen people do stranger things."

Danielle wasn't sure a computer in a bomb shelter made sense, but she liked my idea of checking for anywhere in the Kevs' old neighborhood where a child could be hidden.

"Wouldn't the police have done that?" I said.

"I'm sure they looked at areas surrounding where the Kevs lived and worked. And where your parents did. Not sure if they checked every neighborhood where the Kevs used to live. Might want to ask your friend Highbottom about that."

"He didn't handle the Kev side."

"He still might have heard something. Gotta go, court's going back in session."

I opened a browser and searched for articles on early computer programming. The more I read, the more I wondered if I was way off base. Unlike Steve Jobs, Ted Kev didn't invent a new type of computer. He wrote programs. From what I could understand without knowing the details of Kev's work, early on he probably used something called machine or assembly language. According to the articles I found, many programmers in the 1970s and 1980s wrote their programs in it in pen and ink. Later, they were typed into something called a compiler and run on a mainframe or mid-sized computer.

Kev could have done the first part of his work anywhere. And the second part probably required renting computer time.

I called Lauren. "I might have sent you on a wild goose chase."

"If you did, I caught one. Guess where there's a bomb shelter?"

72

PUTTING THE PIECES TOGETHER

THE EIGHTEEN-YEAR-OLD SALES listing Lauren found showed a vacant lot for sale about five miles from the house where the Kevs lived in the late seventies. Other than the shelter, the lot was undeveloped. It took two days and hundreds of dollars in record retrieval service fees to track the past and present owners. And another couple days to reach the man who owned it in the 1970s.

In between, I worked on my legal cases, barely keeping up. At least nothing required me to return to Chicago.

The former owner lived in Georgia. My people finder databases told me he moved there five years before Vanessa Kev disappeared. He sold the lot decades later to someone who lived in Canada.

Fortunately for me, he was retired, in his early eighties, and had a landline. I claimed to be researching a story about current uses of old fallout shelters. Because I felt I shouldn't lie if I could help it, I made a mental note to put my research together into an article for Lauren's website. She posts all kinds of content about property.

"Oh, I remember the shelter," the man said. "Part of why my

wife and I bought the lot in the fifties. Cold War times. We were afraid we might need it."

"Did you use it?"

"Stocked it with survivalist food buckets. Felt silly a decade or so later when it was pretty clear those shelters won't protect anyone from nuclear fallout."

"Did you do anything else with it?"

"Rented it out in the seventies. For cash. Some local kid wanted a workspace. Had some sort of — what do they call it now? Side hustle?"

I swiveled toward the desk. I was in the attic guest room. "A computer business?"

"Hmm. No. Don't think so. Something with wine. A club? Honestly, didn't ask a lot of questions. Wasn't doing anything with it. Why not rent it out?"

He told me there were no tunnels leading into the shelter, only a hatch and ladder rungs going down. He didn't remember the name of the kid who rented it, but Ted Kev didn't ring a bell. Neither did any of the other names I ran past him. I included my own family members' names as well.

He sold the vacant lot in the mid-2000s to the current owner who lived in Canada, something I already knew.

"Schoolteacher. Bought it as an investment. Didn't care about the shelter, didn't sound interested in renting it. I called the kid — guess he would've been grown up by then — told him to get his things out before the closing date."

"Do you still have his number?"

"Nope. That was three address books ago. Tossed all of that when I moved to a condo."

"And did he get his things out?"

"Tell the truth, never checked. He must have, though, or the realtor or someone would've complained. Charged me some clean up fee or another."

It took me another day to reach the schoolteacher who owned the property now.

She confirmed that she never used the shelter. I asked if anything was left in it when she closed on the property. She didn't know for certain. Her realtor had her power of attorney and took care of all of it for her. The same realtor arranged for a property manager to walk the vacant lot every two months unless something unusual occurred.

The manager checked for hazards like downed trees or power lines. They also made sure the keypad lock on the shelter worked and the door was shut. The owner didn't want anyone, especially any kids out exploring, to accidentally get in.

"I'd love to see the shelter," I said. "Take a few photos. Yours is the first one I've tracked down in the area. I could photograph the whole lot, too, for you. In case you haven't been able to visit in a while."

Before calling, I'd looked into the management company. It filed for bankruptcy reorganization three times during the last fifteen years. Several lawsuits were brought against it in the same time period for failing to repair. All of that made me think the teacher hadn't seen photos of her property in ages.

"I've never visited. I wouldn't mind seeing photos. The agent hasn't sent anything in a long time. The shelter wasn't a big draw for me. I figure sometime down the road a developer will buy it to put up condos or apartments. No one will care about the shelter."

After some back and forth, which included sending her links to my website and a signed letter promising to pay for any damage I caused, she gave me the code.

When I called her back, I asked if the code was the same one the previous owner used.

"Yep. Never changed it. Guy I bought the lot from lived out of state. Didn't see him coming back and sneaking in."

I headed downstairs as I talked, too excited to stay still. "I thought the shelter was rented to someone."

"What? No. Who would rent a fallout shelter?"

"I probably misunderstood. I'll send those photos as soon as possible."

I debated calling the original owner again to ask if he ever shared the fact that someone rented the shelter. But it didn't matter. I planned to check it out either way.

Unless I could convince the sheriff in Edwardsville to do it.

73

STRIKING OUT

"You are not going there alone," Lauren said. "Go next week. When I can come with you."

I adjusted the speed on the treadmill down so it made less noise. It was late Friday afternoon and I was working out in my parents' basement. I hadn't gone jogging since the attack. The treadmill was an old one with only five speeds, but it was better than nothing. I wore earbuds and had my phone propped in front of me.

"That gives whoever took the girls more time to figure out what I'm doing," I said. "Plus I can finally do something besides ask people questions about what happened decades ago. And guess at what happened."

"Shouldn't the police search it?" Lauren said. "That's their actual job."

"I called the sheriff yesterday. But my theories weren't enough. He said, and I quote, 'No judge is going to issue a warrant because "a kid" might have rented a fallout shelter.' And he's not wrong."

There was a moment of silence. I appreciated the chance to catch my breath.

"What if the owner consents?" Lauren said.

"I asked that. Sheriff's not willing to devote the resources to a search when nothing concrete links it to the murders and the owner doesn't recognize any of the suspects' names. Says police might barge in left and right in Chicago. But 'we take property rights seriously here.'"

"But it's so close to where the Kevs lived."

My ponytail whipped into my face and I pushed it away. "Five miles isn't that close. And it was seven years before the murders."

"But you think it's worth looking at."

I shifted the treadmill down again, switching to a fast walk. "Why wouldn't I? The worst that happens is all I find are some expired survivalist food buckets."

"You must miss your favorite Detective Sergeant acutely right about now."

"No kidding. I asked if he could talk to the sheriff there, but he has no pull at all."

I couldn't have gotten a search warrant in my home city, either. But the Detective Sergeant would have done the search himself if the owner consented. He trusted me.

In Edwardsville, I was just a lawyer from Chicago trying to interfere with local authority.

"On the upside, the management company sounds absolutely terrible," Lauren said. "I'd bet my entire year's commissions that no one ever cleaned out that bomb shelter."

"That's what I'm thinking." I wiped my face with my sleeve. "And it's the perfect place to keep a kidnapped child if you know exactly when the management will and won't be on site."

"Which is why you can't go there alone. The aerial views I saw online show the shelter pretty far back in the woods. If anything happens, you'll be isolated."

I took a long drink from my water bottle. "Neither property owner knows the suspects. Who's going to tell them I'm asking around? Anyway, all I plan to do now is walk the property. Find the shelter so we know where it is."

"Oh, absolutely. And once you find it, you're not going to just try the code the owner gave you. No, no, no. Take someone with you."

"Ty's out of the country —"

"Okay, I wasn't suggesting him. Your dad?"

I ended my session, easing into a slow walk as the machine cycled down. "He doesn't need to look at a place where his daughter might've been held prisoner. And killed. And you and Joe are stuck in Chicago."

"What about asking the retired chief to go with you? Or to talk to the current sheriff for you?"

"Thought about that. But then I started thinking — what if he's the killer? As a cop, Q.C. would trust him. So would Vanessa Kev. No one would think twice about him being around the pizza place or a cop being near the school. He'd be almost invisible."

"Huh. He'd know how to cover his tracks. And he showed a lot of interest in your investigation. You really think it's him?"

"Not really." I stepped off the machine and headed upstairs. "The detective in Indiana said the FBI looked into alibis for all the cops. But just in case, I don't want to tell him."

"What about Dylan?"

I stopped on the top step on the edge of the kitchen. "What?"

"You said he offered to help. And Highbottom confirmed his parents' alibi. If Highbottom didn't do it, he'd have no reason to tell you that. And if he did, well, it's not Dylan's parents."

I thought about it. "He is a wrestling coach."

"And he fended off that other attacker. I swear if you don't, I will fly there tonight. And you'll cost me a twenty-thousand-dollar commission, because I've got a buyer who needs one more look to sign on the line."

"All right, all right."

Dylan returned my call after dinner and agreed to help before I finished telling him what I meant to do. My dad, though, urged me to ask Highbottom instead. Or in addition. He pointed out I found no evidence Highbottom was the killer.

I didn't call Highbottom. But to ease my dad's mind, I tried once more the next morning to get the sheriff to do a search. I got nowhere. But at least I tried.

Half an hour before it was time to meet Dylan, I hit the voice command button on my phone and told it to call Ty. But I cancelled before it began to ring, just as I'd done the night before. There was nothing Ty could do from Dubai.

If I filled him in, I'd only worry him. Better to tell him after I either succeeded or found nothing. Plus the next time I talked to him, I wanted a longer conversation. One where I told him I didn't know what the future held, but I wanted it to be with him.

I texted Lauren and Danielle to remind them to watch for texts with photos from me. I meant to document everything. Then I packed the pockets of my leather jacket and jeans with everything I thought I might need and headed out to meet Dylan.

74

SHELTER FROM THE STORM

Dylan stared at the mechanical push button lock on the heavy metal door to the underground shelter. "Someone's still living in the seventies."

"Yeah, not what I expected." When the owner gave me the six-digit code, I imagined an electronic keypad. But those didn't exist in the 1970s. "But it's good. It's the original lock. The code should work."

I pushed the round black buttons in order. With the last one, the lock clicked.

"Guess putting on a new lock would make an under the radar tenant obvious," Dylan said.

"Yes. The property manager must check once in a while."

After Dylan tried to open the heavy round door alone, I grabbed the grimy handle, too. Together we swung it upward and open.

He wiped his hands on his dark jeans. "They really didn't want anyone breaking in during the apocalypse."

I shone a flashlight — a real one I brought so I could conserve my smartphone battery — down the opening. A ship's ladder ran down the side. At the bottom, I saw only a cement floor.

"Stay here." I handed him my nightstick.

"I come all this way and don't get to see the 1950s fallout exhibit? No way."

"I'm not risking us both going in and getting trapped."

He looked around the scrubby field and the wooded areas beyond. "By whom?"

"Crazier things have happened when I've gotten close to a killer."

"You're probably closer to a wine cellar, but I see your point."

I looked at the cement floor only about fifteen feet below us. I'd imagined it going much deeper. Maybe someone could take a computer down there.

Dylan begged for a quick look first. I said okay. I needed to take photos of the lot anyway for the owner.

He left the nightstick with me, took the flashlight, and climbed down. In less than five minutes he climbed out again. "Creepy. Bunks on two sides. Lots of expired food buckets and cans. Not that I checked dates. And a wall of wine racks. Not much wine. Sadly."

I stowed my phone in my back pocket. "I was hoping the wine was a cover."

"Still could be. No cell reception. I'll stay in shouting distance." He took the nightstick from me.

When I got to the bottom, Dylan and I shouted to each other to be sure we could hear. He told me he'd call out every few minutes and to answer so he knew I was okay.

"Got it." I looked around.

The main room was a square about twelve paces per side. Three bunks stacked on one side, three on the other. Spring mattresses lay on each one. They looked old but not dusty or musty. The concrete must have been sealed well.

Metal wine racks sat against a third wall, empty other than a stray bottle in the center right. An old Formica table with metal legs sat in front of the racks, a chair with orange vinyl cushions pulled up to it as if someone had once used it as a desk. A kerosene heater sat next to the chair. I wondered if there had once been a generator.

A hallway led to a smaller room with benches on three sides. Shelves lined the far wall from cement floor to cement ceiling. They held covered plastic buckets, square sealed Tupperware bins, and canned goods.

I took photos in both rooms. My texts to Lauren, Dylan, and Danielle might not go through until I got above ground again, but I sent them anyway.

Dylan called to me three or four times, and I answered. Then I returned to the shelves. Highbottom said the killer might have kept mementoes. If I wanted to hide trophies, that's where I'd do it. The odds were slight that anyone would ever empty the containers.

I ignored the cans. They'd never been opened. I broke two fingernails prying the lids off the Tupperware bins. Inside I found crumbling off-white survival crackers. An article I'd read quoted a former shelter owner who eventually sold similar crackers to pig farmers.

Dylan called to me. His voice sounded faint. But I could hear it. I stepped into the hall and yelled back. "Starting on the buckets."

"Happy to buy you a real dinner."

"Funny."

I sifted through one bucket after another, letting flour, grains, nuts, and dried fruit run through my fingers. I wished I'd thought to bring a sieve or a funnel. By the tenth one out of a dozen it hit me that I hadn't heard from Dylan again. I tiptoed to the opening of the hall.

His voice drifted down from above, but I couldn't make out all his words. I inched toward the main room and the ladder.

"...the owner. Thinking about a field trip for my class."

Another voice spoke. It was fainter. I couldn't tell who was speaking.

"What...go in?"

Only Lauren, Dylan, my parents, and the sheriff knew I'd be here. If it was the sheriff, though, his mind changed, surely he'd climb down to help me. I gripped my phone. My fingers turned icy as I remembered my dad's trust in Highbottom. What if he called Highbottom to tell him where I was going, thinking he was keeping me safe?

"A friend's supposed to meet me," Dylan said. "Didn't want to go down there alone. What brings you here?"

I slipped off my shoes to avoid echoes and hurried back to the storage room. There were two buckets left. Dylan couldn't put whoever it was off indefinitely. And if was Highbottom, though older, he had about forty pounds and three inches on Dylan, making stopping him physically unlikely.

But if I didn't find something now, I had no chance later.

There was no point in hiding my tracks now. I dumped a bucket on the floor.

I ran my hands across the grains and twig-like food. Finally, in the last bucket of flour, along with dead beetles, I felt something hard. I dug it out.

And found five baby teeth in a clear plastic case.

75

NO ESCAPE

I SNAPPED three quick photos of the case, then sealed it in a plastic baggie. After zipping that into my jacket's inner pocket, I shut off the flashlight. As my eyes adjusted to the dimness, I felt my way toward the main room and the faint shaft of sunlight from the hatch.

Dylan kept talking about his students. The visitor must still be trying to get a bead on the situation, maybe assuming I might still be on the way to meet Dylan. But that couldn't last. And if whoever it was brought a gun, I didn't like my odds or Dylan's.

I left my sneakers on the floor to avoid them squeaking on the ladder. Above me, the side of Dylan's leg and butt blocked part of the hatch opening. Smart. He physically sat in the visitor's way. The nightstick stuck out of his back pocket.

Hoping reception would return as I climbed, I typed a quick text to Lauren, Danielle, and my dad to tell them to call 911. But we were too far out for police to arrive in less than fifteen or twenty minutes.

I shifted to the right into Dylan's shadow. Using one hand, I climbed the ladder. In the other hand I held the flashlight by the bulb end. It was heavy enough to use as a weapon. As I eased my body onto the next rung, the voices became clearer.

"You've got no right to go down there. Neither does your friend."

Definitely a male voice. Highbottom's?

"And you do?" Dylan said.

I grazed the seat of Dylan's blue jeans with the flashlight end, aiming right below the pocket the nightstick poked out of.

Dylan flinched, but barely, and the man's voice didn't waver, so I doubted he noticed. "I rent this shelter. You're trespassing. Whatever the owner told you."

Not Highbottom. And it didn't sound like James, who had a southern lilt to his speech. Which left Klaus Erickson or Ted Kev. I didn't know which man scared me more. I doubted either would let us leave after learning I'd been inside.

At the moment, though, his goal must be to get in, get the teeth, and get rid of them before police could find them.

Dylan clutched the edge of the opening with his right hand. "Sorry. Losing my balance here. Didn't know about the rental. Looks like my friend's not going to make it anyway. I'll get out of your hair."

Sun shone straight on my face when Dylan moved. It blinded me. I blinked and hung on. Above me something thudded and a man grunted. Still seeing spots, I scrambled up the last few rungs. I made myself stop when my head was nearly ground level, then inched up to peer around.

The nightstick lay on the grass near the opening. Dylan and a man in a black turtleneck and dark jeans grappled with one another. Face-to-face, arms locked, they both struggled to take the other down. The salt and pepper hair told me it was Ted Kev.

I sprang out of the tunnel and darted across the grass. From behind, I brained Kev on the back of the skull with the flashlight. He clutched his head, howling. Dylan crouched and grabbed Kev around the upper thighs.

I leapt out of the way.

In a move too quick to follow, Dylan slid his knee in, grabbed Kev's left leg behind the knee, and tilted his whole body sideways using leverage to throw Kev to the ground. Kev, on his back and still grimacing in pain, reached inside his jacket pocket.

Fearing a gun, I lunged for the two men as Dylan threw himself on top of Kev. Kev twisted so he lay sideways beneath Dylan. Kev's arm splayed out gun in hand. The barrel pointed toward the trees. I stomped as hard as I could, given my lack of shoes, on Kev's wrist.

The gun, an automatic, went off when it bounced on the ground. The boom hurt my ears but I managed to bear down with all my weight, keeping Kev's arm pinned. Dylan stayed on top of Kev. I wrenched the gun away, keeping my fingers away from the trigger.

"Cuff him, cuff him," Dylan said.

I had zip ties, not hand cuffs. With my free hand I maneuvered one out of my side pocket. But I had to set the gun down to do anything with the tie. I stretched my hand as far as I could without moving off of Kev's arm and placed the gun on the ground.

Kev yelled and tried to flip, nearly throwing me off, but I bore down with all my weight on his lower arm. A crack sounded and he screamed. I ignored it as Dylan shoved Kev's arms together, the right dangling at an odd angle. I wrapped the zip tie around his wrists and pulled tight, a move I'd practiced with my instructor hundreds of times.

Both panting, we secured Kev's ankles, too. I gripped the gun with two hands, keeping it trained on Kev as Dylan, sitting on Kev's torso, dialed 911.

After he finished talking, the corner of Dylan's mouth

quirked up. “Good teamwork.” He nodded at Kev’s bonds. “But you know those aren’t handcuffs, right?”

76

THE SHERIFF

IT TOOK FOUR HOURS, three cups of bitter black tea I held with shaking hands, two local police officers, and one FBI agent later before everyone felt they knew enough to let me leave. My voice hoarse and my body aching, I teared up when I got out to the waiting area. Not only my dad and Dylan but Lauren sat on the benches.

Dylan smiled. "Figured you might like some reinforcements."

My dad hugged me. "Mom's at home with Aunt Cathy. But she said to tell you she's proud of you."

"Really."

"She absolutely actually said that." Lauren hugged me. "Told you I'd hop on a plane whenever you needed me. I was already on the way when Dylan texted. Figured I might be able to help."

"Your commission?"

"You're worth twenty thousand dollars. Plus I got it covered." She held up a blue and white striped bag with the Café des Livres fleur de lis logo. "Carole sent cocoa shavings."

I rested my head against the passenger side of the window, sipping from a bottle of water Dylan handed me. He drove to my parents' house. From the back seat, Lauren explained to Dylan the history of Café des Livres. Dad sat behind me. He kept reaching forward to touch my shoulder as if he wanted to be sure I was still there.

He hadn't, as I feared, called Highbottom that morning, and neither had my mother. Which meant the sheriff must have told Kev or told someone else who did.

No one had seen Gail Kev come into the station. We didn't know if she'd rushed to her husband's aid. But Ted was being held. A detective told me that despite his very expensive lawyers' best efforts, he couldn't get around the court schedule. It didn't hold bond hearings until Monday morning.

At my house, Dylan and Lauren answered my mom's questions. She'd set out cheddar cheese, apple slices, and Ritz crackers. I discovered I was starving and ate more than anyone.

When I felt more like myself, I called the Sheriff's office to try to find out who he told about my plan to visit the bomb shelter. But before my call connected, my phone buzzed. It was Highbottom, so I answered.

He was full of apologies. The sheriff had called him the night before about what the sheriff termed my "cockamamie plan to look at some bomb shelter."

I rarely yell, but I yelled at Highbottom. "And you told Ted Kev? That makes you an accessory to attempted murder. I'm pressing charges."

Everyone in the kitchen fell silent.

"No, no, no," the chief said. "I'd never do that."

"Really. Never."

"My cousin, my second cousin. He's a retired St. Louis police detective. It's how I kept tabs on the task force investigation all those years. I only told him."

I paused in the doorway and gripped the jamb with my free hand. "Accessory to murder."

"I'm sorry. You don't know how sorry. I didn't know he knew the Kevs so well. He wanted to give them hope. That there would finally be an answer about their daughter."

"Pressing charges." I ended the call, suppressing the urge to fling the phone across the room. I couldn't believe anyone could be so careless.

"Are you really?" Lauren said. "Because you seriously should."

"It's probably too much of a stretch." I dropped into a kitchen chair. "But let him sweat for a while."

Gram called not long later. My dad had filled her in earlier on the events of the day. She wanted to be sure I was all right. Normally low key, she shocked me by crying. Between intakes of breath, she told me she loved me and she'd been afraid something terrible would happen to me if I investigated Q.C.'s death. I went upstairs as we talked, tearing up myself.

Gram congratulated me, but warned me not to expect a total personality change from my mother. Knowing who the killer was didn't mean my mother's life, or anyone's, became perfect. Still, she thought in the long run it would be good for everyone. She made me promise to take good care of myself and come see her as soon as I got home.

After we hung up, I filled the antique claw foot tub in my parents' bathroom. Then I dipped into my mother's vanilla bath salts. She might complain later, but as I sunk into the steaming, fragrant water I didn't care. The chill at last left my body.

Forty minutes later, hair still damp, I headed downstairs in faded jeans and a plain white hooded sweatshirt. I was hungry again and thrilled to learn my dad had ordered pizza.

As we ate, my mother said very little, which I understood. I, too, wasn't ready to celebrate. There are a lot of steps between arrest and conviction. Just because I felt Ted Kev's guilt was obvious didn't mean he couldn't go free.

I CALLED Ty the next day. After making sure he wasn't heading to a key meeting, I told the story, downplaying the danger. He wasn't fooled.

"I'm glad you're all right. And thrilled you caught this guy. But Quille, seriously as Lauren would say, you don't have nine lives."

"I didn't use any extra lives. Kev barely got near me."

"You dodged a bullet. Literally."

"The gun wasn't pointed at me."

"It went off near you. I know how scary that is. It's sheer luck no one got killed."

I counted to five in my head. And I reminded myself he was retroactively scared for me. "Not entirely luck."

"No. Sorry. I didn't mean to underplay your skills. You obviously thought things through. Bringing a former wrestler as back up, taking every tool you might need. I just — I can congratulate you and still worry about you, can't I?"

"Absolutely. As Lauren might say."

We caught up on his latest excursion in Dubai, which involved a several hour drive to find a client a certain bottle of champagne. A challenge because local laws prohibited the sale of alcohol in some areas and heavily taxed it in others.

"We need to talk about what you asked me," I said. "About the future."

"Ah, look. I'm so sorry I threw that at you. We can talk when I visit. But, listen, there's no offer on the table. I shouldn't have said anything. Jumped the gun. Not to bring up guns."

I smiled. It was a much better talk to have in person. "No, no, that's okay. We'll talk when you visit. When will that be?"

"In a few weeks. I'll let you know the exact dates as soon as I can. Hey, maybe Kev will confess by then and we'll celebrate your triumph."

"I doubt he'll confess. But I'm all for celebrating."

77

END OF LIES

Lauren and I attended the bond hearing. Lauren was in a good mood. Her sale went through and all she owed was a very large favor to the agent who got it over the finish line.

The prosecutors argued that Ted Kev, with his great wealth and computer savvy, was a flight risk. They said his attack on Dylan made clear he posed a clear and present danger. His attorneys argued that with no forensic evidence in the record yet, there was no way to know to whom the teeth belonged or that they related to any crime. Or, for that matter, that Kev knew the teeth were in the bomb shelter. They painted him as a pillar of the community, unlikely to flee.

The judge wasn't convinced. Perhaps partly because Gail Kev chose not to appear or speak on her husband's behalf.

That suggested to me Gail didn't know about the bomb shelter until now. If she had, unless she was also involved in Vanessa's disappearance, surely she would have told the police to look there for her daughter. But maybe it was only that, like everyone else, she couldn't think of any reason for Ted to bring a gun to the fallout shelter to stop me. Highbottom claimed he didn't know where the shelter was, so Ted could only have known if he'd been there before.

The dominoes fell into place over the weeks after I returned home. Highbottom, no doubt feeling guilty about almost getting me killed, called my law office often to keep me up to date. Dylan texted a few times, too, to see how I was.

Danielle took over representing my parents, saying it was too much for me. Also, there was a small chance the police might try to charge me with some type of obstruction. I felt I could hardly have interfered with them doing nothing. But I was glad to leave things in Danielle's hands. As my parents' lawyer, she was entitled to some information. Police and prosecutors probably talked more freely with her than they would or could to me, a family member and potential witness.

Two of TG Kev Solution's original employees told the police that while they had no idea about the bomb shelter, in the early years Ted often found their crowded workspace too noisy. He disappeared to work in silence elsewhere. At the time the employees assumed he meant at home. But they didn't find it too much of a stretch to think he might have rented a bomb shelter as a soundproof workspace where he could think and write out ideas or algorithms longhand.

They were shocked that he was accused of killing his daughter. They described him as patient and even-tempered at work, the last person they imagined might be violent.

Now that things looked bad for Ted Kev, Klaus Erickson emerged from hiding. On a grant of immunity, he signed a sworn statement testifying that when Vanessa disappeared, he was meeting with James Smith Senior, to sell him marijuana. He asked Eva to give him alibis so he could avoid prosecution for drug dealing.

The statute of limitations had run on any charges against James Smith for possessing marijuana. But he faced obstruction of investigation charges for the murders. Possibly on the hook for that, James made his own deal. He admitted that he had met Klaus the mornings the girls were taken. Fearing being arrested, he asked Ted to serve as his alibi both times. He claimed it never crossed his mind that Ted abducted and killed his own daughter.

Both days Ted joined James at the cabin sometime after James got there. But Ted claimed he'd been out hiking, which wasn't unusual for him. And James had no idea how long he was at the cabin either time before Ted arrived. His habit as soon as he got to the cabin was to start smoking pot. After that, he lost track of time.

Klaus also stated that he spoke at school assemblies. There might have been one at Q.C.'s school, though he didn't remember meeting her and no longer had company records. He confirmed that Ted worked the computer during some of his presentations. He said Ted didn't want his name on the business due to possible conflicts of interest. But as I already knew, he gave money to James to invest for him, which James confirmed.

Because no one connected Vanessa's disappearance with Q.C.'s until later, and because he spoke to at least thirty schools across southern Illinois and in St. Louis County, Klaus never thought about whether speaking at school assemblies related to Q.C.'s disappearance.

Finally, Klaus said that after Ted Kev met me Ted called Klaus. He told Klaus to let him know if I ever questioned Klaus or Eva. Klaus did that. He thought Ted simply wanted to keep tabs on what I was doing, as Ted told him I refused to keep him in the loop about the investigation.

But when Eva was killed, Klaus, a little quicker to grasp the situation than James Smith Senior, took it as a warning. He assumed Ted paid someone to kill his ex-wife, though he had no proof. Not ready to risk his own life, he clammed up.

When Danielle interviewed him, Klaus added that it was

typical of Ted to save time by hiring people on a cash basis to handle tasks for him, especially when both he and Gail were working long hours. Klaus claimed he only knew about legal ones, like picking up food or putting together furniture. The types of tasks people outsource today through apps. But he agreed it wasn't unlikely Kev might have hired someone to plant a tracker in my car, follow me, or throw rocks at me.

Without admitting he knew for sure Ted Kev arranged those things, Klaus guessed that if he did, it was to scare me away from the investigation without revealing himself. He said Kev wouldn't do anything high tech. That would make it obvious he was behind the threats. But, of course, Klaus claimed he was only guessing.

The police weren't able to directly link Ted Kev to the murder of Klaus's ex-wife, Eva. But DNA tests showed that two of the baby teeth in the shelter belonged to Q.C. and Vanessa. Q.C.'s right front tooth was loose when she was taken. My parents knew her body was found without it but assumed it fell out. Vanessa's right front tooth showed signs of having been extracted post mortem. No one told the Kevs that it was missing. The police kept quiet about the fact that both girls were missing the same front tooth. They hoped it might help weed out false tips or catch the killer one day.

Which it did.

The forensic team found DNA in the shelter from Nessa, Q.C., and three other girls who went missing in the following five years. I was surprised Ted Kev was so careless about cleaning the shelter. But Danielle told me DNA wasn't widely used in criminal cases until the early nineties. Ted Kev, ahead of the curve as he was on computer developments, didn't foresee the future of DNA evidence.

The three extra teeth matched the three missing girls. One had lived near Boston, one in New York City, and one just outside Philadelphia. Ted Kev traveled frequently to all three cities for business during the five years after Q.C.'s and Vanessa's deaths. The theory was that he'd started out jealous over the attention his wife gave Vanessa. He wanted a return to their life and work as a couple. Because of that, he planned Vanessa's murder and used Q.C. as a test run to work out any kinks in his plan.

He did his best to make it look like either my parents or a stranger serial killer committed both murders. But the prosecutor believed Ted Kev discovered he liked the experience and went on to repeat it. He couldn't explain why Kev stopped, if he had. He guessed as TG Kev Solutions grew, the business gave Ted Kev a greater thrill and made him less willing to risk everything.

Collie Smith didn't return home to stay. But she did visit and give a statement about Ted Kev paying for her medical care, including surgery, on the condition that she never contact the family again. In addition, she confirmed what she told me about her father's pot smoking and Klaus's drug dealing. And she stated she observed fights between the Kevs over the time Gail spent with Vanessa.

Gail gave a statement saying that however calm and steady he might seem to be at work, Ted often raged at her for her focus on Vanessa. She tried to be understanding given all the strain Ted was under growing the company without her. In fact, she felt guilty that she wasn't there day in and day out at the business.

But she wanted to be a great mom and put her daughter before work. Because she believed Ted had a solid alibi, and because she loved her husband, she never thought that he abducted and killed Vanessa. She claimed she hadn't known about the bomb shelter or about the pot smoking at the fishing cabin. When they started the business as a side project from home, Ted often left to work elsewhere in peace and quiet, but she always thought he went to a library.

The press revived the story of the two little girls and delved into Ted's background and family. They found evidence suggesting his parents abused him. Plenty of armchair psychologists talked about the making of psychopaths.

The publicity caused someone who lived in Edwardsville in the 1980s and worked for the school to comb through old photo albums. They found two photos showing Ted Kev at the computer while Klaus spoke. They were dated four months before Q.C. disappeared. In one, my sister stood only a few feet away, watching his fingers on the keyboard.

Danielle felt sure that Q.C. was, as I originally suggested, a test run for Vanessa. And a way to make police think a random serial killer was at work if the bodies were ever found. She didn't know if Q.C. caught Kev's attention at the assembly and he then researched and learned about her similarities to Vanessa, or if Kev targeted Q.C. first and manipulated Klaus into pitching the school where he hoped to meet Q.C. But one way or another it had to be related.

James Smith still insisted he didn't remember overhearing anything about a fiddle player, my dad, or an affair. Gail Kev, though, recalled her husband going on about musicians and their reckless lifestyles and comparing his long hours and choice of profession to theirs.

I thought it was too much of a coincidence to believe both James and Ted just happened to cross paths with my family. I figured James shared things he heard at the bar with Ted Kev during one of his pot smoking relaxation weekends. That may have led Kev to look into my dad and learn about Q.C.

I didn't share that theory with my dad. He felt guilty enough without thinking his affair set in motion his daughter's death. And there was no way to confirm it. Ted Kev, on the sound advice of his team of lawyers, was saying nothing.

Out of nowhere, a retired FBI agent who was once on the task force visited my parents when I was there for a weekend.

He came to apologize. He said in his opinion everyone on the task force, including him, became so convinced my dad was the culprit they missed clues and didn't press witnesses hard enough. While they questioned people my parents or Q.C. knew personally, they spent very little time focusing on large gatherings like school assemblies where Q.C. might have met a stranger who later abducted her.

"Still, we might've gotten to the truth if anyone knew about the drug connection between James Smith and Klaus Erickson," he said. "But Erickson had no record at the time. Smith struck everyone as shiftless but didn't ring alarm bells. We believed his alibi for Ted Kev. And Kev's for him. Took too much at face value. I just hope we did enough that he'll be convicted now. Finally."

78

THE TIME IT TAKES

IT TAKES MUCH LONGER than they show on TV to bring a case to trial. Or to build enough evidence to persuade a defendant to plea bargain. But the lead prosecutor was optimistic. Despite their tunnel vision, the task force members kept solid records and preserved all the evidence. Combined with what I unearthed, they expected Kev to enter a plea, at least as to Q.C.'s and Vanessa's murders, before the end of the year.

I attended one of the court hearings during a visit to my parents in late April. Like most court dates in any case, not much happened. Both attorneys told the judge their sides were waiting for the other to exchange reports and documents.

The courtroom was on the second floor. When I exited, Dylan Sabatini stood leaning against the polished wood railing that overlooked the first floor. I hadn't noticed him inside. We'd exchanged some texts during the last month, but we hadn't talked.

"So. You doing all right?" he said.

I nodded. "Mostly. You?"

He ran his hand through his hair. "Few nightmares. Guess I'm not as used to confronting criminals as you are."

"You never really get used it."

He gazed into my eyes. As always, the pale blue drew me in. "You're really okay? That wasn't just a criminal. It was the monster that killed your sister."

"I'm getting back to normal," I said. "Meaning too much work and not enough fun. But for now that feels fine. Predictable. And I'll feel better when I'm sure Kev will stay behind bars."

"You in Edwardsville for another few days? I'd love to buy you that dinner before we both leave town."

"You're leaving, too?"

"After I finish the school year. Got a little stuck after my mom died. But it's time to wish my dad well and get on with life."

"I'm glad you can wish him well," I said.

"If you can get past your family issues, figured I ought to try. So?"

I studied his face. "I'd like dinner. But I'm still seeing someone."

"Ty in Dubai."

"Ty in Chicago pretty soon." I was expecting Ty the weekend after next for a ten-day visit.

"It doesn't have to —"

"Be a date. But it sort of would be."

He smiled. This time both sides of his mouth curved up, but only for a second. "Only if we both want it to be. But I get it. Still, nightmares aside, if you ever need an extra partner against crime —"

"I know how to reach you."

He gave me a quick hug. "It's been enlightening."

"That's a five-dollar word."

The lopsided grin came back. "Teacher. Contractually required to use 'em sometimes."

Two days later, Lauren and I were celebrating both catching Ted Kev and the payment of Lauren's recent commission. She and her boyfriend Joe, who was also my long-time friend, got us a reservation at Oriole, a fine dining restaurant in the West Loop. Its prices ensured I'd never check it out on my own.

I'd wanted to wait until Ty was visiting, but reservations were next to impossible to get, so Lauren insisted we go and plan something else with him.

When the cab dropped me off, I thought I was at the wrong address. It looked like an old warehouse. Inside, it still looked like a warehouse with brick walls, dim lighting, and worn hardwood floors. I felt out of place in my short cocktail dress and heels. To my right was a large open freight elevator with a metal floor, benches on either side, and a closed corrugated overhead door opposite the entrance.

But a young woman in a stylish black dress stood behind a podium. Joe and Lauren arrived as she was taking my coat. She ushered us to the benches, then brought us mugs of hot lemongrass tea with ginger and some type of liqueur. As I drank, warmth spread through my body. I leaned back against the brick wall, feeling more relaxed than I had in months. I was finally caught up at my office. Everything looked good for Kev's prosecution. Ty was visiting soon.

And I was here with my friends.

A server took our empty mugs and another closed the overhead door to the entryway so we were secure inside the freight elevator. But rather than it rising, someone opened the opposite door.

Inside was a wide room with more brick walls, a candlelit bar on one side, sleek couches on the other, and small square tables with more candles lighting them.

A slim man in a dark green turtleneck and black pants stood at the bar. He turned as we stepped in.

"Ty." I rushed to him.

He pulled me close for a kiss. "Surprise," he said after we broke apart.

With his arm still around my shoulders, I turned to Lauren. "You know how to throw a good celebration."

We ate our first appetizer at the bar. It was a bite of tuna tartare on a thin wafer with some sort of citrusy herb leaf that brought out the flavor.

Lauren raised her champagne glass as we finished. "To Quille — and me if I may humbly give myself credit — solving another crime. The most important crime."

Joe wound his fingers through hers. He wore a dark suit, with a starched white shirt and monogrammed cuffs. He was in his forties, the oldest of all of us, and a little more traditional about fancy restaurants. "It's not humble if you brag, Lauren."

"I was being ironic."

Ty clinked his glass with mine. "To Lauren and Quille. And to Ted Kev behind bars forever."

The arrival of the server interrupted our toast. After another small bite, we followed him to an island near the open kitchen.

As we all stood around the chef's table for foie gras flavored with blueberry and anise, I told the others that the prosecutor thought they were near a plea deal with Kev.

"What kind of a plea deal do you offer someone for multiple murders?" Lauren said. "They're not ever going to let him out are they?"

"Missouri still has the death penalty," I said. "So does Pennsylvania, but there's a moratorium on carrying it out. Danielle's guess is he'll end up with consecutive life sentences from five states, not death, if he pleads to the murders of all five girls. And gives enough information so the bodies of the three missing girls can be found. Plus another sentence for assaulting Dylan and me and unlawful use of a weapon."

"And he'll never get out?" Joe said.

"He'll never get out," I said.

Everyone toasted.

I'm not normally a fan of champagne, but it tasted wonderful with the next dish — caviar with tomato and fragrant olive oil. Twenty minutes later we were ushered to a four-top table for the rest of the courses and wine pairings.

"Did your mom finally tell you thank you? Directly?" Joe said. He's known me and my family forever.

I tasted the latest white wine. It had a faint pear aftertaste I liked. "Not exactly. But sort of."

Ty set his wine glass down. "She told me on the phone how much she appreciates what Quille did. And that Quille's amazing. I told her she ought to tell Quille that, but she said Quille knows."

"Which means it's up to you to pass it on," Lauren said.

"Which I happily did." Ty squeezed my hand beneath the table and kissed my cheek.

I filled my friends in on the changes I saw in both my parents. My dad started a new band, one where my mother sang back up on a few songs. They recorded some YouTube videos and took two jobs in the area. None of it required traveling more than a half hour, and they both seemed to be having fun with it.

That was a major step for my mother. For most of my life, her anxiety kept her from riding in cars or on trains or planes. And from going almost anywhere beyond the back yard. But the combination of her newer medication and some relief over Q.C.'s killer being found seemed to have allowed her to try some new things.

Unlike my mother, Kendra specifically called to thank me. Knowing who killed Q.C. didn't change her day-to-day life that much. But she told me she found herself dwelling on the past less often.

The final meat course was medium rare Miyazaki Beef, which the server said was the finest quality beef from Japan. I enjoyed every bite as Ty shared tales of Dubai. He kept them light and made all of us laugh. He and Lauren competed for most outlandish client request. After dessert, they argued over splitting the bill. Finally, Ty let Lauren pay but said next visit he got to choose the restaurant and buy the meal.

Lauren and Joe caught a cab to his place, which was only a mile away. I took out my phone to request a Lyft for Ty and me.

"Before you do that," he said, "we should talk."

I shifted to face him. "That's in no way an ominous statement."

IT WAS in the high sixties, warm for mid-May, with no breeze. We took a Lyft to Buckingham Fountain. The colored lights danced over it. Behind us, lit up pedicabs squired tourists around Grant Park in the dark. We sat on one of the benches.

Ty held my hand. "I got an offer for a longer project in Dubai."

"But you said nothing was on the table," I said.

"It wasn't earlier. I knew there was still a chance. But I realized it wasn't fair to put the decision on you."

"You didn't put it on me. You asked me how I felt about a future together."

"I was trying to make you decide for me if I could do this huge thing. And that wasn't right. We both took things slow from the start. Both wanted to have fun, not look ahead. Then I leave and ask you to make some sort of commitment, when I hadn't done that."

I glanced toward the lake but couldn't see it. There was only a vast expanse of dark beyond the lights of DuSable Lake Shore Drive. "I never asked you for a commitment. But I thought it was more than just fun."

He brushed my hair away from my eyes. "I didn't mean it that way. Of course it was. Is. But neither of us talked about the future, then I sprang it on you."

"You did surprise me. But you said — I mean, I did. Think about it. The future. What I see. What I want. And I can't imagine it without you."

Ty shifted so we nearly faced each other and took both my hands in his. "It's not that I don't feel that way. I do. I miss you all the time I'm there. I miss you right now just because I know I'm going back."

"Then don't go. I mean, go, but don't stay forever."

"This is the type of work I've wanted for so long. Dubai is where it's happening. And it's not forever."

"How long is it?"

"Two years. After my four months is done, which is end of June."

"And after that? Are all the great opportunities going to be somewhere that's not here?"

"There'll be some in the United States. And for now, they'll pay for me to fly home for two weeks every three or four months. Or for you to fly to me."

"Two years," I said.

The flight to Dubai was thirteen and a half hours one way. That plus the time change meant closer to three or four days devoted to travel or recovering from it for each trip. Going back and forth to St. Louis, with less than an hour flight time, had been intense.

"I want to be with you," Ty said. "If you can't fly there, I'll go back and forth to visit. But I can't — I don't want — to pass this up."

"I wouldn't ask you to." I squeezed his hands. "Any more than I could close my practice."

"Or stop investigating crimes."

"Or stop investigating crimes."

"Could you move your practice, though?" he said. "Down the road?"

"Not to another country."

"No, in the U.S. Another state maybe. Is it hard?"

A light breeze started and blew my hair into my eyes. I tucked the stray strands behind my ear.

"It depends on the state," I said. "California, everyone wants to live there. You've got to take a three-day bar exam no matter what. Other states, I could get admitted based on my Illinois experience and license. But my clients are here. And all my contacts who send me business are here."

"But you know lawyers in other parts of the country."

"Some."

My Gram, though, was here. And Lauren and Joe. And Carole.

We both stared at the fountain.

"I can't ask you to put your life on hold for two years," Ty said. "But I want to see you. I want to visit."

"I want that too."

"So we'll take it day by day. It may not work but —"

" — we'll do our best," I said. Because there was no other good end to that sentence.

"MAYBE HE WON'T LIKE it once he knows he's there permanently," Lauren said. I'd called her the second Ty got into the shower the next morning. "Semi-permanently."

"Maybe." But I didn't want to wish Ty unhappiness. I just wished he could be happy being here. With me.

My phone rang early one Saturday morning in mid-July. It was Carole. "Quille, *cherie*, someone is here for you."

"At the café?"

"*Ah, oui*. He says it's a surprise."

Lauren's words ran through my mind as I took a quick shower and put on blush and mascara. Ty hadn't said anything in our last call, but maybe he'd decided Dubai wasn't worth it.

My normal early summer wear is jeans or jean shorts and a tank top. But lately I'd started buying more colorful, fun clothes. I pulled on a magenta sundress that set off my olive skin and dark hair and added an emerald Lucite bracelet. It was only two blocks, so I went with low-heeled sandals.

One quick look as soon as I stepped into the café showed Ty wasn't there. Carole stood behind the counter. She nodded toward one of the round tables at the window. A man with sandy brown hair and a wiry frame sat with his back to me.

"Hello?" I said.

Dylan Sabatini turned around and gave me that half smile. "Your dad told me this was the best place to find you. Besides your office."

I slid into the chair across from him. "When did you see him? And you could have texted me."

"Ran into him at an open mike. When I told him I was coming to Chicago, he suggested I surprise you. Said you might need a little help taking a break from work."

"Really."

I wasn't sure why my dad thought that. Other than that the last three or four Sunday mornings when he'd called I'd been at the café writing briefs on my laptop. Several of my cases were in full swing.

"Yep." Dylan studied me. "But sorry, I thought a surprise would be fun."

"I — normally yes. But Ty — I thought he might have decided to surprise me. He did it once before."

"Ah. Sorry. I'm not the man you were looking for."

"No. Not your fault."

He gave me that one-sided smile. "Hope it won't keep you from doing me a favor."

"Hmm. It's not like you've ever done anything for me. Except put yourself in the path of a serial killer just because I asked. What do you need?"

"Tips on navigating your fair city. And on where to live. I don't know the neighborhoods."

"Live?"

"You are looking at a brand new, very happy University of Chicago grad student. I'm getting a degree so I can teach at the college level. And in music theory. And I hope picking up some studio work while I'm here."

"Which is for how long?"

"Pretty long. At least two years."

I smiled. "That's not such a long time."

ABOUT THE AUTHOR

In addition to the Q.C. Davis Mystery series, which includes *The Worried Man*, *The Charming Man*, *The Fractured Man*, *The Troubled Man*, *The Hidden Man*, *The Forgotten Man,* and the novella *No Good Plays*, Lisa M. Lilly is also the author of the *Awakening* supernatural thriller series.

A resident of Chicago, Lilly is currently working on the next Q.C. Davis mystery. In addition, she hosts the podcast *Buffy and the Art of Story,* and her stories and poems have appeared in numerous publications. Under L. M. Lilly, she writes the Writing As A Second Career series and teaches fiction writing.

Join Lisa M. Lilly's Reader's Group at LisaLilly.com to receive *No Good Plays (A Q.C. Davis Mystery novella)*, short stories, an author e-newsletter, and updates on sales and new releases.

ALSO BY LISA M. LILLY

Q.C. Davis Mysteries

The Worried Man

The Charming Man

The Fractured Man

The Troubled Man

The Hidden Man

The Forgotten Man

No Good Deeds (Short Story for Readers Group members)

No New Beginnings (Short Story for Readers Group members)

No Good Plays (A Q.C. Davis Mystery Novella - also available for download by Readers Group Members)

The Awakening Series

The Awakening (Book 1)

The Unbelievers (Book 2)

The Conflagration (Book 3)

The Illumination (Book 4)

Other Fiction

www.ingramcontent.com/pod-product-compliance
Lightning Source LLC
Chambersburg PA
CBHW060855210726
48293CB00006B/1811

* 9 7 8 1 9 5 0 0 6 1 4 3 3 *